KARL'S KINGDOM

BOOK 3: IN MEMORY OF...

MARK BOUTROS

Edited by
NICOLA HODGSON

MARK BOUTROS

Cover art by Ivan via Miblart

Edited by Nick Hodgson: www.root-and-branch-editing.com

Proofread by: Amanda Rutter

This book is written in UK English

Print ISBN: 978-1-9162974-9-4

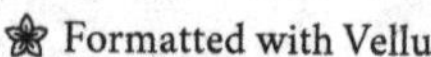 Formatted with Vellum

This is dedicated to the Laurens, who claimed to love this series, but then told me they had lost their copies, only to then find those copies in the bin.

Thanks for all the encouragement. You are the true heroes of this series. I hope the books were at least in the recycling bin.

CONTENTS

WELCOME TO THE REST OF YOUR DEATH

*I*f the afterlife was this bad, Karl hoped Sabrinia and his friends would find a way to live forever.

He lifted his pickaxe over his head and swung it into the shallow purple seawater. The pick clacked against the mauve rock, dislodging a purple nugget. Each swing became heavier and his arms ached that little bit more.

Karl unclipped the net from his belt and scooped several nuggets out of the water. He dragged his feet through the sand over to a barrel. The clack of a hundred more pickaxes intensified in the miserable air.

Karl dropped the nuggets into the barrel and peered in. He huffed. He'd need hundreds more before this boredom would end.

This had been his existence for the last forty sunsets. Wake up, get pushed and prodded by guards until he was on a ship, arrive at the shore, stand in the hot, stinking purple water and chip at stones for no particular reason, get prodded and pushed back onto the ship and all the way back to the island, eat some weird sludge, sleep, repeat.

What were these nuggets even for? If he'd known the Realm

of the Dead was this painfully dull he might have reconsidered risking his life to save the others.

He glanced out at the island, a short journey by ship away. It was more like a prison. The spike-shaped castle poked out above the high walls, which were lined with ballistae and guards.

They called the place the Sea Spike, because sea surrounded the island, and the castle resembled a spike. What else would they call it? The Pointy Faraway Place? The Impractically Shaped Castle?

On top of a cliff, workers rebuilt a broken part of the wall. Karl assumed there had been a battle before he arrived, or maybe it was just poor construction. There was only one proper entrance: a huge iron gate, with one way into it, by boat and up to the docks within the kingdom walls.

Karl stepped back into the purple water, careful to avoid getting it inside his boots. He missed the water in the Land of the Living, refreshing and cool. This water stank of rotting flesh and burned his skin.

Everything about the Realm of the Dead confused Karl. There were three suns, yet darkness characterised everything from the dull purple water to the grey stone and strained faces. The leaves on the trees were more rotten than vibrant.

He had always imagined the afterlife as a place of joy and peace, where he could sit on the grass by a waterfall and eat unlimited honey-covered beans. Everyone in his imagination was friendly and approachable and he could define his own purpose. But in reality, this place was miserable, and his purpose was to survive long enough to figure out what was going on.

There were only two positives. One, was that he didn't recognise anyone among the other prisoners. The other, was that he hadn't come across any man-hawks. He wondered if he would meet others from his previous life. His mother, Sags, King Sastin, Hargon; he hoped they were in better circumstances.

Karl stared at the forest, some distance from the shore. He

thought about escaping. Every day he stared at the trees - the unknown.

Freedom.

There had been chances to run. There were enough people to try that someone would get through. But then Karl would take one look at the ghostly figure between him and the forest and fear would choke him stiff.

If the Realm of the Dead were a person, she was that person. Numbing, mysterious, and mostly terrifying.

Two bizarre creatures climbed around her. They were some sort of combination of bat and human. It was as though someone had taken the torso and limbs of a small child and stitched a bat's head, claws, wings and feet to them.

Karl felt as though insects were crawling underneath his skin. He shuddered.

One bat-human pulled on the strands of stringy hair that clung to the ghostly woman's face. The other bit into her shoulder, yet she remained still.

While her eyes were dull and her gaunt face expressionless, it was that stillness that terrified Karl. It was on the edge of ferocity. How many lives had she ended?

Every day she stared while guards in leather armour maintained order.

Why was she so still?

Karl was sure she put her finger in her ear once, but he probably imagined it to try to make her seem less weird.

She only moved when the work was done and they returned to the Sea Spike. Some nights, Karl spotted her hovering above the kingdom, probably looking for something to bite chunks out of.

Karl felt sorry for who or what had scratched her steel armour.

Even if he outran her, those little flying annoyances would catch him and probably shred him with their filthy claws.

Maybe he would become braver as the sunsets passed. But he had thought that yesterday, and the sunset before that. He hoped one day she would be too busy to come and watch them. Perhaps she would take some sunsets to go on a lovely holiday?

Maybe diminishing her would boost his confidence. Instead of calling her Terrifying Armour Lady With Hungry Bat Creatures Who Could Rip My Eyes Out And Eat My Insides, he renamed her to something gentler that made him smile: Bat Lover.

Karl wiped the sweat from his brow and carefully aimed his pickaxe at another stone nugget, mindful to avoid the bubbles that formed on the rocks.

A prisoner to his right, with a belly that suggested a previous life of feasting, whacked carelessly at the stones.

'Be careful. You don't want to hit a bubble,' Karl warned through his dry mouth.

The man wiped his long hair out of his eyes and pointed his pickaxe at Karl. 'Do I look like I need the opinion of a scrawny runt?'

Karl raised his arms apologetically and stepped back. 'Understood.' Then under his breath he muttered, 'Idiot.'

It was that level of friendliness that made Karl avoid interacting with anyone.

'That's right,' the man said. 'Dumb kid. Can barely lift a pickaxe. Telling me to be careful.' He whacked the stones furiously. He was probably desperate to finish quickly enough to get on the first ship back and get his hands on some barely edible sludge.

Karl didn't want to watch but was compelled to. He shuffled away as the man's pickaxe came down.

Karl winced.

Rather than a clank against the rocks, water exploded into the man's face and thousands of purple water-ants swarmed his body.

The man screamed while Karl and everyone else fled.

'Help!' the man begged, but nobody did.

The ants covered every inch of him. They entered his mouth, nose and ears. His eyes reddened and bulged. He fell to his knees and crawled out of the burning water, but his screams became chokes and he coughed ants.

Face down in the sand, the waves washed over him, and the ants feasted on his body. He stopped squirming and exploded into ash, sending ants flying at everyone.

Karl ducked. He would never get used to how people died here. It was so final.

Bat Lover remained motionless, but her bat-humans smiled at the spectacle.

'Get back to work!' a guard said. He waved his sword at everyone.

An old man further along the shore threw his pickaxe on the sand. 'I ain't goin' back in there with them things.'

The guard tapped the point of his sword against the man's forehead. 'Yes, you are.'

A muscular, middle-aged woman used the distraction to nudge Karl. She gripped her pickaxe and whispered, 'If enough of us rush 'em, we can take the ship and sail away from this.'

Some other workers nodded and gathered around: about twenty of them.

This could be it. Karl stared at Bat Lover and his insides turned colder than when his life had drained out of his chest. There was something about her. Something he wasn't ready for.

'I think I'll get back to work.' Karl turned.

The woman squeezed the top of his arm. 'In the Land of the Living, a drunk witch saw my future. She said I would become the ruler of the Realm of the Dead. It's my destiny.' She released Karl's arm. 'So, you can join Team Destiny and be part of the new world or go your own way and I might remember it if we cross paths again.' She raised a bushy eyebrow.

Karl nodded and considered the offer. 'I never met a drunk

witch, but I knew a bar witch before I died. She regularly called me an idiot.' He smiled at the fond, albeit insulting memory. 'I think she'd tell me to get back to work. Good luck.' Karl walked back to the shallow water. He had no need to go from a prisoner to a follower. His escape would be on his terms.

The woman kicked sand in Karl's direction. 'Pathetic.' She turned to Bat Lover. 'For destiny! Kneel before the ruler of the Realm of the Dead!' She charged at Bat Lover.

Twenty prisoners followed, pickaxes raised, some throwing rocks.

The bat-humans screeched and flapped above Bat Lover. Their eyes shone a dark blue and they poked their nails into Bat Lover's head. Her eyes shone blue like theirs.

Karl's heart raced and his body tensed.

Bat Lover unfolded her arms and placed a hand under her chin. She blew a blue mist into those charging at her and their shouts disappeared under an icy cloud. The mist rose, revealing the rebels as frozen statues.

Karl swallowed.

Bat Lover walked among them, her bat-humans back on her shoulders, screeching.

She casually stomped the frozen knee off a man. She back-handed an icy woman's head off and tossed it into the sea. The woman's body exploded into ash.

One by one, she dismembered the attackers – an arm broken here, two feet shattered there. Bat Lover snapped the ears off another woman.

She stopped at the self-proclaimed ruler of the Realm of the Dead. Bat Lover blew on her and the woman unfroze. She noticed the destruction around her and fell to her knees.

'Please! I'm so sorry. It wasn't my idea, I swear it.' The woman grabbed Bat Lover's crusty, stain-covered right foot and kissed it.

Bat Lover didn't glance down.

One bat-human lifted the woman into the sky and flew her back to the Sea Spike.

Bat Lover stared at Karl. For the first time since she had found him in the Realm of the Dead, Karl felt as if she had noticed him. He wished she hadn't. It was as though someone had squeezed his heart.

Karl bent down by the frozen death. 'I'll clear up some of this mess.'

Bat Lover gave no acknowledgement and walked onto the nearest of the three ships.

Karl grabbed a frozen pickaxe. He stomped the head off it and tucked it into his boot and under his trouser leg.

The ruler of the Realm of the Dead had given him the opportunity he needed.

He had no idea how much worse the rest of this land was, but he had to escape. He had to find somewhere better than this, and it had to be soon.

THE DAILY GRIND

Karl rolled his heavy barrel of nuggets off the boat and up the muddy hill, trying not to slip.

He lowered to his knees to push the barrel. If he closed his eyes, he could easily fall asleep against it.

'Hurry up.' A stocky guard with a face as welcoming as a flaming sword poked a baton into Karl's back.

Karl strained against the barrel. 'Do you think I'm kneeling in this filth because I like how soft it feels on my knees?'

The guard kicked Karl's ribs and pushed the barrel back down the hill. 'What a tragedy.' She grinned.

Karl coughed and wearily stood, slipping on the mud then regaining his footing. 'Well done. That's the opposite of what you wanted.'

Her grin vanished. 'Just hurry up!' She shoved him onto his back and he slid down the hill. Mud was everywhere, even in his ears. His trouser leg came loose from his boot and the pickaxe head poked out.

Karl yanked his trouser leg over the pickaxe head to hide it again.

He glanced up the hill hoping nobody saw. Luckily the guard

was gone, getting on with whatever pointlessness she was involved in.

This place was full of idiots.

Karl pushed the barrel up the hill until he arrived at the town's entrance. Wooden huts were cramped together along narrow paths of sloshy mud, all in the shadow of the shiny Sea Spike. This was not a home he had ever dreamed of.

Karl rolled the barrel through the town. There wasn't much to the place. There were fields of dark mushrooms towards the east side of the thick wall, and a row of blacksmiths directly ahead.

The blacksmiths hammered away, making weapons and more barrels. The smell of coal and molten steel helped to dampen the whiff of mud mixed with toilet bucket.

Karl stopped rolling his barrel outside his wooden hut. He waited for the guard to turn a corner, then pulled the icy pickaxe head from his boot and buried it in the mud underneath his doorway.

He pushed the barrel until the narrow paths opened into a busy stone square that hummed with functionality. Sure, some people seemed happy, but it was probably because they had given up and had settled for a life of servitude.

People rolled barrels into a stone storage area, took two buckets of good water from a row of tables and then disappeared into their huts.

Karl was thankful to be out of the mud. The rattling of nuggets as the barrel rolled on the stone was music to his ears. It was nearly the end of another day.

He arrived at the barrel store. There must have been hundreds inside.

A guard commanded a giant, twice Karl's size, to take the barrel and pile it on top of the others.

Karl would normally fear giants, but this one's bones poked through her skin as though she had been starved. She was more like a skeleton with a skin sheet hanging over her than a full being.

Karl felt sorry for the giant and nodded at her. A prisoner like him. She sniffed and moved more barrels.

Karl took his water buckets and walked by the western wall. A line of huts faced into town, so nobody had a view of the path from their window hole.

Along the walls, guards chatted around the ballistae and a few archers patrolled.

Karl came to the broken wall. A hairy, bored guard sat on a stool and watched the workers piece together the destruction. One worker tied a chain around a stone slab, linking it to the pulley system atop the wall.

Their hammers, pots of mortar, loose chains and ropes messily dotted the ground.

The purple sea must have been about sixty feet below, but Karl couldn't be sure.

Was this his way out? He'd likely burn in the water before making it to the distant shore.

Karl stepped towards a length of chain and put his buckets of water down.

'What you looking at?' the guard asked.

'Nothing. Just a nice view from here, isn't it?' Karl edged closer to the chain.

'Well, don't get used to it. These lazy idiots will have it fixed by tomorrow, won't you?' The guard turned to the workers.

A couple of workers on the wall pulled the stone slab up to the top of the wall. The worker on the ground chuckled as he polished another piece of stone.

'That better be a confident laugh instead of a rude one.' The guard strained off his stool and walked over to the worker, towering over him.

'Of course.' The worker smiled.

Karl grabbed the chain and hid it in one of his water buckets.

'Of course, confident, or of course rude?' the guard asked.

The worker grinned at him and said nothing.

'Just get on with it! I'm sick of being out here.' The guard scowled and returned to his stool. 'Stinks.'

Karl nodded. 'Well, I can't wait until it's finished. It'll make us all feel safer.'

He returned to his hut and checked the path was clear. He pulled the pickaxe head out of the mud and entered his home.

The hut was okay. It had a bed, a box of tatty clothes, a table and a chair he could sit on to stare at the damp wooden wall. But it was a mess. Mud was smeared on the wood and dirt always blew in. Karl refused to clean it. To clean was to accept this was home.

He caught his breath, dreading this routine tomorrow. Everything felt heavy. He thought back to his death. That was the worst thing about this place. When he chipped away at rocks he was distracted by how tedious it all was. However, when he had a moment to pause, all he could do was replay when Ryza drove that demonic blade into his chest.

The sensation returned. The lightness in his body, the pain flooding through every inch of him, moment by moment, as Ryza twisted the Grave Blade, and the smaller blades welded to it sliced his insides.

Karl touched his hand to his chest where the wound should have been, but it was gone when he appeared in this realm.

He pictured Oaf's eyes turning from angry to terrified. He heard Sabrinia's cries. He remembered Ryza's beak curling into an irritating smirk and the feeling of death's grip tightening around his heart.

Could he have saved himself instead of giving up his life? Could he have trained better to have stood a chance against Ryza? Should he have killed Arazod when he had the chance and not listened to his friends?

Every day Karl went through this. He was only twenty-two. It wasn't fair. He had to find meaning again, and it wasn't here.

Karl walked over to his table. He took his clothes off and soaked them in a water bucket and hung them on the hooks by the door. He dipped a cloth in the other water bucket and wiped the mud from his body.

He dried himself with another cloth then grabbed a shirt and tatty trousers out of the box.

He pushed his bed against the door and pulled up a loose plank of wood, retrieving a length of rope and chains he'd tied together and hidden.

He lay on the wooden floor and lined the length of rope and chains up. Karl was just under six feet, so he folded the length over itself; with his new addition he had about fifty-five feet. He tied the rope through the pickaxe head. He stared at what he believed would be his climbing device to freedom. Hope filled his heart: an unfamiliar feeling.

A dull horn sounded for longer than was necessary. Karl hurriedly put the rope and chains back in the hole and covered it with the plank. He dragged the bed back over it.

He opened the door. Other exhausted prisoners seemed equally confused.

'Everyone to the west wall!' a guard ordered, his face red with fury. Karl's heart battered against his chest and his throat dried to the point where swallowing hurt.

Had someone seen him take the chain? His neck heated up. He worried that Bat Lover would freeze him in front of everyone as an example then break pieces off him one by one.

DEATH IS WHAT YOU MAKE IT

Karl and about a hundred other inhabitants of Mud Town bunched together on top of the west wall. He was about a foot away from falling off and into the hot purple sea. If the wind blew one person over, many more would topple with them.

The shore to the unknown was a long swim away. There was no chance he would make it. He'd burn to death. Or a ballista bolt would rip through him. Yet, that little voice in his head willed him to try. Dying out there would be better than the slow death here.

Karl planted his left leg firmly and leaned into the crowd. If he fell, it would be away from liquid misery.

'Stay still!' the large guard commanded. Her voice was as beastly as her frame, and her furrowed brow suggested she'd had enough of everyone.

She tapped the base of her spear against the stones and nodded to the tower. A guard opened the door and out stepped Bat Lover. She stood to the side of the door with her bat-humans perched on her head and shoulders.

A sinewy man in a vest and loose trousers followed. Scars

covered every exposed part of his skin. They criss-crossed his head as though a man-hawk had tried to scratch its way into his skull.

The man yanked a chain and the self-proclaimed ruler of the Realm of the Dead stumbled out, chained by her neck. Her face was bloodied, her arms were slashed, and she struggled to stay upright.

Karl turned away from the mess.

Some of Karl's fellow sufferers referred to the scarred man as Messiro, an Ugphan. Frong had told Karl of Ugphans in one of his long, boring stories.

He would love to hear a boring Frong story right now over a nice drink in any setting other than this. Even in a volcano.

Frong had said that the Ugphans were raised in a culture of discipline and bred as warriors to be hired out to the rich to commit crimes for them. It allowed their kingdom to prosper, but then they were wiped out, because by committing the crimes they became the targets for retaliation. They probably should've thought about the consequences of their prosperity strategy.

But, while they killed for money, they understood the sanctity of life. For every murder they committed they carved a wound into their body so the scar would remind them. The head would be the last place they wounded.

Karl swallowed his terror. Messiro must have killed hundreds.

His only relief was that this event probably wasn't to do with him stealing the chain, so he wouldn't become a scar. He shook his head at his stupidity. Why would anyone care about what he did? He was insignificant. If they categorised beings in the Realm of the Dead there would be rulers, lunatics to avoid like Bat Lover, workers, and nothings. He was firmly rooted to the bottom of the nothings category. That was his space, and nobody would take it from him.

Bat Lover and Messiro walked towards the group, then Karl's

new owner emerged from the tower door. She didn't have the psychotic excitement of Arazod, nor did she look at people with disdain and disappointment like Ryza and Lord Ragnus. Her face seemed kind, unblemished by fear or misery.

Zianfer.

This was the first time Karl had seen her. Her thick blue robe obscured her physique and was so fluffy she could probably use it as a blanket to sleep anywhere.

She walked towards the crowd with the calm of someone who didn't have to hammer at rocks and pick nuggets out of burning water every day.

The beastly guard pointed her spear at the front of the crowd. 'Kneel, you fools!'

Some tried to kneel, but there was no room. A couple of people at the other end of the wall fell into the mud below.

Karl pushed back against people. 'There's no space, you idiots. We'll all fall.' He stayed on his feet.

Zianfer stopped near the crowd. 'No need to kneel. The stone is hard on the knees.' She glanced at the beastly guard, who looked down at the stone.

Zianfer shuffled her arms under her robe. 'I'm sorry for bringing you up here, and I'm sorry for making some of you feel that you need to escape to find a better life.' She looked back at the ruler of the Realm of the Dead, who spat blood on her robe.

Messiro yanked the chain as a warning.

Zianfer stared at the spit on her robe and shook her head.

One of the bat-humans flew over and sucked the spittle off Zianfer's robe, then drifted back to Bat Lover.

Zianfer grimaced and turned to her people. 'I'm sorry the situation isn't as good as it should be.' She inhaled and stared at the horizon. 'I promise, life in our deaths will improve. The work you're doing is necessary and is the foundation of a great eternity. It may seem unrewarding right now, but you will benefit.

Your death is what you make it, and you can find meaning in what you do here. And reward.'

Zianfer loosened her robe, revealing light armour that shone with the purple nuggets.

It was great that Karl's hard work and aching limbs allowed Zianfer to be the most fashionable person in the Realm of the Dead. What a reward.

She pointed to the broken wall. 'If you need proof of reward, then look at that. That is all an army was able to do. Now their ships lay at the bottom of the sea and their lives have ended.' She sighed, almost sad. 'Here, you are secure. And I hope we don't need to fight others anymore. But I will keep you safe from the ultimate end.'

Karl shook his head. Here, people were meaningless. At the mercy of someone else's desires.

Zianfer puffed out her chest and raised a finger. 'Your huts are temporary. We have already captured more territory and with it, resources. Soon you will have stone homes!'

Some of the crowd roared approval. Their optimistic energy made the hairs on Karl's neck stand up, but he had his doubts.

'Inspiring, isn't she?' a pale man with branches for limbs said. Karl had never seen a being like him, part human and part tree. 'I love it when she visits us. Reminds me of my purpose.'

Karl smiled and nodded politely, not willing to buy into it just yet.

Zianfer faced them. 'It pains me that someone felt so mistreated that they needed to run away. For that, I'm sorry. For not paying enough attention.' She scratched her chin.

King Sastin built a great Flowforn on the back of some bad decisions and mistakes. Maybe this was the same. And maybe this was the safest place for Karl. He could wait for his friends to live their lives and then join him one day.

Zianfer nodded to a guard, who offered her a quiver of arrows.

She took an arrow in her right hand and spun it between her thumb and forefinger. 'All I request is that you follow the rules. I was a ruler in my past life, and I had a kingdom where people lived freely, because we worked together.' She placed her left hand over her chest. Her fingers were covered in jewels. Stones of all colours sparkled under the three setting suns. 'But we had rules. Because without rules there is chaos, disorder and, worst of all, surprise. Not nice surprises like when someone carves you a flower of stone on your birth anniversary, but the kind where you're working through your tasks one idle sunset and suddenly find a knife stuck in your spine.' She tugged at the hair behind her ears then nodded to Messiro.

He handed her the chain.

'Some of you may think you want to leave. It's normal to wonder what else could be out there. Is there a better, easier existence? But I assure you, the world outside these walls is terrible. Giants, dragons, creatures nobody has a name for, and worse; other beings like us, all ready to hurt you. Even the water wants to hurt you. With me, you are working hard, but towards a goal. Out there, your only goal is survival.' Zianfer twisted the chain around her left wrist bringing the woman towards her.

The ruler of the Realm of the Dead punched Zianfer in the face. Zianfer took it and smirked.

Some in the crowd gasped.

Zianfer shook her head and released the chain.

The ruler of the Realm of the Dead stumbled towards the tower door, but the bat-humans flew after her, grabbed her shoulders, flew her back and dropped her in front of Zianfer.

The woman wept. 'Please. Please...'

Zianfer clamped her left hand around the woman's throat and lifted her into the air as though she were a stick.

Karl had only seen this kind of strength in Oaf and Lord Ragnus, the strongest beings he had ever come across. He wondered if the jewels gave her power. He dreaded a world with more magical relics.

Zianfer turned to the crowd as the woman kicked the air and tried to pull Zianfer's hand away.

'I'm sorry to be brutal,' Zianfer said, 'but this woman is a poison in the minds of hard-working people. Twenty of your friends are now ash because of her negative actions. Because of this ruler of the Realm of the Dead. Her words would drive people into battle and have them slaughtered for nothing.'

Bat Lover remained expressionless as her pets screeched. One of them flew around the crowd. Karl was sure it pooped on someone.

Zianfer stared at her prisoner. 'You want to be free?' Zianfer walked to the edge of the wall and held the woman over the drop.

She struggled and her eyes pleaded.

'Be free.' Zianfer released her grip and the woman coughed as she fell, until a splash silenced her.

The crowd remained silent.

Karl's eyes shot to the water. The woman resurfaced gasping for air. She swam towards the shore. Smoke rose from her skin. Her screams sent a tremor through Karl, while onlookers groaned and turned away.

It was as though there were screams within her screams. She barely made it halfway before she thrashed in the water and her skin bubbled.

'I'll end her suffering.' Zianfer stretched her left hand out to aim and drew the arrow back in her right. She threw the arrow faster than any bow would launch it. It pierced the back of the woman's neck.

Karl held back his tears. He ran through a list of things that made a lunatic ruler. Scary calmness. She had that. A message of unity that sounded like nonsense. She definitely had that. Showing off power in a cold manner. Karl gazed at the arrow sinking with the woman. Confirmed. And the worst yet -

believing you are doing something good. She ticked every box. Full lunatic.

The ruler of the Realm of the Dead was nothing more than ash on the water that burned into nothing.

Karl's heart pounded. He wanted to be reunited with his friends when their time came, but not here. Maybe he could make the swim. He wasn't beaten to the point of exhaustion.

Zianfer stared emptily at the sea and shook her head. She turned back to the crowd but her calm face was heavy with regret. 'For your safety, we will conduct nightly searches of your huts.'

People groaned and complained.

Karl's eyes widened and his breath hitched to the point where he coughed.

The tree-man, concerned, turned to him.

'I'm fine,' Karl said. 'Swallowed a fly. Quite tasty, though. Lovely sensation when it bursts into ash in your mouth. Never got that in the Land of the Living.' He smiled at the tree-man.

Zianfer opened her palms. 'If you've nothing to hide it won't be a problem. And to ease the intrusion, I'm welcoming you all into my castle now. We have many foods. Berries, mushrooms, leaves, soil. Whatever you like.'

'What about mushroom brew?' an idiot yelled from the other end of the crowd.

'Plenty of mushroom brew,' Zianfer said. 'Tonight, relax.'

'I love you, Zianfer!' the tree-man shouted. A chorus of appreciation for Zianfer sounded and people cheered her name.

She smiled. 'Kindness works both ways, so please be kind to me by trusting what we are building.' She clasped her hands. 'Let us look after each other and we shall all have better deaths. You are neighbours. Speak and share. Build your futures. Find the joy in your work.' She turned and left with Bat Lover and Messiro.

The guards gathered in a line, ready to search the huts. Karl couldn't dawdle any more. He had to leave right now.

SOONER THAN EXPECTED

Karl pulled the rope and chains out of the hole under his bed. He covered the hole with the wooden plank and pulled the bed back over it.

He tried to stuff the chains and rope down his trousers, but fifty feet of it and a pickaxe head made him look as though he were pregnant with triplets.

His head was light, and the guards wouldn't be far. He rolled his equipment in his spare clothes.

He opened his door and was blocked by the tree-man. 'Hello.'

Karl stepped back. 'Hi.'

'I'm Salmat.' He extended his twiggy hand.

Karl shook it gently, worried he'd break something. 'I'm Karl.'

'Don't worry,' Salmat said. 'If it comes off it'll grow back.' He smiled. 'I thought I'd do what Zianfer said and talk more. I've seen you looking glum all this time and feel bad we haven't spoken much. I'm only in the next hut along.'

Karl nodded, desperate to leave. Guards searched nearby huts. 'We'll definitely talk more. I'd like that.' Karl smiled, knowing that would not be happening.

'Do you want to walk over to the castle together?' Salmat asked.

Karl nodded. 'That would be great, but I actually have to get changed. These clothes are a bit sweaty and itchy, and I want to make an impression.'

'I can wait,' Salmat said.

The guards left another hut and were two away from Karl's.

'No, no. Please. I'll only end up rushing so you don't wait long, and then I'll have a terrible evening. But we will definitely talk in the castle.' Karl nodded and shut the door.

'I look forward to it!' Salmat shouted through the door.

Karl waited until the squelching of branches and twigs in mud faded. He opened his door and left his hut.

He walked among others as though headed to the castle but slowed down and turned towards the west wall.

He pulled each torch off the wall and stubbed it out in the mud. He waited until the path fell quiet. Guards were at the huts furthest away and fellow inhabitants climbed the steps to the castle.

Every part of him tensed as he approached the broken wall. The pulley chains were hooked around a stone slab on the ground. Karl's hands shook, unable to grip the hooks.

He stopped and took a breath. He closed his eyes. He could do this. He could be free. Or dead, but he preferred to think free. Hopefully the night air made the purple water cooler and less likely to cook him.

He steadied his hands, grabbed a hook in one hand and the chain in the other and unlinked them. One by one, he released the chains from the stone slab.

He took his rope and chains out of the pile of clothes and threw the garments through the gap in the broken wall and out of this place. At least his clothes were free.

He secured the pickaxe head to the pulley hooks and let the length of rope and chains hang. It was too dark to work out how far down it went. He hoped he wouldn't have to jump too far and waste precious moments underwater.

Cheers erupted from the castle and ear-offending flute music tormented the night. Karl took a breath and grabbed the chain.

'Oi!' a voice said.

Karl froze and tried to still his nerves. He turned to face the beastly guard.

'What are you doing? Get in the castle!' she said.

Karl released the chain and turned, his hands clasped. 'I... I was just waiting. I like to arrive late and make an entrance. Get everyone's heads turning. You know?' Karl shrugged.

The guard grabbed Karl by the collar and pushed him away. 'Just move.'

Karl stumbled through the mud. 'I can walk on my own.'

The guard pushed him into the square. 'Shut up and go.' She pointed her spear at the steps.

Karl rushed up the steps and turned back, hoping the guard would get back to whatever she normally did. She watched him all the way.

FRIEND TO THE END

The inside of the spiked castle caused Karl to feel even more meaningless. He could see right to the pointy top and it made him nauseous.

Rooms were built all the way up the spike's walls, connected by walkways and stairs. Railings were all that protected those on the upper floors from falling to their deaths.

Karl stood by the grape table and picked away at them, waiting for the right moment to go back to his rope. He had a good view to the outside through a rectangular window.

Guards patrolled the walls and paths and searched huts. A guard walked past the broken wall and stopped, and so did Karl's heart. The guard spat on the ground and moved on, relighting the torches Karl had put out.

Karl's emotions were controlled by every step other people took. If they found his rope there was nothing linking it to him, though. Unless that miserable hairy guard found it.

'There you are!' Salmat said and stood next to Karl.

He forced a smile. 'Yeah, ended up just wearing the same thing in the end.'

Two more guards entered and stood at the door.

'Glad I don't have that problem,' Salmat said. 'Biggest decision I have to make is whether to twist my branches around each other or leave them straight.'

Karl chuckled politely.

Salmat grew a branch out of his back and leaned on it. 'So, how did you die? Might as well get it out of the way. But be ready to answer that question with anyone you speak to tonight.'

Karl nodded. It was more interesting than talking about Hastovian weather when he was alive. 'Sword through the chest during a battle with a tyrant.' He hoped his answer would satisfy Salmat.

Salmat grimaced and the twigs around his face stretched. 'Brutal. Much more heroic than most of the people here.' Salmat pointed a branch at a cyclops. 'That's Wendar. She died in an apple-eating contest. Ate nine hundred and eighty-two, one away from the record, then a pig-fly flew into her mouth. Choked. Death.'

Karl shook his head and glanced through the window. The hut area emptied and the guards on the walls left their posts. They headed towards the castle.

Salmat pointed his branch at a slender man with a single fang at the front of his mouth, whose arms stretched to the stone floor. 'He's Rejansa. He heard a rumour that if you stood on top of Mount Sistemila when the night sun perfectly aligned between two distant peaks and then jumped off, you'd grow wings. He didn't grow wings. Welcome to the Realm of the Dead, Rejansa.'

Karl chuckled. 'This is all pretty morbid.' He knew Salmat wasn't going anywhere, so he might as well engage while he waited for his chance. 'And you?'

Salmat scratched a twig against a branch. 'And me? Sold as a pet to a giant. He got bored of me and set me on fire.'

Karl winced. 'I'm… that's horrible.'

'Kind of why I like Zianfer. In terms of rulers I've had, she's amazing. She's going to make all our lives great.'

Karl forced a smile. He could see the value in following someone who was the least terrible. But what made someone want to be a ruler, anyway? Was it to have the misguided or false love of hundreds? Was it to be talked about by people for some time after you died? Karl doubted it was to give everyone a better life, as people mostly liked to complain. He realised it was probably to have the nicest room in the kingdom.

'You died at a good age, though,' Salmat said. 'In your prime.'

Karl ate another sour grape. 'That's a good thing?'

A lute joined the flute music, creating a screeching mess.

'Ah, you don't know.'

Karl shrugged. 'There's a lot I don't know. Normally it's for the best.'

Salmat stretched a branch around Karl's face and squeezed his cheeks. 'You, like this, is you forever. What are you? Seventeen? Eighteen?'

'Twenty-two,' Karl said through squashed cheeks.

'Well, that's you forever here. Twenty-two.' Salmat let Karl's cheeks go.

'What?'

'Yeah. You have mothers who died and are now younger than their daughters, babies who remain babies forever. Everything that dies, from creatures to trees, ends up reborn in this realm but stuck as it was.'

Salmat grabbed a grape. 'Someone burns a vine of grapes. Up it pops somewhere here.'

Karl tilted his head. 'You think I'm an idiot, don't you?'

Salmat laughed. 'No. It's true. You'll see as sunsets pass. In the Land of the Living, you're the body. Your spirit grows inside it until it's freed in death. Good thing is, death is healing. That's why there's no hole in your chest and I'm not a load of burnt sticks. I know someone who lost an arm in life, got it back in death!'

This world was too weird.

'You're in a good place. I've been here for what must be three hundred or so sunsets now. Zianfer's kept me fed, and the place has improved.'

But at what cost? There was always a cost. In Flowforn the cost was not understanding the rest of the world. It was a closed existence. What would it be here? At the moment it was having no control over your own life. What next? Being on the front lines of a meaningless war over some grapes?

The guards at the door lined mugs of mushroom brew on the floor and tried to throw apples into them. A guard with armour too big for his frame threw an apple into the furthest cup and knocked it over.

'Off the floor! Off the floor!' the others chanted, and the skinny guard lowered to his hands and knees to lick up the spillage.

Another guard kicked him while he was down and the skinny guard lay on his back in the beer, laughing like an idiot.

A bell rang and the shouting, singing, music and clanging of cups and plates died down.

'She's going to make another speech. Two in one day!' Salmat said with too much excitement. 'Come on. Let's get to the front.'

Karl watched the drunken guards sway away from the door to join the back of the crowd.

'I'll follow,' Karl said. 'Just need the toilet bucket.' He nodded and smiled.

Karl sprinted through the mud. A drunken guard with a bear's head and lizard's legs, and his trousers around his knees swayed in the path towards the hole in the west wall.

It was too risky to run past him.

Karl crept into the next path of Mud Town. All clear. He

edged past a couple of huts, careful not to squelch his steps too much.

The turning to the west wall was beyond the next hut. His heart raced as he approached, but guards wrapped in each other's arms fell in front of him. He slipped into the narrow gap between two huts and hoped they hadn't spotted him.

Their passionate slurpy kisses suggested they were too busy to have noticed him.

There was no way around them.

The male guard straddled the woman and awkwardly unstrapped his armour. 'I love you.'

'We've only just met,' the woman underneath him replied.

They both laughed.

'Shall we use one of the peasant huts?' she suggested.

They were welcome to use Karl's if it meant they'd get out of the way.

'I quite like it in the mud,' the man said. They both giggled and the kissing continued.

Karl grimaced. His only chance was to go up. He pressed his foot into a gap in the hut's wooden planks. He pushed up and grabbed the roof, pulling himself onto it and laying there for a moment. Why was climbing so tiring?

Cheers erupted from the castle. Karl stood and studied the area. The bear-lizard swayed in the square. Karl's path was clear. He leapt onto the next hut roof and jumped down into the mud.

He faced the gap in the wall and allowed himself to feel hope-ful. The rope and chain were still there.

'What are you doing?' a voice said.

Karl's stomach cramped and his neck tensed.

Salmat faced him, the twigs around his legs stirring the mud. 'You're trying to leave?'

Karl raised his palms. 'I don't belong here, Salmat. Please. It was great chatting to you, but I'm just going to get out of here, okay? I hope you're right about Zianfer.' Karl reached for the chain.

Salmat stretched a twig out of his right arm and wrapped it around Karl's wrist. 'You knew while we spoke.' Salmat pulled Karl out of the gap in the stones and pressed Karl's wrist against the wall. He stretched twigs from his left hand over Karl's face and pinned him against the stone.

Karl strained through the twigs that invaded his nostrils. 'It's fine. You'll get a better neighbour. One who wants to be here.'

'Zianfer wants us to build together. To all be in it *together*. To look after each other. You'll learn to like this place. It really is good. Guards!' Salmat yelled.

Karl pulled the twigs away from his face, but Salmat overpowered him.

Karl spotted the torch to his right. 'Please, Salmat! Let me go.'

'Guards!' Salmat repeated. 'You'll thank me, Karl. I promise. You just need time to appreciate Zianfer.'

Karl had no choice. He grabbed the torch and pressed it to Salmat. His twigs caught fire. He shrieked, released Karl and rolled in the mud. Karl hoped he'd survive.

'I'm sorry, Salmat. I really am.' Karl grabbed the chain, jumped over the edge of the cliff and climbed down. His heart pounded.

He wouldn't look down until he was far enough away from the top. Any sign of a guard above and he'd have to let go of the rope and crash into the water.

The flicker of Salmat burning lit the gap in the wall. If the guards knew, arrows would no doubt rain down on Karl.

A strong hand gripped his ankle from below. 'Out of the way, fool!' a woman's voice commanded. She tried to yank him off the rope.

Karl kicked at her. 'Get off!' How was someone beneath him? He kicked again, but the woman held his leg and sank her teeth into his calf.

Karl screamed and fell, crashing into the water.

The tingling heat attacked every inch of him. He rose from the depths and coughed up water that burned his insides. He'd never make it.

He took a deep breath. He had to try. Sadness filled his stinging eyes. He'd never see Sabrinia or his friends again. He didn't deserve such a grim death.

The heat choked him, but as he swung his arm to swim his wrist bashed something solid and pain shot through his arm.

A rowboat.

He climbed onto it and lay there a moment. His body throbbed and burned. His shirt and trousers were like burning towels, but he couldn't waste a moment.

He fought the pain, grabbed the oar and rowed towards shore, coughing through the agony.

The woman climbed up to the broken wall. Why would anyone want to enter the kingdom of misery? He was thankful she did. Without her boat Karl would be exploding into ash about now.

He took slow breaths.

As Karl's former prison shrank into the dark horizon, his heart lightened, although he felt like an army had battered him.

'Farewell, Kingdom of the Crazies.' The boat hit sand. He removed his clothes, grabbed the oar and fell onto the sand. It clung to his wet body.

He touched his skin, covered in blisters and itchy all over.

He stumbled towards the forest, his oar raised to whack any creatures that might be looking for a meal.

A familiar, shadowy figure hovered in front of him. Her bat-humans held her off the ground by her hair.

Bat Lover stared down at him.

Karl dropped the oar, fell to his knees and cried, 'Just kill me! Please.'

BRINGING PEOPLE TOGETHER

'You're an idiot!' shouted the woman who had chewed into Karl's calf. She pointed through her cell bars. 'That was my chain!'

Her dark hair looked like it had been cut by a parrot with a dagger in its beak. She seemed slightly older than Karl, but her brown eyes could have held a hundred years' worth of anger. She was too tall for the tiny cells and her muscles burst through her leather armour. She breathed so fast that Karl thought she might explode. He hoped she would.

Karl stepped to the front of his cell opposite hers and stared back at her. 'It was my chain! What kind of idiot tries to come into a place like this? You run away from places with crazy rulers, not towards them!'

She spat towards his cell. It landed a few feet from his wet boots.

'Charming.' Karl turned away. He rested his head against the stone wall and cursed his failed escape.

He scratched his back against the bricks. His body stung and his skin was red raw.

He sat on the stone floor. The guards had given him an oversized shirt and loose trousers, seemingly offended by his burned body. He took his shirt off and lay down to feel the relief of the cold against his back.

The woman paced her cell, which was about three steps wide. 'I can't believe it. It was my damn rope!'

'It wasn't your rope, Rimala,' a woman strained. She poked her head out between the cell bars, two cells to Rimala's left. She was slight, thin and pale. Her face had fresh cuts and bruises, but the most striking thing was her one working eye. The other was scarred and burned.

'Freyu?' Rimala tried to squeeze her head between the cell bars, but it was too big. 'But the rope was the signal. I watched for days.'

'I couldn't finish preparing. I'm sorry.'

Karl sat up and glared at Rimala. 'You can apologise to me whenever you're ready.'

She ignored him.

Karl shuffled across the ground and sat back against the stone wall. Bat Lover's face attacked his mind and he shuddered.

'Is he here?' Rimala asked and gripped the cell bars.

'He was.' Freyu coughed. 'He left tonight. Towards the west to a port.'

Rimala's eyes widened. She shook the cell bars with more hate-filled energy than Karl had ever witnessed. 'Let me out! Let me out now!'

Karl couldn't take his eyes off her. Either she'd rip the bars out of the stone, or her veins would burst out of her arms.

But the shaking slowed, and the shouting died down. Her anger faded into a sadness Karl had seen only once before, in Oaf. The sadness of revenge. Karl had felt it too when Arazod killed his mother. That deep, blinding anger followed by desperate emptiness because you could do nothing.

Rimala retreated to the back of her cell and sat against the wall. She buried her face in her knees.

'I'm sorry,' Freyu said. 'We were so close.'

Karl wanted to point out that breaking into a kingdom full of guards to find someone was a terrible idea from the start, but he restrained himself.

A key turned in a lock and a door opened.

A wiry old man limped in wearing a thin, open robe. Three tiny red hairs clung to the barren land on his head, and he carried a tray with four bowls on it. His face was gentle, but Karl doubted it matched the man. The tools and the keys on his belt rattled against each other.

Rimala shot to the front of her cage. 'Let me out. Please. I have to go now!'

The man bent down and placed the tray on the ground. He lifted a bowl of dark liquid with leaves in it and offered it to Rimala.

'Let me out!' she commanded.

The man placed the bowl on the ground in front of her cell. 'Is that against my orders?' he asked.

'Please! I have no interest in harming this place or innocent people.' Rimala clasped her hands together.

'Would Zianfer be upset if I let you out?' the man asked.

'Stop answering me with questions!' Rimala snatched at him through the bars, but he stepped back and turned to the tray.

She reached out and grabbed her bowl. She flung it at the man's back. The liquid soaked his robe and the bowl clattered against the stone.

He winced and rubbed his back. He stared at the bowls and shook his head. He turned to Karl and brushed his three hairs down the side of his head. 'Is my hair okay?'

Karl shrugged. 'They're still there.'

The man nodded appreciation, picked up another bowl and approached Karl.

'Don't ignore me!' Rimala yelled.

The man offered Karl the bowl.

Karl took it and inhaled the steam. It smelled like an unchanged washing bucket and looked worse.

The man's eyes lingered on him. Maybe he wanted Karl to taste it.

Karl obliged and slurped the leafy black liquid. He swallowed the bitter, acidic taste. 'Lovely,' Karl forced out. The lumps of leaf stuck in his throat and burned.

'Do I recognise you?' the man asked.

Karl stared back at him. 'I think that's something only you'd know.' He raised the bowl to thank the man and slurped some more.

'Do you want to know what's in it?' the man asked.

Karl stared into the bowl a moment then back at the man. 'Probably for the best that I don't.'

The old man smiled and returned to his tray. He picked up Rimala's upturned bowl and placed it back on the tray, then took another bowl to Freyu. Then another bowl to a cell a few to Karl's left. Whoever was in there remained silent, and Karl couldn't see them due to the cell's stone walls.

'Let. Me. Go. Please,' Rimala asked again, her voice breaking.

'Will I get in trouble?' The man picked up his tray to leave.

Rimala gritted her teeth. 'If you ask me another question in response to one of my questions, when I get out of here, I will kill you!'

'Am I sorry?' the man asked.

Rimala screamed.

Karl's hands trembled. The man did only seem to ask questions. He couldn't be.

The man turned and cast one last glance at Karl, then walked towards the dungeon door.

Karl grabbed the cell bars. 'Are you an Inquiso?'

The man stopped but didn't turn around.

'Do you know Questions?' Karl's heart raced. 'Red hair, asks questions about absolutely everything, but is one of the best people I've ever met.'

The man dropped the tray and ran to Karl's cell. His eyes teary, he placed his hands on Karl's. 'Did you save her from the rock people?'

Karl's body felt light. He had sacrificed the Hat of Invisibility in order to protect her. 'She saved me more times than I could ever repay her for.' A lump formed in his throat.

The man wept and Karl knew in that moment the man who touched his hands was Questions' father, Quizmal.

'She always spoke about you, Quizmal, and your book of tales.'

Rimala stretched her arms between the bars. 'So, we're all friends. Great. Let us out!'

Karl stared past Quizmal at Rimala. 'Please shut up.' He turned his attention back to Quizmal. 'How do you know about what happened at Mount Alseed?'

Quizmal released Karl's hands and opened a pouch on his tool belt. He removed a small jar of water that contained four bizarre yellow creatures that looked like fish, but had the wings of a fly, little scaly legs and big eyes. They had orange bumps all over them. 'Did you ever listen to a seashell?'

Karl nodded. After they saved Flowforn the first time, Oaf took everyone to Reech. Karl and Sabrinia listened to seashells together and the sounds of the world. 'I have. It sounds like the ocean.'

Quizmal shook his head. 'Does it sound like the Realm of the Dead? Are they the ears between realms?'

Karl wanted to express doubt, but the fact he had died and now stood in a land of dead people who didn't age stopped him questioning things.

Quizmal held the jar closer to Karl. 'Are these light flies the eyes?'

'What?' Karl stared at the flies, flapping away in the water.

Quizmal smiled. 'Do they let you see the Land of the Living?' He put the jar back in its pouch. 'Is it how I saw you save my daughter?'

Karl smiled. 'You've probably seen that Questions has children now. With a kind creature called Oaf. They named the boy after you, Quizmal.'

Quizmal gripped the bars and hung his head. He wiped his arm over his eyes and nose. He stepped back and took a vial from inside his robe and handed it to Karl. 'Will this help the burning?'

Karl turned the vial of green syrup between his thumb and forefinger. 'Thank you.' Karl bit his lip. 'I don't suppose there's a chance you'll let me out, is there?'

Quizmal sighed, his eyes full of desperation. He gazed at the floor. 'Does Zianfer give me light flies if I'm good? Will she help me give Questions a good life when her time comes to join me?'

Karl nodded. He would likely do the same in Quizmal's position. 'Do you really want you and Questions to live a life on Zianfer's terms?'

Quizmal wiped away the last of his tears. 'Am I thankful for what you've done for Questions?'

Karl understood. 'I hope you get the life you want.' He reached a hand between the cage bars.

Quizmal pressed both his hands over Karl's and touched his head to them. He let go, nodded, put the bowls back on the tray and left.

Karl rubbed the chilled ointment into his skin. It smelled of wet grass and soothed the pain. Rimala's teeth still marked his calf.

The door opened again. Karl hoped Quizmal had had a change of heart, but it was Zianfer.

Rimala shot to the front of her cell again.

'No, Rimala,' Freyu pleaded.

Rimala looked Zianfer up and down, but listened to her friend and stepped back.

Zianfer approached Karl's cell and stared at him. 'I'm sorry you felt the need to leave the kingdom.' She clasped her hands. 'Can I ask why?'

Karl stood far enough from the iron bars that she couldn't reach him. 'It's nothing against you. But I don't really love the whole "work hard for someone else's goals" thing. I'd quite like to find my own way in the world, maybe have some of my own goals.' Karl opened his palms. 'But I hope it all goes well here. A lot of people seem to love you.'

Zianfer's eyes shot around Karl's face. 'I understand. Freedom of choice is important.'

'So, I can go?' Karl asked.

Zianfer chuckled. 'I was hoping you would see the value in what we're doing here. We're working hard now, but that will change. New people will arrive, and those who've dedicated themselves will move up in this system. But if you really want to go, I won't stop you.'

'Really? You're not being sarcastic?'

Zianfer smiled and nodded at the door.

Salmat, his body resembling a charred forest, limped in on a burnt branch.

Karl's chest twisted. 'I'm so sorry, Salmat. I didn't want to do that.'

'But you did.' He stood next to Zianfer.

Zianfer placed a hand on Salmat's twiggy shoulder but kept her gaze on Karl. 'I am happy for you to go free. What was your name?'

'Karl.'

'I'm happy for you to go free, Karl. But you did a bad thing to someone in my care. So it's really Salmap's choice—'

'Sal*mat*, not Salmap,' he interrupted. 'Salmat. Think of salt and a mat, and put them together.'

'Of course,' Zianfer replied. 'Salmat. It's Salmat's choice.' She turned to him. 'Would you like this man to go free? Or would you like me to make an example of him? To show your fellow hard workers that we need to stick together?'

Salmat stared into Karl's eyes.

Karl hoped Salmat understood why he burned him.

'I enjoyed our chat, Karl,' Salmat said.

'So did I,' Karl replied. 'If I wanted to stay here, I'm sure we would've been great friends.' He meant it.

Salmat nodded. 'But I can't believe a word you say.' He picked a burnt twig from his body and threw it at Karl. Salmat turned to Zianfer. 'Make an example of him.'

Zianfer grinned at Karl.

WHEN TWO WORLDS COLLIDE

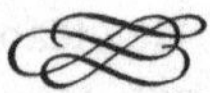

Zianfer studied the giant maps carved into the basement wall. On the top half of the wall was one of the Realm of the Dead. On the bottom half was a map of the Land of the Living.

She dipped a steel arrowpoint in a bowl of hot purple liquid, blew on it, then marked a circle on the map of the Realm of the Dead, across the sea to the west of the Sea Spike. 'Messiro will secure the area. Then we'll be the first to claim the dead from Flowforn.'

The bat-humans crawled around Cyrilla's head and shoulders. One picked her ear and ate the wax.

Zianfer studied the map. Both her forts were in the south. The first matched the beach town of Naymaro in the Land of the Living. They hadn't had many new dead come through that fort recently. There was one day where thirty dead people had arrived, so Zianfer wondered if Naymaro had been destroyed in a battle.

The second fort was further south and slightly to the west. It matched with the Sylfa Mountains. They hadn't found many dead there, either. But those that came through were great warriors.

The Sea Spike matched with the position of her former home, Ghazri village on an island in north Hastovia. Zianfer swallowed the sadness that struck her whenever she thought of her old home.

It was one of her proudest discoveries, though, that locations in the Land of the Living matched those in the Realm of the Dead. It allowed her to capture new arrivals before anyone else and to remember where she had passed fields, so they could be the first to find food.

A knock at the door drew her away from her planning.

'Who is it?' Zianfer instinctively moved her hand inside her robe and grabbed her dagger.

'It's Lae.' Lae opened the door, a smug grin across her face. Everything about her was smug. She was smugness in human form, and she held her chin so high it was a miracle she didn't fall backwards.

'I take it from that smile you found it?' Zianfer asked.

Lae pointed at Cyrilla. 'What the filth is that meant to be?'

Zianfer wanted an answer, not questions, but she figured the sooner she answered the sooner she would know if her goal was closer. 'After those peasants told us of the portal and you left, Cyrilla attacked us. She killed seven guards but the moment I suggested working together to find the portal she dropped to her knees and has given me no reason not to trust her.' Zianfer smiled at Cyrilla who nodded back. 'She doesn't talk, so I call her Cyrilla, after a friendly monster from a story my father used to tell me.'

'No need to share that story. Just keep her away from me,' Lae said.

Zianfer folded her arms. 'So, do you have good news or annoying news?'

Lae smirked. 'Follow me.'

Zianfer grinned and turned to Cyrilla. 'Soon we will control life and death.'

THE WATCHER

Karl sat against the back wall of his cell and waited. It was all he could do.

Would Zianfer throw him back in the burning water and make him swim to his demise? Or would she have Salmat jam branches in his nose, ears and mouth so he died a twiggy death?

Rimala stretched. She was incredibly flexible for someone so beastly. He could barely touch his ankles, but she folded like a piece of parchment.

She stopped stretching and tried to pull the bars off her cell again.

Karl admired her persistence, but hoped she'd accept that she was going nowhere. Mostly because her grunts and screams were loud, and he wanted some peace before he died.

The door clicked open. Karl took a breath and stood, ready to go. He'd had enough of this realm and hoped when his friends died they would manage to avoid Zianfer and the Kingdom of the Crazies.

Quizmal, carrying a bucket of water, approached.

'Let me out!' Rimala yelled again.

Quizmal ignored her.

Karl approached the front of the cell. 'Does she want me clean for my death?'

Quizmal held the handle and base of the bucket, ready to throw it.

'Fine.' Karl closed his eyes and braced himself, but the water only chilled his ankles.

He opened his eyes. Water covered the cell floor. 'I don't know what weird customs Zianfer has introduced, but I hope you don't expect me to wash by rolling in it.'

Quizmal opened the pouch on his tool belt and removed the jar of light flies. 'Do you want to see your friends?'

Karl's body felt weak. He nodded and his eyes welled up. 'More than you know.'

'Can you open your hands?' Quizmal asked.

Karl formed a bowl with his shaking hands and took slow breaths.

Quizmal opened the jar and gently pinched a light fly. He placed the half-fish, half-fly in Karl's hands. The fly's tiny, scaly legs poked into Karl's palm.

'Can you close your hands without crushing it?' Quizmal asked.

Karl nodded and carefully made his hands into a closed ball.

Quizmal closed the jar and returned it to the pouch on his tool belt. He held the cell bars. 'Can you picture who you want to see in your mind?'

Karl did that.

'Can you open your hands?' Quizmal asked.

Karl did and the orange bumps on the yellow light fly glowed. Its wings buzzed and it flew off Karl's palm and shot straight into the puddle on the cell floor. It vanished.

Karl dropped to his hands and knees and stared at the puddle. 'Where's it gone?' He studied the puddle and poked at it.

The water clouded and an image formed. Karl was seeing the world through the light fly.

It swam through a blue sea, avoided two jelly-sharks, then swam through a group of octo-whales, evading their slimy tentacles.

It was so fast that Karl's head throbbed, but he couldn't take his eyes off the puddle.

Rocks appeared in the distance and the light fly headed straight for them and then up. It burst through the water and into the blue sky. The land below stretched forever. Forests and grass bled into dark mountains and blue water.

Karl recognised the black rocks of Mount Hastovia poking above the horizon, and there it was: Flowforn. Home. He wished he could jump through the puddle and go back there.

The fly descended. Karl swallowed the lump in his throat. Flowforn was still being rebuilt from the battle with Ryza and the man-hawks.

Karl took a breath, ready for the fly to land, but it continued past Flowforn.

'Hey, turn back,' Karl told the puddle. It obviously didn't respond.

The fly continued over the bendy white trees of Herbis Forest. It avoided a lionbear's swipe outside the Red Mountain and flew towards a cliff edge.

Karl sighed and wished he was still part of that world and all its weirdness. At least the weirdness there was sometimes friendly.

The fly skipped along the water's surface and towards a waterfall. It got closer to the thrashing water and Karl's body tensed as though he was headed for it.

The fly burst through the waterfall and into a cave.

A rowboat knocked against a rock and a partially ruined temple was built into the cave wall and ceiling.

The fly entered, flew along the crumbling corridors and burst through a couple of spider webs before it ended up as a meal.

Karl caught glimpses of dusty weapons and skeletal remains on the stone floors. His heart thumped against his chest.

He looked through his fingers as the fly entered a hole and crawled towards the flickering of fire or candlelight. This place didn't seem like a happy place and Karl worried that what he was about to see would crush his heart.

The fly stopped and fixed its gaze on her.

Tears streamed down Karl's face.

Sabrinia sat on an old wooden chair in a destroyed library. It looked as though there had been a war and the only weapons were books and bookcases.

'Sabrinia!' Karl called out. But she couldn't see or hear him.

Her bow was on her lap and her quiver of arrows by her feet. She turned the page of a book. A tear fell from her chin and onto the page.

Karl wanted to comfort her. He pressed a finger to her watery face and the puddle rippled.

Sabrinia's eyes shot up from the book. Had she felt it?

She looked beyond the fly, put the book down and raised her arms. Panic washed over her face.

'Turn around!' Karl ordered the fly so he could see what she looked at.

Sabrinia stood and her bow fell from her lap to the floor. She took a couple of steps back towards the wall.

A creature fell at her feet. It had the face and tail of a fox, but the body of a gorilla. Sabrinia leapt over it, grabbed an arrow out of her quiver and jammed it into the back of the creature's neck.

She picked up her bow and quiver and threw the book towards where she looked.

She ran and the light fly's gaze followed her. She joined Frong, who put the book in a sack, Marlens and Death.

Gorilla-foxes blocked their path. More disturbing than the idea of a half-gorilla, half-fox was their half-rotten, shaggy hair in patches and loose pieces of flesh often withered to the bone.

Sabrinia shot an arrow into one's eye, while Frong speared another. Death scratched a couple of the beasts across the chest with his long nails. Their wounds burned with black and white flame.

The group rushed along the corridor. The fly followed, but a couple of gorilla-fox swipes blew it into the wall.

The creatures burst out of every crack and crevice, growing in number.

Marlens fiddled with her potion belt as they sprinted through old banquet rooms and past a statue of a two-headed gorilla-fox, one head a fox, the other a gorilla.

'Faster!' Karl yelled at the puddle.

A gorilla-fox grabbed Sabrinia and knocked her to the floor. Death turned back, but a swarm of gorilla-foxes obscured the fly's view.

'Sabrinia!' Karl punched the puddle and hurt his knuckles.

The fly flew up into a crack and crawled towards sunlight.

Karl rocked, waiting to see what the fly saw. His heart tightened as though it was being twisted. 'Hurry up.'

The fly flew out of a crack in the temple and landed on the cave wall. It watched the temple entrance and waited. It felt like an age.

A cloud of dust exploded from the entrance and the temple toppled. Karl took deep breaths, waiting for the dust cloud to clear, seeing only broken stone and rubble through the haze.

'Please.'

A gorilla-fox emerged and Karl's heart sank. Then an arrow-point poked through its neck and it fell forwards.

Death, Marlens, Sabrinia and Frong ran out of the temple rubble, covered in a dull yellow dust and coughing.

Marlens turned and threw a potion bottle. It smashed and a wall of flames repelled the beasts that followed.

A giant, two-headed gorilla-fox like the statue emerged from the rubble. Its left arm was all bone with shreds of flesh and its left leg was stripped of hair.

The image in the puddle flashed orange and yellow.

'Is it fading?' Quizmal asked.

'No. It can't yet!' Karl pleaded.

The two-headed gorilla-fox walked through the flames unscathed and stalked the four.

The fly followed the four to the rowboat.

Karl wanted to see how close the beast was, but the fly was fixed on Sabrinia.

Frong rowed towards the waterfall and the fly followed. Boulders flew past the fly and smashed the side of the boat, sinking it.

The four swam through the waterfall and the fly burst through the water with them.

Karl willed it to turn around so he could see if the beast was close.

His friends swam to shore.

The fly flew around Sabrinia and watched her, the waterfall in the background. The silhouette of the two-headed gorilla-fox lingered behind the falling water.

The group ran into a forest, rested and patched up their wounds.

Frong tipped out the contents of a sack. Sabrinia took the slightly wet book and continued reading. She stopped to watch Frong put a blue, feather-lined belt on. He jumped and whooshed past the light fly and to the top of a tree. The group smiled and laughed.

Another magic relic. Karl laughed with them, wishing he could be there.

Sabrinia showed Death a page from the book. He tore it out and took a potion bottle from Marlens. He poured an orange syrup on the page, lighting it. It burned and crumbled in his hand, then he released it into the air.

The ash and fire floated and formed into a fiery crow. It flew towards a mountain castle. The group followed its flight and walked in the same direction.

The puddle flashed yellow and orange and the fly settled in the grass. The image faded and a puddle remained.

Karl cried. He was glad they were okay, but terrified of where they might be going.

'Are you okay?' Quizmal asked.

Karl shook his head. 'Yes and no.'

He turned around. The keys to his cell were on the stones in front of him.

Quizmal sat outside Karl's cell. He scratched a nail against the side of his head, drawing blood. Tears filled his eyes.

Karl picked up the keys and stared at Quizmal.

Quizmal slashed the nail across his robe. 'Did you attack me and take the keys?' He smiled.

Karl chuckled through his tears. 'You put up a good fight, though.' He stood and unlocked the cell, then knelt and hugged Quizmal. 'Thank you.'

Quizmal squeezed him. 'Do I wish you good luck?'

'I hope you and Questions are reunited.' Karl realised that didn't sound so great. 'But obviously not soon. When the time is right.' He released Quizmal and faced the door out of the dungeon. He took a breath.

'Do you need to go right to avoid the guards?' Quizmal took his hammer from his tool belt and handed it to Karl.

Karl accepted it and nodded. 'I'll try not to use it.'

'Free us!' Rimala ordered.

'You need to learn to ask for things nicely,' Karl said.

Rimala glared at him, her breaths louder than a bull-ogre's.

'Staring isn't going to make me help you.' Karl shrugged.

Freyu poked her head out of the cell. 'Please. We have a way out. I swear. I was working on an exit for when Rimala took her revenge. You can come with us, then we'll go our separate ways when we're safe.'

Karl studied Freyu's face. While Rimala was every kind of anger and misery, Freyu seemed gentle.

Karl pointed at Rimala. 'And you won't knock me out and throw me back in my cell?'

Rimala shook her head. 'My anger and violence are reserved for another.'

'Good to know.' Karl unlocked both cells.

Rimala looked him up and down and smirked.

'Pleasure,' Karl said.

'Free... me...' a voice strained from another cell.

It sent chills through Karl's body.

He walked over to the cell and saw his beaten foe curled up on the ground. Her spiked wings were mostly featherless, and her right arm was snapped at the elbow. Her body would have regenerated like his when she was reborn, so this must have been Zianfer's doing.

'I... can help. We can work... together,' Ryza said.

Karl's neck burned and he gritted his teeth. He remembered her driving her demonic sword through Sags' chest and doing the same to him.

Anger flooded his body. He took in every one of her struggling breaths as she stared at him, her only hope of escape.

Freyu joined Karl. 'She could fly us to freedom.'

Karl's body tensed. Freyu had a point, but mercy had ended Karl's former life.

He put the dungeon keys in his pocket and walked away, ignoring Ryza's pleas.

MEMORIES OF THE FUTURE

Zianfer turned the sharp golden stone, the size of a lemon, in her hand. It shone under the sunrise and was unimpressive, yet she could feel its power.

Her three prisoners lay on the garden grass. The old man's arms were behind his back and inside a sack tied around his wrists. Rope bound his ankles. Blood soaked his cloak and a snapped arrow stuck out of his shoulder. A hood obscured his hairy face.

The young creature next to him, also tied with rope, wept. She had a human body covered in scales, a lizard-like face and claws. Her spiky ears fluttered and she was abnormally tall.

Blood seeped out of a wound on her cheek and a chunk of her hair was missing as though it had been ripped out. A scar marked her left shoulder.

A frog-woman lay next to her. Her slimy arms were tied behind her back and she was gagged. Slashes crossed her frog legs.

Zianfer turned to Lae and gestured to the wounded trio. 'Was this brutality necessary?'

Lae smirked at the lizard-creature. 'She tried to bite me and scratched me. Toady thing slapped me in the eye with her tongue. And that old fella punched me in the back of the head.' Lae brushed her long hair behind her ear.

Such a lack of remorse. Zianfer turned to the lizard-creature. 'How old are you?'

The creature groaned and shuffled but avoided Zianfer's gaze. 'Sixteen.'

Zianfer turned to Lae and shook her head.

Lae shrugged and removed her quiver of arrows. 'Need a rest. Been a long journey.'

Lae walked away, but Zianfer put her arm out to stop her. 'Don't you want to see how it works?'

Lae scoffed. 'Don't care. Job's done. Time for a wash, a drink, and whatever fun the drink brings.' Lae pushed Zianfer's arm down and walked towards the garden gate where Cyrilla waited.

Zianfer took a breath and nodded to Cyrilla.

Cyrilla stepped in front of Lae.

'Get out of the way, you big freak.' Lae waved the back of her hand.

A bat-human scratched Lae's face. The other grabbed her hair, yanked her to the grass and dragged her along it to Zianfer.

'Get off!' Lae pleaded, her cheek and left eye bleeding.

Cyrilla planted her foot on Lae's stomach while the bat-humans held her arms down.

Zianfer knelt by Lae's head and turned to the prisoners. 'Let's see exactly what happened.'

Lae's panicked screams drowned out her smugness.

Zianfer dug the sharp point of the golden stone into Lae's forehead and cut along it. She placed the stone on the blood and the gold glowed. A cloudy red filled the stone and then a crack formed in it. A spider's little legs pulled its body out of the crack and a long tail followed, connected to the stone. An eel-spider, red and gold. This was the first one Zianfer had seen.

It crept down the stone and squeezed itself into the cut on

Lae's head. It vanished under the blood and shuffled under her skin.

Lae's eyes rolled into the back of her head. The screams stopped and her mouth foamed. Her body spasmed and her legs kicked wildly. A light black and white glow pulsed through the tail and into the stone.

Zianfer smiled at Cyrilla who remained motionless while her bat-humans shrieked.

The eel-spider pushed out of Lae's bloody cut and whipped back into the stone. The crack sealed.

Lae's body became limp, and the stone stopped glowing.

The bat-humans and Cyrilla released a motionless Lae.

'Light the pit please, Doran,' Zianfer commanded a guard by the entrance. She then approached the old man, the toad-woman and the lizard-creature. 'I'd prefer it if you told me where the portal is so I don't have to do that to you.'

Zianfer walked to the firepit and threw the stone in. Nothing happened for a moment, but then, in the flames, Zianfer saw Lae's memories.

As a child, as well as doing nothing but playing in mud all day, Lae had witnessed her mother shoot her father with an arrow. Lae was abused by her mother until she was old enough to use a bow and arrow herself, but opted to poison her mother instead of giving her a swift death. Then Lae sold herself for food and money until she could sell her archery skills. Her life was normal for some time, but then Lae fell in love and got married. However, she lost her husband to a flesh-eating sickness. Then she took her own life.

It reminded Zianfer of her own tragedies and her mind drifted to Hermin, taken from her too soon. Her heart suddenly weighed more.

Doran brought over a couple of swords and planted them in the ground next to the firepit.

Zianfer watched Lae's early memories of the Realm of the

Dead. She mercilessly ended the lives of people for no reason, basking in the ash explosions. Then a few nights ago, she had approached the old man and girl as they camped.

She fired an arrow at the man while he slept, kicked the lizard-creature in the face and dragged her around by her hair. She found the toad-woman asleep in a lake near the camp and slashed the backs of her legs.

Zianfer had seen enough. She nodded to Doran, who used the two swords to try to grab the stone out of the fire, but he struggled.

Lae squirmed, inhaled and opened her eyes. 'What's this? Who are you?' She sat up and looked around. 'In fact, who am I?' She stood and nodded at the surroundings, impressed. 'I hope I live here.'

Zianfer approached her. 'You do live here.' She turned to Cyrilla. 'Show Lae to her room, please.' Zianfer smiled.

Lae smirked. 'Lae? Great name.'

Cyrilla walked towards the garden exit and Lae followed.

'Do I have a big bed?' Lae asked Cyrilla. 'And why do you look so unfriendly?'

Zianfer knelt by the old man. 'Last chance to talk.'

The old man exchanged glances with the lizard-creature and the toad-woman. 'Very well.' He struggled for breath. 'Please.'

He sat up as best he could with his arms tied behind his back. 'We are simple travellers who one night stumbled upon a battle-field, long deserted.' He coughed and glanced at Doran.

Doran nearly got the stone out of the fire but dropped it again. He stabbed a sword into the grass and cursed himself.

Zianfer shook her head. 'Ignore him.'

The old man coughed blood. 'There were only the stains of ash, the dead. No injured, no living checking the battlefield. Just the lingering smell of loss. No weapon or crumb of food in sight. But the night suns revealed a crack in the mountain. Above it were markings in a language none of us understood, and I reached in and found a sack with that stone in it.' He winced and shuffled. 'Our plan was to sell it for food. We didn't realise it was so precious. I promise you. We are unaware of any portals. We're just peasants looking for bread and board.'

The toad-woman nodded.

Zianfer smiled. 'Well, I appreciate your honesty.'

She turned to Doran, who still struggled.

'It's too slippery!' he complained.

Zianfer sighed and walked to him. She grabbed the mind stone in her hand. One of her rings glowed red and the stone's heat had no effect on her. The stone shone gold once more.

She approached the old man. 'The problem is I don't quite believe you.'

The man's eyes widened. 'But it's the truth!'

Zianfer knelt by the toad-woman. 'I'd prefer to be certain.'

PART-TIME FRIENDSHIPS

Karl followed Freyu and Rimala. They snuck out of the castle and crept around its side, moving towards the northern wall. They pressed themselves against the stone to avoid the eyeline of the guards above.

Karl's nerves jangled. Freyu put her hand out to stop them all by a ladder that led up to the wall. She gestured for them to wait.

Karl stayed still. Footsteps tapped against the stones above. He worried the guard was directly over him. Freyu continued and pointed up.

Rimala climbed the ladder.

Freyu gestured with her finger for Karl to follow her. They crept along the bottom of the wall.

They came to a tower in the northeast corner. An archer stood on top and faced the sea.

Freyu gestured for silence and pressed her hands and head against the door.

A guard walked along the eastern path. If he turned towards them, they would be caught. Karl's heart raced and he wiped the sweat from his neck.

'Someone's coming,' he whispered.

'Hold on,' Freyu said.

The guard turned the other way, thankfully. Karl exhaled. But then the guard stopped.

The door clicked open and Freyu entered. Karl sped in, hoping the guard hadn't seen them.

Freyu led him down the stone steps until they came to an arched brick room. The walls were lined with barrels that covered alcoves.

Karl stood in the doorway and Rimala barged through him. 'Watch yourself.'

She had a bow and quiver of arrows. 'We'll have no problem getting out now.'

Freyu smiled and walked to the far wall. She moved a barrel. 'This is where they store the good water from their port base, but it's also an emergency escape room for Zianfer.' Freyu moved another barrel, revealing a hole in the wall.

Karl caught a glimpse of a rowboat and the purple water.

Freyu nodded to some barrels in the corner. 'Rimala, there's a crank there.' She pointed to Karl. 'Keep an ear open.'

He stood in the doorway.

Rimala shifted some barrels away from the wall and found the crank. She turned it. A gate creaked open beyond the hole in the wall.

Karl listened into the stairwell and his chest tightened. He closed the door and pressed his back against it. 'Footsteps! More than one person.'

Freyu crouched to go through the hole. 'We have to go, now!'

'Wait!' Karl said. 'If they see us on the boat they'll call to the other guards and it'll be arrow time.'

Freyu nodded. 'Rimala?'

Rimala shrugged. 'One, easy. Two armed, trickier and it'll give them time to shout. Three, we've blown our chance.' She stared at Karl. 'How many more than one do you think?'

Karl thought about it. 'It was like a clop, clop, clop clop, clop, clop clop clop, clop.'

Rimala and Freyu stared at him as though he was an idiot.

'I'd say definitely more than one.'

Rimala took aim at the door with her bow and arrow. 'We'll have to chance it.'

'Or,' Karl said, hoping to redeem some credibility, 'we create a distraction to occupy them. It'll give us enough time to be far enough away so that when they do realise, we're out of range.'

Rimala nodded and turned to Freyu, who also approved.

'Great idea,' Rimala said.

Karl sighed, relieved. He turned to grab a barrel. 'I'm not sure exactly what it should be, but let's work with what we have. Barrels.'

'I've got an idea,' Rimala said.

'Great.' Karl turned to face her.

She grabbed his head and smashed it against the wall.

MEMORIES OF A GENIUS

Zianfer stared into the fire and watched the toad-woman's memories. A life spent evading capture and losing her fellow toad-people to hunters.

Toad-people were famed for the healing properties of their blood, and it wasn't long before she was in a net and being drained of hers.

In the Realm of the Dead, it was more of the same until the old man saved her.

It seemed the old man was correct. They had spent their days seeking food and trading what they could find. But then they met the lizard-creature and watched a castle for many sunsets.

In the next memory, the toad-woman leapt into the castle in the middle of a chaotic night battle. Towers fell, fiery explosions demolished walkways and it didn't rain arrows, it rained snakes, but her agility was dizzying, and she evaded the mess of war around her.

The toad-woman leapt into a half-collapsed throne room, where a king kneeled and sobbed over the corpse of a baby before it exploded into ash.

A knight stood above the king and raised his glowing green sword, which was covered in snakes.

The toad-woman spotted the mind stone among the debris of a broken statue.

The knight noticed her and charged, but she lashed her tongue towards the stone, grabbed it and jumped out of the window and into a moat.

She swam and leapt away from the kingdom, not daring to look back.

She returned to a tavern and met with the old man and lizard-creature. They cast the stone into a fire and watched the memories. Whoever owned the memories spent a lot of time eating, drinking in taverns, and curled up next to a toilet bucket.

The memories became disjointed. Flashes of a stone forest. Running through bushes. Eventually a memory settled and the person stopped outside a mountain cave. A figure Zianfer had only heard about revealed herself.

Zianfer grinned.

From her giant form to the white hair and the dragon bite on her neck, it had to be her, the genius giant Ulago. She would know how to find the portal, because she created it.

Ulago angrily pointed for whoever owned these memories to leave.

Zianfer watched for anything distinct in the surroundings to locate the place. Two mountains. Useless. That could be anywhere. The memory owner turned and faced more mountains. They were surrounded, in a circle of mountains.

The toad-woman lashed her tongue at the stone and flicked it out of the fire.

Zianfer tensed. She needed more.

The old man placed a map on the tavern table and marked it. Zianfer's eyes widened. The circle of mountains was to the west, not far from Port Larken.

The memories ended with the toad-woman here in the

garden. Zianfer turned to her prisoners. The old man cried while the lizard-creature's eyes carried nothing but fury.

'I'm sorry I had to turn her into this shell.' Zianfer stood above the old man. 'But when she regains consciousness we'll tell her she has always lived here and loves it. She'll have a great future. As will you, as I'll keep you all together.'

The old man refused to look at her.

Zianfer took the stone out of the fire. 'Or, when I take your memories, when you regain consciousness you'll have never met.' She stared at the old man. 'So, how do I find Ulago?'

The man shook his head. 'Find out in my memories. I no longer care.'

Zianfer shrugged, turned to one of two guards and pointed to the toad-woman. 'Take her to a cell.'

Another guard rushed in, out of breath. 'Zianfer… there's a…' he wheezed. 'Escaping people. Northeast tower.'

Anger rose through her, but she swallowed it. 'Not again.' She touched the guard's shoulder. 'Stay and keep watch.' Zianfer gazed into the sky. 'Cyrilla!'

Zianfer sped towards the garden exit.

THE PRICE OF FREEDOM

When Karl regained consciousness, someone was dragging him by his feet along a stone pathway towards the castle. He'd gone from a prisoner to a glorified broom.

His wrists were bound with rope and his captor had a companion.

Bat Lover flew away from the castle, likely chasing Rimala and Freyu. Karl felt as though they deserved to be hunted by her, but then regretted the thought and hoped they would be okay.

The weedy male guard dragging him turned to the muscly one. 'Do you reckon Zianfer will let us move up to another floor in the castle for this?'

The muscly one scratched the back of her neck, under her helmet. 'Definitely. We'll be her favourites for sure.'

Karl was oddly comforted that at least his life had some value.

'Wait!' the weedy one said and stopped. 'We can't share him with the others.'

The muscly one nodded. 'Hide him while I distract them.' She moved to block the path.

The weedy man dragged Karl to a wall and rolled him to face

the stone. He knelt and placed a hand over Karl's mouth. 'Shush,' the weedy guard said.

What was the point in trying to shout anyway? To go from one captor to another?

The muscly guard spoke to someone. 'I've not seen the prisoner. Heard he ran towards the south-west tower, though. If I see him I'll definitely call for you, captain. Yes, I already cleaned your quarters. I swear I have.'

Karl wanted to weep. He hated this place so much. Maybe the Realm of the Dead had a cruel energy where if someone hated something enough, they would have to experience it over and over.

The guard released Karl's mouth. Two arms wrapped around Karl, pulled him to his feet and turned him around.

Quizmal faced Karl and pressed his finger to his lips.

Karl felt light-headed and noticed the weedy guard asleep on the stone tiles.

Quizmal placed a bottle of yellow liquid back in his tool belt and waved Karl to follow him.

Thankfully, the muscly guard still spoke in the path entrance.

Karl mouthed a thank you to Quizmal and followed him.

'Are you sure we should be inside the castle?' Karl whispered as Quizmal sped along a corridor and waved him over again.

'Is there a secret passage in the garden?' Quizmal asked.

'Of course,' Karl replied. 'What obsessive ruler doesn't have multiple secret passages and escape routes?'

Quizmal pointed into the garden. It was like Flowforn's garden before Arazod had ruined it. Bright flowers and statues provided peace and colour. It didn't match Karl's struggles.

A guard stood by a firepit, right at the back of the garden. He spun his sword into the air and tried to catch it, failing, nearly cutting himself several times and cursing.

Two statues stood in the far corners on stone plinths by two large trees. One statue was of Zianfer, obviously. Why would a ruler not have a statue of themselves? The other was of a thin man, far too average to have a statue. Maybe it was to make Zianfer's stand out even more.

Quizmal held Karl's shoulder. 'Will I distract the guard while you enter the passage?' Quizmal pointed to the statue of the average man.

Karl nodded. His heart was heavy but bursting with thanks. This time he would surely escape. 'Thank you, Quizmal. Just like Questions, you're my hero.'

Quizmal's eyes shifted to the ground then back up to Karl. 'Is the switch the man's left hand?'

'Got it.'

Quizmal approached the guard, who threw the sword into the air and failed to catch it again. 'Do you want me to teach you, Limpus?'

'Please. I need to impress Zianfer.' Limpus handed Quizmal the sword.

Quizmal turned Limpus to face the statue of Zianfer. 'Will she motivate you?'

Limpus nodded.

Quizmal threw the sword into the air and caught it.

'Wow! How?' Limpus asked. He took the sword from Quizmal and tried again. He failed and the sword pierced the soil by his foot.

'Do you need to flick your wrist more?' Quizmal asked.

Karl snuck behind the bushes and crept towards the statue of the average man. The plaque read:

Hermin. An angel among devils. I only wish you could see our vision realised.

Karl reached for Hermin's left hand, but caught something in the corner of his eye and covered his mouth as sickness rose up his throat.

Maybe Rimala's whack to his head was making him imagine things. He closed his eyes and hoped that what he saw would be gone when he opened them.

No such luck.

An old man and a young lizard-girl were tied up and on the grass. They stared up at him.

The old man mouthed, 'Help.'

Karl's neck tensed and he massaged it, trying to rub the fear away.

He caught Quizmal's eyes over Limpus' shoulder. Quizmal's face willed him to hurry.

Karl trembled. He pulled Hermin's left hand, shook it, but nothing happened. He twisted it and something clicked behind him. The trunk of a large tree opened and revealed stairs.

He needed to go, but the arrow sticking out of the man's shoulder suggested he was probably a victim. Or maybe the pair had done something bad to end up in this situation. It was unlikely, though.

Karl gazed at Quizmal and pointed down behind the bush. He had no idea what the gesture was for 'two people tied up and in pain, likely victims of a horrible attack,' so he waved his arms around and crept towards the old man and the lizard-girl.

He knelt by the old man and untied his ankles.

The man rolled around so Karl could untie his wrists, too.

Karl whispered, 'Last time I freed someone they smashed my head off a wall, so we'll keep that there for now.' He helped the man to his feet.

Quizmal saw the man and his eyes widened.

Karl shrugged. What was he supposed to do? He untied the lizard-girl and helped her, too.

Limpus flicked the sword into the air again. He missed again.

'Maybe I was just born the wrong way and can't do it.' He stabbed the sword into the soil.

Quizmal shook his head. 'Can you do anything you put your mind to?'

Limpus took a breath and nodded. 'Clearly not. But okay, one more try.'

Karl waved the old man and lizard-girl towards the secret passage.

'Wait,' the old man whispered. 'We need the stone in that firepit.'

Karl gazed at the firepit. It was right next to Limpus who stretched. Karl grimaced. 'Is it essential? Or is it something that's just nice to have?'

The man stared into Karl's eyes. 'It could be the most important item in the Realm of the Dead at this very moment. And if Zianfer keeps it we are all doomed.'

Karl clenched his fist and tapped it against his front teeth. He whispered, 'I wish you'd said anything else. Get in that tree and get ready to run.'

Karl crouched and crawled over to the firepit. He was so close he could smell the smoke from the previous fire and Limpus' stale sweat mixed with mushroom brew.

Limpus flipped the sword and caught it. 'I did it! Thank you, Quizmal!'

Karl grabbed the stone and turned. He crawled back.

'Who are you?' Limpus asked.

Karl froze, raised his arms and turned around.

The sword point was under his right nostril.

Karl shuffled back, but the sword followed. 'I'm just a collector of stones like this lovely one. Definitely not a big fan of smelling the tips of swords, though.'

'Stand,' Limpus ordered.

Karl obliged.

'What shall we do with him, Quizmal?'

Limpus turned to Quizmal, whose face fell.

Quizmal reached into his pouch and took out the bottle of yellow liquid. 'Shall we make him smell this?' Quizmal opened the bottle and held it under Limpus' nose.

Karl stared at Quizmal and bit his lip. He had already created so much trouble for the poor old man.

Limpus inhaled. 'Oof. That's some powerful stink. Yeah, definitely make him…' He collapsed to the grass.

More guards appeared in the doorway.

'Quizmal!' one of them yelled. 'What are you doing?'

Karl put the stone in his pocket, picked up the sword and offered Quizmal an apologetic look. 'I'm sorry, Quizmal.'

'Who is going to give me light flies?' he asked, full of sadness.

'Not anyone here anymore, come on.' Karl pulled Quizmal's arm.

Quizmal groaned and followed Karl into the secret passage.

ICY STONE

The spiral stone steps went on forever. Karl and the others must have been below sea level. The light from the tree entrance had vanished long ago and Karl was going as fast as he could while feeling his way through the darkness.

'I promise I won't harm you. Please, untie my arms,' the old man requested.

Karl waved the sword in front of himself. It scraped along the wall. 'When we get to freedom. Not a moment before.'

'What do we do about Lamarza?' the lizard-girl asked the old man.

'When we can, we will return for her, I promise.'

A light appeared at what looked like the bottom of the tedious staircase, but growling accompanied it.

Karl stopped. 'Do you think that's a friendly growl or an "I'm going to chew your head" growl?'

Quizmal squeezed past Karl and sped towards it. 'Is it Goblo?'

Karl shrugged.

He followed and found Quizmal at the bottom of the steps feeding rocks to a dog-sized, round goblin in a cage. Goblo's belly glowed with each breath.

'What is that?' Karl grimaced.

Goblo growled at Karl.

'Nice to meet you, too,' Karl said.

Quizmal held the cage up. 'Is she a light goblin to illuminate Zianfer's escape? Do I come here and feed her every thirty-two sunsets?'

Karl nodded.

The lizard-girl approached the cage. 'Hello, Goblo. I'm Luro and this is Paliun.'

Goblo nodded and pointed at Karl. 'Idiot man?'

'My name is Karl, actually.'

'Idiot man,' Goblo repeated.

Karl huffed. 'We should hurry,' he told Quizmal.

Quizmal nodded and fed Goblo another rock.

Her belly shot a beam of light along the stony corridor that went on and on. One way.

The group ran.

Karl stayed at the back. Every time he glanced over his shoulder his heart felt as though it could explode.

In the distance, Goblo's light hit some stairs.

'Are we nearly there?' asked Quizmal.

Karl took a breath, relieved, his legs throbbing. Then he realised there would likely be hundreds of steps up.

A shriek echoed behind him, and a blue glow grew stronger. 'Keep running!' Karl yelled.

The blue light caught up with Karl.

'Smells bad,' Goblo grumbled.

They came to the bottom of the stairs. They'd never make it up fast enough.

'Please take Luro out of here,' Paliun told Quizmal.

Quizmal looked back at Karl, who nodded his approval.

Paliun held his arms out to Karl, the sack tied around his wrists. His eyes screamed seriousness. 'Please. Otherwise we're all dead.'

Karl cut the ropes and freed Paliun's hands. He looked over his shoulder and Bat Lover hovered towards them, held by her bat-humans. Their eyes glowed a deep blue.

Paliun sat on the floor, closed his eyes and pressed his hands to the stone floor.

'This isn't the time to meditate!' Karl moaned.

Paliun took a long breath. 'My wound slows me down, so you must grant me time.' He released a low hum.

Karl's stomach knotted and he puffed out his cheeks. He stood in front of Paliun and held his sword towards Bat Lover, more in hope than any kind of defiance.

The bat-humans lowered Bat Lover. She placed a hand under her chin and blew a thin line of blue mist that swirled and solidified into a spike.

Karl tightened his grip around the sword. 'Great.'

Bat Lover's eyes pulsed, and the icy spike shot at Karl. He leaned to his side and knocked it with his sword. It chipped against the stone wall and fell to the ground.

Karl took a breath and readied himself. 'Any progress back there?' he asked Paliun.

The deep humming intensified.

'I don't need terrifying sounds to go with this,' Karl said.

Bat Lover prepared another icy spike and shot it.

Karl blocked it again. 'This is going to be fine,' he told himself.

Bat Lover walked towards him and created another spike.

'You can stay back there. This distance works,' Karl said.

She created another spike, then another. She was about twenty feet away now.

Karl readied his sword, but how would he block three spikes?

Bat Lover's eyes throbbed, and the spikes flew.

Karl held his sword in front of his body, trying to cover as much as the thin blade was able.

Paliun leapt in front of Karl. Clumps of stone covered parts of his body. The icy spikes crashed against him. 'Stay back!' he ordered.

Bat Lover stepped closer, but Paliun raised his arms. 'Erato,' he whispered.

Rock arms burst out of the tunnel and grabbed Bat Lover's arms and her bat-humans.

The bat-humans screeched and scratched at the stone.

Paliun stretched his arms out, touched the stone walls to his sides and whispered, 'Terrana.'

The tunnel shook.

A small crack appeared above Karl's head and grew wider towards Bat Lover, who bit into the stone hand that gripped her left arm, her teeth grinding against it. It sent chills through Karl's body.

Blood poured out of her mouth and the stone broke.

Karl's heart clenched.

Bat Lover placed her hand under her chin. A blue mist swirled and covered the rocky restraints. She headbutted them over and over until they cracked then shattered around the bat-humans.

They lifted her by her hair and flew her towards Karl and Paliun.

'Avalanta.' Paliun pounded the walls and the stone ceiling collapsed on Bat Lover and the bat-humans. Purple seawater gushed into the tunnel.

Paliun raised a rock barrier to close off the tunnel, keeping him and Karl from being burned.

'You did it!' Karl sat back on a step and took a breath. 'Thank you.' Whoever this magic old man was, Karl was happy he was on his side.

Paliun turned around and blood dripped from his mouth. An icy spike was wedged into his stomach between clumps of rock. He stared at it and fell to his knees.

Karl's stomach tightened. He rushed over to Paliun.

A SMALL FAVOUR

'You need to slow down!' Karl called out.

Paliun stumbled through the forest, towards the base of a mountain.

The three setting suns resembled bloody eyes that wept a reddish glow over everything.

'He's right,' Luro said.

Paliun gripped the icy spike sticking out of his stomach and took a breath. 'Nearly there.' He walked up the mountain until he found a cave.

Quizmal lifted Goblo's cage and fed her a rock. Her stomach illuminated the entrance.

Paliun sat against the cave wall and wiped the sweat from his head. The rocks on his body shook then shrank. His normal form returned.

Luro grimaced. She rubbed her scaly, slimy forearm across her eyes. 'What can we do?'

'He's going to be okay,' Karl told her.

'Looks bad,' Goblo grunted.

Karl stared at the creature. 'Maybe stay quiet for a bit.'

Goblo spat on Karl's trousers, which was not the expected response.

Karl huffed and helped Paliun to remove his cloak.

Paliun took a breath and turned to Quizmal. 'At the base of some of those trees grows a mushroom. It's brown with a red line running over the top of it. Could you and Luro get me a handful, please?'

Quizmal nodded and followed Luro into the forest.

Karl stood over Paliun. 'Okay, so I'm going to pull that spike out and then cover the wound until they come back. Does that sound like a good plan?'

Paliun shook his head. 'There's no point. The arrow's poison is deep in me now, and with the magic from this spike... we don't have long before they meet.'

Karl swallowed and lowered to his knees. 'Your magic seems pretty strong.'

Paliun coughed. 'I'd need to connect my energy to clean water, but it will take us the night to walk to the nearest source.'

Karl buried his head in his hands. Surely there was a solution. 'What if I suck the poison and magic out? It's weird, but I'll do it.'

Paliun laughed, but then held his stomach and gritted his teeth. He exhaled. 'I need you to look after Luro. She's important.'

Karl nodded. 'I plan to find a place that isn't full of crazy people. I'll take her with me.'

Paliun shook his head. 'You have to take her to Ulago, the genius giant.'

Karl grimaced. 'What's wrong with a quiet village?'

'Ulago created a portal to the Land of the Living. Luro is needed in Hastovia to stop a great war.'

Karl's arms and legs tingled. He had been in this position before. 'Are you sure? I was once told I was from another world and that there was a portal home. Turned out the portal didn't exist and was made up to spare a kingdom embarrassment. Mages searching for portals was a cover for them to hunt my mother and I went through a lot of hassle before finding out is was all nonsense.' He clasped his hands.

Paliun nodded. 'Ulago, and the god of nature, Naturais, created a portal with a dragaur, Klarsa. It is deep within a maze. While nobody has seen Naturais or Klarsa in thousands of sunsets, Ulago is here and knows the way.'

Karl winced. 'Maze sounds dangerous.'

Paliun chuckled. 'It will be. Especially as Zianfer seeks the portal, too. Warn Ulago about her. If Zianfer has control of the portal, she will command both worlds and life and death will be miserable for everyone.'

Karl took a breath. It felt as though a boulder had been placed on his shoulders.

Paliun shuffled against the rocks and sat up higher. 'Luro is aware of her burden. It is for her to share or not, but please don't make her feel more of a hindrance.'

Paliun held his frail hand out to Karl. His skin was ice cold.

'Any chance you can teach me how to do that magic?' Karl asked.

Paliun chuckled.

Quizmal and Luro returned with a handful of mushrooms.

They handed them over and Paliun nodded. 'Thank you.'

'Will these make you better?' Luro asked.

Paliun coughed. He shoved a couple of mushrooms into his mouth and spoke through a mouthful. 'No, but it's a nice final meal.'

Luro's eyes reddened.

'We'll give you a moment.' Karl walked Quizmal and Goblo away.

Quizmal stared into the dense forest, torment etched on his face. 'What am I going to do? Should I go back and apologise? How will I get light flies?' he asked himself.

Karl leaned against a dull tree and watched him for a moment. Quizmal had risked his afterlife to help him. 'I'm sorry,

Quizmal.' Karl stabbed his sword into the soil. Maybe he could take his mind off things. 'You know, Questions always used to talk about the *Is This the Book of Tales?* you gave her, and she filled it in on many of our adventures.'

Quizmal welled up and glared at Karl. 'Do I care right now?' he shouted.

Karl stepped back and raised his hands. 'I'm sorry, Quizmal.'

Quizmal's eyes lowered. 'Am I sorry for shouting?'

Karl shook his head. 'Don't apologise. I wrecked your after-life. However, apparently there's a portal back to the Land of the Living. So, how about we go on an adventure and when you see Questions again you'll have some new stories for her to add to the book?'

Quizmal approached Karl and stared at him. Karl worried Quizmal might punch him.

Quizmal squeezed Karl's shoulder and nodded.

Karl put his hand on Quizmal's. 'I'll do all I can to make this right.'

They returned to the cave and found Luro hugging Paliun.

'Karl, I need you to do something,' Paliun said.

Karl huffed. 'You have a lot of requests, don't you?'

Paliun smiled. 'The stone. It's a mind stone.'

Karl shrugged. Those words meant nothing.

Luro reached her hand out and Karl passed her the stone.

Paliun lay on his back. 'It was created for people to hold onto the memories of a lost loved one. But evildoers thought a better use would be to steal the memories of people who had informa-tion they wanted, and to eradicate their minds.'

Karl shook his head. 'Of course.'

'The creature within can hold one person's memories at a time.' Paliun coughed blood. 'You can watch the memories in a fire. It's the person's most memorable moments from joy to pain. Don't judge my younger years. I was foolish.' He smiled.

Luro knelt by Paliun and held the sharp edge of the stone over his forehead. She hesitated.

Paliun closed his eyes. 'Don't be scared, Luro. My memories will guide you to the Land of the Leaf where you'll find a plant. Under the night suns, free the frozen berries to light the way. Then you will find Ulago and your way home.'

Luro tensed. 'I love you like a proper grandpa.' Luro dug the stone into his forehead and cut across it.

'I love you like a proper granddaughter.' Paliun squeezed her hand.

A weird-looking spider crawled into the bloody slit on Paliun's forehead. Karl winced.

'Disgusting,' Goblo said.

Karl nodded.

'Eel-spiders are a marvel,' Paliun said. His body jerked and his eyes rolled into his head. He foamed at the mouth.

The eel-spider crawled back out and vanished into the rock.

Luro wept and Quizmal put an arm around her.

Paliun's chest rose and fell, until it rose no more.

'We should turn around,' Karl said.

Everyone apart from Luro did. Paliun exploded into ash. Only his cloak remained.

Luro's silence was worse than a grieving scream. Karl had no idea what to say to her that would make this moment better. Nothing would.

He promised himself he would get them out of the Realm of the Dead, and he would find his way back to Sabrinia.

STONE RUSH

Zianfer stared at the secret entrance to the escape tunnel and took slow breaths.

She turned to Cyrilla, whose body and expressionless face were burned by the sea, but her eyes were drowned in anger.

One bat-human snapped the other's wings back into place. The creature shrieked.

Limpus stared at the grass.

Zianfer approached him and placed a hand under his chin. 'It is not your fault that people attacked you.' She hugged him. 'I'm sorry I wasn't here to protect you.'

His body shook against hers. 'Thank you, dear leader.'

Zianfer released him. 'For the next three sunsets I need you to double the load of purple nuggets. Then get the barrels on a ship to Port Larken.'

Limpus nodded. 'I'll make it so.' He left.

Zianfer turned to Cyrilla, who yanked a clump of her hair out of her head and fed it to the bat-humans. 'I leave for Port Larken. As soon as you're able to fly, find the thieves and bring me the mind stone.'

Cyrilla bit into her lip. Blood leaked out of it and ran down her chin.

HASTOVIA'S HOPES

Karl, Luro, Quizmal, and Goblo in her cage sat around Quizmal's campfire in a clearing. Rays of light from the three rising suns burst through the canopy as they watched Paliun's memories.

His childhood had been terrifying. He was trained to align his energy with elements by coming into contact with them.

An angry-looking old woman buried him alive and brought him to the brink of death before freeing him. She repeated it daily until Paliun was able to free himself.

Then she dunked his head in a lake until he faded, repeating it daily until Paliun was calm and could exist underwater.

Then she left him in a cage over lava until he was able to open the cage, swim through the molten rock and climb out of the volcano.

Next, she carried him into a tornado and held him in it until he could stand inside it alone.

Karl was thankful for his childhood of sitting around eating bread while poking sticks in mud.

He wished Paliun was with them on this quest. He would be much better than a sword Karl didn't want to use.

Paliun's life was full of travel and trouble. His traumas included him watching a teary-eyed woman and child walk away from him while he threw chopped wood and cups at them. He must have been kicked out of every tavern in Hastovia. At times he was so drunk his memories swayed and blurred.

He used his power over mud and rocks to build homes, and people loved him for it. He was celebrated, but it was all momentary. There was so much loneliness and moments sat on shores watching the sea. More often than not, interactions with people showed groups pointing and laughing at him.

In another memory, Paliun stared at his bare feet and shuffled towards the edge of a cliff, then he looked into the distance where fire ravaged a castle. He threw an empty bottle off the cliff and peered at the drop.

Karl's breath caught in his chest. 'Maybe you should look away, Luro.'

She ignored him.

Paliun leaned forward and fell towards the rocks.

Karl rubbed the back of his neck.

Paliun considered doing the same in the Realm of the Dead, but he spotted a girl running from a cyclops. He climbed down the peak, battled the cyclops and saved her. It was Luro.

Karl glanced at Luro, who stared at the fire, her eyes full of anger. Karl couldn't find the words, so patted her awkwardly on the back.

Luro ran her claws through the soil. 'Can I watch alone a moment? I'll tell you when it gets to the part with the map.'

Karl nodded. He, Quizmal and Goblo left and picked any mushrooms they found, staying close enough to see Luro.

'We can't be far from the water source Paliun mentioned,' Karl told Quizmal. He chewed a mushroom, which filled his mouth with a bitter taste. He retched.

Luro turned from the fire and wiped her eyes. 'It's coming up.'

Karl and Quizmal returned and watched the memories of a map being marked. Quizmal took Karl's sword and marked lines in the dirt.

Karl worked out where they currently were, and where a river was. They would need to travel along it and then through a forest until they came to a shore where they could see two mountains. Between them would be the entrance to the Land of the Leaf, whatever that was, where the plant Paliun had mentioned would be.

Luro watched the rest of Paliun's memories and then buried her head in her knees.

Quizmal threw dirt on the fire while Karl knelt next to Luro.

'It's my fault he's dead,' she said. 'He was trying to help me.'

Karl shook his head. 'You saw his life before he met you. You gave him meaning.'

She raised her head and smiled at Karl. 'It's hard to believe that at this moment. I'll get back to the Land of the Living and save Hastovia. For him.' She stood and wiped the soil off her trousers. 'I'll miss his stories the most.'

Karl stood with her. 'I had a friend who told lots of stories.' He smiled at the thought of Frong pulling on his filthy beard as he rambled through another tale. 'They were the longest, most boring stories you could ever hear.' He swallowed. 'And I miss them every day.'

Luro nodded.

'But that's how people are always with us, through the pieces of their lives that they share.' Karl swallowed.

Quizmal threw more dirt on the fire. 'Shall we go?' He rolled the stone on the grass and soil, then handed it to Luro to keep. She tucked it into a deep pocket on her trousers.

Karl stared at the map marked in the mud. 'Let's all try to remember this. River. Lots more forest. Shore. Split mountain. Land of the Leaf. Plant.'

The other two nodded. Quizmal handed Karl the sword, picked up Goblo's cage and they walked into the thick forest. Karl chopped at the branches that blocked their way.

He was unsure if he should ask, but it was probably important to know. He turned to Luro. 'I have quite a lot of people I care about in Hastovia, so, just out of interest – and I understand if you don't want to tell us – but, what exactly are you saving Hastovia from?' He hacked another branch out of their way.

'I'm a dragiant,' Luro said.

Karl turned to her. 'What you'll learn on this journey is that there are a lot of things I need explained to me.'

Luro opened her palms. 'The child of a dragaur and a giant.' She put her hands together.

Karl raised a finger and she nodded.

'A dragaur is half-dragon, half-human. And if you're confused, there are even more hybrids, like a drag-dog and dragoshark.'

Karl turned and chopped through a thick, rotten bush. It broke easily. 'I hope to never meet a dragoshark.'

'They only eat plants,' Luro reassured him. 'But why am I this symbol that I don't want to be? You see, giants and dragaurs were at war with each other for… well, always. Annoyingly, it came from a moment of peace. Dragaurs welcomed giants to their kingdom for a feast and the giant queen, Zubta, walked through a crowd. Her beautiful golden hair flowed and the dragaurs were thrilled to see it from so close. Then a drunk dragaur, Desmond, a true idiot who loved a boozy berry, hiccupped. A burst of fire burned Zubta's hair. She was so embarrassed that she threw a punch, but hit the wrong dragaur, who happened to be the dragaur king's son, who had snuck into the crowd. Broke his jaw, and so, hello war.'

Karl shook his head.

Luro sighed. 'And being big and usually clumsy, their battles damaged a lot of places and hurt people who had nothing to do with them. A stray breath of fire to the east and it's goodbye village of innocents.' She mimed smoke. 'A slightly inaccurate boulder throw to the north and it's farewell lovingly crafted castle tower and everything inside it.' She mimed crumbling.

'The nonsense of war.' Karl hacked another branch and paused a moment, his arm throbbing.

Luro reached for Karl's sword and he handed it over. She took the lead. 'Then finally, a giant and a dragaur used their brains for a moment and made peace. And better than that, they fell in love.' She hacked at branches. 'I'm the result of that love and I'm the next ruler, the only dragiant, supposed to keep the peace and all the things that come with being born into a duty you didn't ask to be born into.'

She carried the same curse of responsibility as Sabrinia.

She stopped. 'Listen.'

'What is it?' Quizmal asked.

'All I hear are leaves in the wind,' Karl replied.

She shook her head. 'Leaves sound crunchier, while rivers sound runnier. Plus, my ears are better than yours.' She waved the sword around to break through a cloud of annoying flies. She led the group slightly to the left. 'Anyway. Not everyone wants peace, because how can you show off your power with peace?'

Karl shook his head. 'Idiots everywhere.'

Goblo pointed at Karl. 'Idiot man.'

'Everywhere outside of this group,' Karl said to Goblo.

Luro choked up. 'When my mother was ill, it was a matter of sunsets before I would rule and keep the peace. But my aunt hated the idea of peace. She never got over a battle that wrecked her village and killed her husband. She read about history and how dragaurs were hunted by all other kinds of beings long before the Battle of the Burned Hair. She was broken by experience.' Luro stabbed the sword into a mushroom and bit it off the point. She offered another to Karl and Quizmal, but both shook their heads.

'Me,' Goblo said.

Luro fed Goblo. 'All I remember about my death is waking up with two swords buried in my stomach. I recognised the masked murderer as my aunt from her bone bracelet, and then she slit my throat.' Luro stopped a moment.

Karl exhaled. It was all so heavy. 'I'm sorry.'

Luro shrugged and continued hacking at branches but with a bit more anger in each swing. 'So, with Aunt Grausel in power, the giants and dragaurs are at war as we walk. But as soon as the dragaurs wipe out the giants, which they will – because, you know, breathing fire is a bit stronger than boulders and big fists, Grausel will turn her attention to all other parts of Hastovia. She's scared, so she needs to kill the fear. Which means people do as she says, or likely they will be burned. Your friends included. So yes, I need to get back and reclaim the job I don't want, so I can sit on an uncomfortable chair most days and tell people to stop being stupid.'

Karl's body numbed. The responsibility was suddenly a lot bigger, and he wished he hadn't asked.

'Can you breathe fire?' Quizmal asked.

Luro shook her head. 'Most of me is from the giant side. Only thing I seem to have gotten from the dragaur is my hearing. I can handle a bit of heat and I'm tall enough to grab fruit that's higher up a tree, which is useless in this place as it seems all we ever get are mushrooms.' She shrugged.

'Well, if we're going to help you get back, I guess it's important we stick together,' Karl said.

Luro nodded and handed the sword back to him.

Karl wanted to elaborate. 'So, we'll make thorough plans before we do anything and take group decisions.'

A blur rushed past, swiped Goblo's cage and ran into the forest.

Quizmal snatched Karl's sword and gave chase. 'Can you give back Goblo?' he yelled.

'Hey!' Karl complained.

Luro followed Quizmal.

Karl threw his arms into the air. 'That is not a group decision!' He ran after his companions.

TRUST YOUR TEAM

*T*he trio chased the creature as it scurried deeper into the forest. It had a baboon's body but a crocodile's head and kept clicking. Its red bottom was covered in crocodile scales and released puffs of green smoke as it ran.

Karl's eyes shot around the trees, hoping no more of these creatures would emerge.

Quizmal threw the sword at the croco-baboon but missed. 'Can you stop?' he asked it, but it ignored him.

Karl picked up the sword and continued chasing his allies.

The croco-baboon leapt and kicked itself off one tree to the next.

Karl gained on them, but a body smashed into Luro and fell on top of her.

'Luro!' Karl ran towards her, but she easily overpowered the person who crashed into her, rolled over them and pinned them. She wrapped her hands around their throat.

Freyu.

Karl's eyes widened and his chest rose and fell. 'You.' He held his sword to Freyu's neck. He hoped he wouldn't have to use it.

Freyu gazed at Karl, her one eye wide. 'Sorry… Karl,' she strained through the choking.

'Let her go, Luro,' Karl said.

Luro squeezed Freyu's neck tighter.

'Luro?' Karl said. She seemed in a trance. 'Let her go.'

Luro snapped out of it. She released Freyu, got up and stood by Karl, as did Quizmal.

Karl stared at Freyu. It wasn't her who had smashed his head, but she was friends with Rimala, and that didn't help her cause.

Freyu coughed. 'There's a pit. I was saving her. I'll prove it.'

Karl used the sword to gesture for Freyu to stand. He kept it pointed at her.

Freyu took a few steps ahead, knelt and pulled a net covered in leaves, sticks and mud towards her, revealing a pit about twelve feet deep. 'That croco-baboon is part of the group who took Rimala. It stole her–' Freyu looked at Quizmal and corrected. 'The hammer you gave Karl that we took from him. Rimala chased it and then–' Freyu pointed to the pit. 'Maybe we can help each other to get back the things we've lost?'

'That didn't go so well last time.' Karl turned to Quizmal and Luro. 'How much do you really want to risk your safety for the creature?'

Quizmal folded his arms. 'Did I risk my life for you?'

'We put her in danger by taking her,' Luro said. 'And we need all the allies we can get.'

Karl huffed. He lowered the sword.

Freyu smiled. 'There are a few more pits and traps, so follow my steps.'

Karl nodded and Freyu walked on. Karl turned to the others. 'It's not just traps we need to be careful of.'

PEACE BE WITH YOU

Karl crouched by Freyu. She pointed towards two huts on the riverbank.

Goblo, in her cage, was in front of the left hut.

Rimala emerged from the right hut with rocks tied to her ankles and wrists. She turned and tried to swing her fists at the middle-aged man behind her, but the rocks weighed her down.

The man poked an arrow into her back and made her kneel on the riverbank. He placed his hand over her face and raised his head to the heavens.

'Water worshipper,' Freyu said. 'At sunset they'll mortally wound her and offer her and your friend to the water, so it keeps flowing.'

Karl huffed. The bottom of the three suns met a mountain peak. 'If there are a few of these worshippers along the river doing this, doesn't it mean the water they drink has someone's blood in it?'

Freyu scrunched her nose and nodded. 'Not much makes sense here. Let's sneak up, kill him and save them.'

She edged forward, but Karl put his arm out. 'Wait.'

Three middle-aged women emerged from the other hut. One carried a sack with four small stones tied to it. Another had the croco-baboon on a rope, while the third held a curved sword and a roll of rope.

'Maybe we can do this without violence,' Karl suggested.

Freyu raised the eyebrow above her working eye. 'In the Realm of the Dead, it's serve death or eat death.'

Karl shook his head. 'Of course it is if that's what everyone keeps saying. How about, in the Realm of the Dead, it's serve conversation and find mutually beneficial ways to avoid death and serious injury?'

Freyu grimaced.

Karl placed his sword on the mud. 'Not the smoothest, but it's better. The first step is a grown-up discussion. Then, if things get out of hand, we try to knock them out and restrain them, so we can leave and they can reflect on their actions. If that fails, then yes, reluctant stabbing. But it needs to work in stages of seriousness.'

Freyu scratched her head. 'You won't last long here.'

The woman with the croco-baboon and the one with the curved sword walked towards where Karl and Freyu watched from.

'Just let me try something, okay?' Karl requested.

Karl waited in the pit. He tried to find a muddy spot that was clear of bloodstains from previous victims.

The croco-baboon's clicks hinted they were coming.

Karl took deep breaths. Now it was up to the others.

'Shut up!' one of the women said.

The croco-baboon continued its clicks.

'Maybe he has wind again,' the other woman slurred.

They stood at the rim of the pit and looked down at Karl. Their teeth were stained with the world's filth and their rags didn't cover enough of their sun-wrinkled bodies.

'Hi,' Karl said and smiled. 'How are you both?'

One of the women tied the croco-baboon to a tree. The other pointed her sword at Karl and spat at him.

He sidestepped it. 'Does that mean you're well, or that you're a bit under the weather and want me to check the consistency and colour of your saliva for abnormalities?'

The sword wielder turned to her friend and handed her the roll of rope. 'If there's any left, jam it in his yap.'

Freyu's forearm wrapped around the sword wielder's neck. 'Drop your weapon.' Freyu poked her sword point into the woman's cheek.

She dropped the curved sword.

Quizmal picked up the sword and pointed it at the other woman. She dropped the rope.

Luro took the rope and lowered it to Karl and pulled him out of the pit.

'Please don't hurt Doggy,' the slurring woman slurred.

Karl glanced at the croco-baboon and couldn't quite connect the logic. 'Doggy?'

'I wanted a dog as a little girl. Mama said no but kidnapped other kids for me to have as pets.' She shrugged.

Karl wished he hadn't asked. 'Doggy will be fine if you coop-erate.' He tied the women to each other.

Karl took the curved sword from Quizmal. He and his group marched the women and Doggy back to the river.

The middle-aged man used an arrow point to smudge muddy eyes onto his cheeks and placed the sack on Rimala's head, muffling her abusive shouts.

He walked Rimala into the river up to her thighs while the middle-aged woman carried Goblo's cage.

Goblo growled, but the woman shook the cage to quiet her.

'Hey!' Karl whistled to get their attention and walked towards them.

The man and woman turned around. On noticing their tied-up friends, the man pointed the arrow at Karl.

'Release my wives!' he commanded.

'I'll free your wives if you give me back that pet and the unnecessarily aggressive person with the sack on her head.'

The man turned to the woman.

She shook her head. 'The water demands an offering.'

'Does it really? Did it tell you that in those words?' Karl asked.

She shook her head at the man.

He pushed Rimala onto her knees. Water flowed at her neck.

Rimala, panicked and tried to stand up.

Karl nodded to Freyu, who pressed her sword against Doggy's neck.

Doggy clicked erratically.

Karl walked into the warm water. He pointed the curved sword at the man. 'If you kill her or that weird creature—'

'Rude,' Goblo interrupted.

Karl continued, 'You harm them, then your wives and you will become the next offering. We could even kill you right now, but my offering to the water is a peaceful exchange with no blood.'

The man looked at the woman again. She stared at Karl and his companions, and her look shifted from anger to defeat. She nodded.

The man pulled Rimala out of the water and walked her to the riverbank. The woman placed Goblo by Rimala and stood back.

The man removed Rimala's sack. Her eyes burned and she tried to bite at him.

He stepped back. 'Bring me my wives.'

Karl walked out of the water and stood between his friends in the forest and the water worshippers on the riverbank. He nodded to Quizmal, who brought the women and Doggy forward.

Karl jammed the curved sword into the soil to mark the middle ground. 'There. Now send the creature and the grump to me.'

The man hesitated, then pushed Rimala towards the sword.

Rimala stared at Karl. On spotting Freyu, her hardened shell showed a crack of relief.

The man picked up Goblo's cage and approached the line, but walked beyond it.

Karl pointed at the man. 'Too far.'

The man stared at Karl a moment, stopped and placed Goblo's cage down.

'Now go back,' Karl said.

The man wouldn't move.

Karl held his palms up. 'We have a deal. No blood.'

The man walked backwards, but kept his eyes on Karl.

Karl glanced at Goblo and smiled, hoping this marked progress in their friendship.

'Idiot man,' Goblo said.

Clearly not. Karl sent the women and Doggy back to their lives. He pulled the curved sword from the mud and nodded at the water worshippers. They nodded back.

Karl lifted Goblo's cage while Rimala dragged herself to Freyu.

'See, Freyu.' Karl smiled, relieved they had avoided bloodshed.

'Maybe you're right.' Freyu smiled back at Karl, then hugged Rimala. She cut the ropes that bound Rimala to the rocks.

Karl joined Quizmal and Luro. He took a big breath. 'Right, let's keep going.'

Quizmal beamed at Goblo.

'Rimala!' Freyu yelled.

Karl turned around.

Rimala, armed with Freyu's sword, charged at the water worshippers. She chopped the man's head off and sliced the unarmed women across their backs. 'There's your offering!'

Freyu pulled Rimala's arm, but Rimala shoved her away.

Doggy clicked at Rimala. She beheaded him and kicked his limp body towards the water.

The dead all exploded into ash.

Karl trembled and threw up.

PORTAL HUNTERS

Karl and Luro stood in the river and drank water under the sunsets. It should have been refreshing, but Karl was too angry to enjoy it.

'It's kill or be killed,' Rimala said.

Karl stared back at her and at Freyu behind her.

Freyu avoided his gaze.

'Not all people are awful and should be hacked to death,' Karl said.

Rimala chuckled. 'Then you've not met enough people.' She walked towards the huts.

Freyu approached Karl. 'I'm sorry.' She hesitantly placed a hand on his shoulder. 'She's obsessed with revenge. Anything that gets in the way or tries to is seen as a threat.'

'That doesn't make it okay,' Karl said.

Freyu nodded. 'You should get as much water as you can to drink and to trade. It's this realm's gold. Then get away from here before someone else comes to set up camp.'

Karl nodded his appreciation.

'I'll search the huts for anything to carry water,' Luro said.

'Thanks,' Karl replied.

Luro walked towards the huts. It hit Karl how this journey would be full of casualties. Was it worth going home if he had to kill others to get there? Was Luro really that important to Hastovia? Maybe she had oversold her role.

Karl approached Quizmal, who knelt over a bucket of water and stared into it. Quizmal's bottle of light flies was by him. He cried.

Karl looked into the water. Questions and Oaf walked through the middle of Reech with their children. Karl's heart filled with hope.

'Is that you?' Quizmal asked.

Karl noticed a sculpture in the background. Oaf had sculpted Karl and his friends.

A warmth filled Karl's body. 'Yeah, it is. But he's not really captured the definition in my arms.'

Quizmal chuckled through his snotty tears. He wouldn't take his eyes off the water. 'Am I scared?'

Karl placed a hand on Quizmal's back and looked around at the trees and the unknown. 'It's okay to be scared. But we'll be okay.' He gave Quizmal his privacy.

Luro emerged from a hut with a couple of waterskins and buckets. 'Not much else in there.'

Karl searched the other hut. There were bloodstained fur mats on the floor, a bowl of rotten berries, Quizmal's hammer and a jar with three light flies.

Karl left the hut and approached Rimala, who washed in the water. He held out the jar of light flies, hoping a peaceful offering would chip away at the shell of misery and rage. 'Do you want one? You can check on your loved ones in the Land of the Living.'

Her eyes met his. 'I've nobody to watch.' She turned away.

Karl remembered how he felt when Arazod killed his mother. The boiling hatred inside him. Even now when he thought about it, the residue of revenge remained, never to be washed away. 'I had a friend in my last life who was obsessed with revenge.'

Rimala dipped her hair in the water and ran her hands through it.

Karl stared at the light flies. 'He was an Oaf, the last of his kind, after his mother and entire village were slaughtered by a man named Lord Ragnus. Miserable beast of a man with stone fists. Oaf vowed to be the first of his kind to ever kill and he hunted Lord Ragnus for years.'

Rimala splashed her face with water. 'Did he get his revenge?'

'He did, but he didn't kill Lord Ragnus. He threw him off a cliff that causes petrification.' Karl thought about it a moment. 'Not too dissimilar really, but it meant Oaf stayed true to his people. He didn't sacrifice who he was for that awful mess of a man. He found a new way to live. He found someone to share his life with.'

Rimala nodded. 'That's a lovely story.' She squeezed water out of her hair. 'But I'd appreciate it if you stopped boring me with your tales.'

She walked towards Freyu.

What a miserable idiot.

Karl returned to Quizmal and gave him one of the light flies and his hammer. He offered a fly to Luro.

She stared at the jar a moment and twisted her ear. 'I'd rather not know. If my aunt is killing everyone I'll rush and get us killed, and if she's dead I'll get lazy thinking everything is okay.'

Karl chuckled. 'You're very wise for someone so young.'

'Or you're not so wise for someone so old.' She grinned and scratched the scar on her shoulder.

Karl nodded. 'Good point.' It was nice to see a real smile in this world of misery.

Luro's face dropped and she held a finger up.

Karl stared at her.

Her eyes widened. 'Chirps. Hide.'

'I don't hear anything,' Karl said.

Luro pulled on her superior ears. She nodded up at the darkening sky at a shadowy figure.

Bat Lover.

THE BEST LISTENER

Luro, Karl, Quizmal, Freyu, Rimala and Goblo gathered in one of the huts.

Luro counted the gap between bat-human chirps.

Everyone else stared at her, their eyes full of confusion.

She gestured for them to stay silent. They needed to follow her lead.

Karl scratched his head and Luro glared at him. She froze to make the point that they needed to stay still.

Karl nodded apologetically.

The chirps quickened. Luro's head throbbed. She closed her eyes to squeeze the pain out, but it got worse.

Chirp… chirp… chirp.

She opened her eyes. Karl's face wore concern.

Goblo frowned and covered her ears.

Luro opened her palms and gestured calm.

The chirps continued as though a sharp fingernail repeatedly poked her head.

Something splashed in the river.

Everyone else heard that. Rimala reached for the curved sword, but Luro waved her finger.

Rimala glared back as though she was going to ignore Luro, but Freyu caught Rimala's gaze.

Rimala rolled her eyes and froze.

She seemed the kind of person who would only bring trouble and chaos.

Footsteps slapped on wet mud. The group's eyes shifted between each other.

Sweat formed on Luro's brow and she had an itch she wanted to rip out of her shoulder scar. She focused on her breathing.

The bats screeched and Quizmal's eyes welled up.

Luro held her finger up again and hoped the group would trust her to remain still.

What would she do if the monster appeared in the hut door? The chirps were deafening and the screeches worse.

Everyone's eyes stayed on Luro. This was her situation to control. She wished she were powerful enough to fight her way through it. She wanted to kill the demon. Thanks to her, Paliun was dead and her chances of getting what she wanted were in the hands of much weaker beings.

The demon must have been only steps away. Luro had to decide. Would they attack or wait?

Rimala met Luro's eyes and drew them to the sword.

Luro opened her palm. She would either wave her finger or point to the sword.

The chirps grew sharper, the screeches more piercing. It was as though a hurricane bashed around inside Luro's head. She tensed, trying to remain still. Her breathing quickened and she was about to scream.

Then the chirps, and screeches stopped. The footsteps stopped shortly afterwards.

Rimala tilted her head at the sword again. The demon was close.

If they attacked, they might get the upper hand. But Luro couldn't risk their lives here. She wouldn't risk anyone unless there was no choice. She needed the numbers to get to that portal.

She waved her finger, and everyone waited. She hoped it was the right choice.

Rimala gritted her teeth.

The demon's breaths filled Luro's ears. Maybe she needed to let Rimala attack. Losing her wouldn't be the worst thing.

One more breath and she would indicate to the sword. She stared into Rimala's eyes and was about to nod, but the breaths stopped.

The chirps started again and faded away.

Luro fell to her knees, wiped the sweat off her brow and dug her nails into her scar.

Everyone stared at her.

'She's gone,' she said.

Relief filled the tent.

Freyu looked out of the hut then turned to Rimala. 'It's best to camp here for the night then leave at sunrise.' She turned to Karl. 'You should do the same. We'll keep watch.'

'What?' Rimala said, irritated.

'They saved you. We owe them,' Freyu replied.

'Thanks,' Karl replied. 'But maybe me and you keep watch. I'll be a lot more comfortable if General Grump is asleep.'

ONE TEAM TWO DREAMS

Karl and Freyu sat by the river. Karl clutched his sword and Freyu kept the bow and arrows handy.

Luro paced. She seemed bothered by what had happened, as if she doubted herself.

Karl picked some dirt off his boots. Keeping watch was boring, but boring was better than terrifying. 'So, why do you follow the Lord of Happiness around?'

Freyu dabbed water on her burned, scarred eye. 'She saved my life, so I guess you could call it dumb loyalty.'

Karl nodded. 'Just don't get yourself killed for her problems.'

Freyu stood and stretched her arms behind her. 'Once she kills Messiro she's promised we'll find a village and live a calmer life. There's a great person behind the rage and sword swinging. Sadly, as she gets closer to Messiro that person makes fewer appearances.'

Karl bit his lip and leaned back on his elbows. There was no way he, Luro, Quizmal and Goblo would make it through this weird world alone. 'I think we might be going the same way but for different reasons.'

Freyu nodded.

'Do you promise you won't let her knock me out again?' Karl asked.

Freyu shrugged and smirked. 'I can promise I'll try to stop her.'

The suns rose above the mountains and the group gathered on the riverbank to fill their waterskins.

Karl and Luro had shared their stories with Freyu and a less interested Rimala. The mention of a portal meant nothing to her. It was all about revenge.

Quizmal wet his hand and stroked his three red hairs against the side of his face. 'How's my hair?'

Karl nodded. 'Still there.'

Quizmal smiled appreciation and carried Goblo's cage to a tree stump and fed her a mushroom. Her stomach glowed. 'Would you like to be free?'

'Cage boring,' Goblo said.

Luro knelt by the cage and opened it. 'Be free.'

Goblo ran into the forest without a goodbye.

'You're welcome!' Karl called out after her.

Quizmal smiled in Goblo's direction as she disappeared.

Rimala strapped on her quiver of arrows and picked up her bow.

Karl handed his curved sword to Freyu and the other sword to Luro.

He picked up a rock for himself. 'Let's get away from here.'

Freyu pointed into the forest. 'Best to stay away from the river and keep under the trees.'

They followed Freyu.

Luro scratched her shoulder again.

Quizmal reached for his tool belt. 'Do you want an ointment?'

She shook her head. 'It's fine, thanks.'

Goblo scurried back to Luro. 'Got no friends. Come with you.'

Luro lifted Goblo onto her shoulder. 'Of course you can.'

Karl shook his head. 'You got scared, didn't you?'

Goblo spat at him.

'Spitting is not okay!' he moaned.

Goblo spat at Karl again.

Quizmal stifled a laugh.

Karl folded his arms. 'You shouldn't encourage her.'

Rimala huffed. 'Less moaning, more moving.'

Karl swallowed his annoyance and they all continued. 'I can actually move and moan at the same time.'

Karl thought about his friends in Hastovia. He wished they were with him, but then he wished they weren't, as being with him would mean they had died. He swallowed his sadness and hoped he could find something similar in this group.

He doubted it.

DIRECTIONLESS

Zianfer paced Port Larken's storeroom.

The giant, beaten up, his wrists and ankles chained, refused to speak, but his heavy breaths suggested he may talk soon.

Zianfer grabbed two fingers from his large right hand and squeezed them. She stared up at his eyes as the bones cracked.

The giant's groans echoed around the room and he fell to his knees.

'How do we get through the stone forest?' she asked.

The giant wept. He yanked at the chains but couldn't break free.

Zianfer turned to Messiro. 'Has he answered anything?'

Messiro shook his head. 'Not even his name.' Messiro dipped his bloody knuckles in a bowl of cold water. The blood clouded the liquid.

Cyrilla pushed the storeroom doors open and approached Zianfer.

'Hopefully you have better news?' Zianfer asked.

Cyrilla shook her head.

Zianfer huffed. 'We can't delay.' She turned to the giant. 'Tell us how to find Ulago's home, or others will suffer.'

The giant smiled through his blood-covered teeth. 'You will never find her. The stone forest will drive you mad.'

Zianfer turned to Messiro. 'We will find a way. Make a symbol of suffering out of him.'

Messiro seemed hesitant. 'There is no need.'

Zianfer glared at Messiro. 'It is his fault some of our own will suffer. So he must suffer, too.'

ONE-WAY PATH

Karl and the group walked, walked, then walked some more. The only time they stopped was to rest for the night and to find a discreet bush in order to go to the toilet.

It had been four sunsets of the same routine. The only variety was in the noises. Grunts, growls, squeaks, and screams. Each made Karl nervous, but luckily he had avoided anything horrible.

Everything about Karl stank. His clothes, his hair, his breath. Whenever he blinked a waft hit him and he wondered if eyes could stink, too. Was this the smell of death or just being unwashed in the heat and filth for so long?

His legs throbbed and the trees never ended. The same brown and dull green leaves. He forgot if any other colours existed.

'Keep pushing,' Rimala said in her charmless way.

Was there any point? Zianfer would be days ahead and probably had found the giant, the portal and was relaxing in Hastovia sipping on some ale. She likely didn't even drink ale. Maybe she preferred the blood of rare creatures to soothe her throat.

'Why does the Realm of the Dead exist?' Quizmal asked.

'I don't know,' Karl said.

'Why not?' Quizmal pressed.

'Because nobody told me.' He pulled a branch out of the way.

'Why?'

Karl huffed. He could see where Questions got her curiosity from. 'Because I know very little.'

Quizmal nodded and stared at him a moment.

Karl hoped that would be enough.

'Why do you know so little?'

Karl sighed. 'You should ask Rimala. She'll know.'

Quizmal walked over to Rimala and Karl chuckled to himself.

Thankfully, Freyu distracted Karl for a lot of the journey. She taught him more about this stupid realm. The reason the sea burned was because a dragon born of rot and sickness decided to make the sea its home. Its every breath released heat and hot air bubbles, polluting the water.

In Hastovia the dragon existed in the open, but it was hunted and killed. So, it seemed sensible that the dragon protected itself here by living underwater.

Freyu also taught Karl that dragons all had one scale that was the source of their power. Not everyone knew of it, but her village was built on the magic of one and that's why many hunted the beasts.

Freyu was a world student in her past life. Well, a thief who stole books to learn about Hastovia and its history. But world student sounded less thief-like.

The ground shook.

Freyu pulled Karl to the side.

'Afterbirth!' Freyu called out to Rimala, who rushed over and nocked an arrow.

Soil and grass sank and a paw emerged from a muddy hole.

Karl stepped back and a horned wolf's head squeezed through the soil. It growled and scratched against the dirt. It emerged into this world, like Karl had when Bat Lover found him.

Rimala released the arrow into the wolf's neck and an ash explosion followed.

Karl's heart clenched. It was bad enough having to navigate this miserable land, but if random creatures could emerge anywhere, it made things twice as awful.

What if they were asleep in a cave and a man-hawk emerged?

They walked on and Freyu sipped from her waterskin. She shook it above her mouth, but nothing came out.

Karl offered her his waterskin, but she seemed apprehensive, as though it were a trick.

'I'm sure,' he said.

Her eye welled up and she drank. 'Thank you.' She handed it back.

Karl took a sip.

Luro stopped. 'I hear water. Lots of it.'

Karl turned to Freyu. 'My gesture feels a bit meaningless now.'

Freyu chuckled.

They followed Luro to the edge of the forest, finally. Mud met stone and then stone took over. They stood on a horseshoe-shaped cliff. Across it, water gushed down into a river. It snaked towards the sea but split off. One path continued into the sea, where it fought with the purple water, while another path routed fresh water into a reservoir.

A port town with guard towers surrounded the reservoir. Two ships were docked. People loaded barrels onto one and it left the dock back in the direction of the Sea Spike.

The other ship remained.

The town was almost as busy as the Sea Spike, and people wore armour made from the nuggets Karl had spent sunsets picking out of the burning water.

The town blocked the path towards the split mountain in the distance.

'Is there another way?' Karl gazed around the horseshoe cliff, but they would have to climb up a mountain and back down to get around the base.

Freyu shook her head. 'It's too dangerous up there.'

Karl pointed at the packed town. 'More dangerous than people with weapons who love a crazy person?'

Freyu pointed at the top of the mountain. 'Air webs.'

Karl squinted and made out what looked like small clouds with stringy, dangly bits. There were hundreds, all the way along the mountain.

'Touch one and you're temporarily paralysed. Body totally numb,' Freyu said.

Karl shrugged. 'Temporarily doesn't seem too bad.'

'Then an air-webber swoops down and feasts on you. It's like a bald albatross with spider legs. A fascinating creature,' Freyu said.

Karl hoped to never see one.

'I'm not sure if being numb to it makes it better or worse,' Freyu added.

Karl grimaced and spotted Bat Lover flying around the mountains. 'An awful option just became impossible. Guess we go through the town. Maybe they'll welcome us as travellers.'

Rimala stared at the place.

Freyu approached her. 'We'll rest and sneak through the base at night.'

'What if Messiro is there now?' she said.

Freyu took Rimala's hand. 'Then you won't get to him. If the tower guards don't stop you with their arrows, then those with swords and axes will. Please, Rimala.'

Rimala pulled her hand away, took a breath, walked towards a tree and sat on the ground. She folded her arms and rested her head.

Freyu turned to Karl. 'I suggest you all get some rest. I'll be on Rimala watch.'

Karl nodded and studied the town. He hoped they could avoid bloodshed, but was worried Rimala would slaughter anything that stood in front of them.

DRIVEN BY DARKNESS

Karl struggled to rest. He had struggled the entire journey, always on edge, waiting for either Bat Lover to swoop down and eat his head or a creature to emerge from the soil and eat his feet.

How could everyone else sleep so easily? Luro snored with the mind stone in her hands, Quizmal drooled, and Goblo had a grin on her face and her eyes wide open. It was probably some kind of animal thing to terrify predators. Freyu, who was meant to watch Rimala, was asleep stood against a tree.

Even while asleep, Rimala seemed grumpy.

How would they beat Zianfer? They were outnumbered by her followers, plus Zianfer was stronger than everyone, and Bat Lover had whatever that weird magic power was. Karl hadn't seen much of Messiro, but assumed if he was in that group, he was probably unnecessarily strong and violent.

Maybe it would be better not to look for the portal. He had had his time in Hastovia. Why should he get another chance while other people might not?

He stood, picked up his waterskin and crept to the edge of the cliff. The mountain rocks glowed under the night suns. It would be beautiful if everything wasn't so terrifying. He poured the last drops of water from his waterskin onto the cliff to form a small puddle.

He took the jar of light flies from his pocket, opened the lid and removed one. He cupped the yellow creature in his hands and imagined Sabrinia. The fly's bumps glowed orange. It flapped its wings, flying out of Karl's hands and shooting into the puddle.

As the image of the Land of the Living formed, the fly rushed through the sea and burst high into the night sky. Karl recognised none of the setting this time.

The fly descended. Flames tickled the horizon and tents formed around a gigantic pit. Hundreds of people dug, watched by armoured guards.

Karl hoped his friends weren't enslaved.

Knights on horses rode out of the camp. The fly buzzed between them and then dipped left into a forest.

It weaved between trees and slowed down by a lake. Sabrinia, Frong and Marlens slept. Death kept watch and drank ale alone. He might have been sad, or that might just be the way his face always was. He raised his pouch of ale to the fly and drank.

Karl was relieved they were okay, and that Death was with them. By saving Death from Ryza's command, they had gained a powerful ally.

Karl's heart was heavy, though. Watching Sabrinia was both beautiful and terrifying. He wanted to be there. He feared the next time he sent a light fly it would find her in danger, or worse, not find her at all.

He watched her sleep for a while and was glad nothing happened. It was peaceful. The fly flickered and disappeared.

Karl buried his head in his hands. He needed to get back to Hastovia. He just hoped his friends were alive when he got there.

He raised his head and Rimala was staring down at him.

'Let's talk,' she said.

Karl followed Rimala further along the cliff and sat on a rock opposite her. She gazed at him and took a breath, then leaned back on her rock.

'The person you watch in the water. You love her?'

Karl's eyes welled up and he nodded.

'Messiro killed the one I'd like to watch.'

Karl swallowed. 'I'm sorry.'

'I was born into a stupid community,' Rimala said. 'It was so stupid that we all have 'mala' at the end of our names. Me, Rimala. There was also Simala, Timala, Limala, Bamala. The place was even called Sagmala. It's totally pointless and nobody could tell you why it was the case. Nobody bothered to question it.' She laughed. 'It's just a beach town in southern Hastovia, but there were so many rules, traditions and expectations. May as well have been a beach prison.'

Everywhere seemed terrible for different reasons.

'Our ruler was a proud idiot. A shrivelled man desperate for control. His wife ran away with another woman, so he decided rules were needed, so that old ugly men could keep their wives and their power.'

Karl shook his head.

Rimala clenched her fists. 'His main rule was that he chose who married who. Supposedly to keep community balance. He wanted me to be with some fool called Jasmala. The man was useless. He tried to make a fire but set his trousers ablaze. Then he ran into the sea to cool off, but it was peak jelly-shark season and one bit his right buttock off.' She laughed.

Karl grimaced and shuffled on his rock.

Rimala bit her lip and gazed at the dark sky. 'My parents obviously adored him. They were told they had to. But I loved someone else. My neighbour, Mamala. When I spoke to her, it was the first time someone wanted to know me. She taught me that I was someone beyond the person Sagmalans wanted me to be.' Rimala leaned forward and ran a hand through her hair.

'She sounds like a good person,' Karl said.

'The best person. She had a saying. "Show me a man who doesn't get confused when thinking, and I'll show you a donkey with a head made of cheese."' She chuckled.

Karl folded his arms. 'I've seen weirder things, so that man likely exists somewhere.' He pointed to himself and smiled.

Rimala chuckled. 'We snuck out of town one day and visited the hot spring.' She stared at the stones beneath her feet. 'Had our first kiss.' She grinned. 'The heat between us made the hot spring jealous.'

Karl chuckled and remembered his first kiss with Sabrinia. It was buried in nervousness and then relief that she didn't punch him in the throat.

Rimala stood, planted one foot on the rock and leaned on it to stretch. 'I told my parents I wanted to marry Mamala and they were surprisingly supportive. My mother asked the elder and his face turned redder than a tomato dipped in blood. He said Jasmala was my destiny and shamed my parents as failures. They turned on me and demanded I marry Jasmala.' She shrugged. 'I told them where they could shove destiny and I ran away with Mamala.'

'I'm glad you escaped the misery,' Karl said.

Rimala gazed off the cliff. 'We were sixteen and travelled Hastovia looking for a new home. We learned a lot together. How to bargain. How to fend off bandits. How to suffer. How to hunt. Who to trust. But the best thing we learned was that it didn't matter where we were. We, together… we were home.'

Karl swallowed the lump in his throat.

'At twenty-four years old we built a hut by a lake and felt settled in the world.' She scratched the back of her neck and said nothing for a moment. She coughed and turned back to Karl, tears in her eyes. 'One night, three idiots attacked us. They were drunk and pathetic, so I roughed them up but spared them. Then I went out to collect some berries.' Her voice cracked. 'When I returned, Mamala was on the grass, neck snapped. No breath.'

Karl exhaled into his fist.

The hatred returned to Rimala's face. 'There was a note from my parents. It simply read: "Come home." I found the three idiots. They confessed that a scarred man was looking for people who fit mine and Mamala's descriptions. I killed them and returned to my village. First, I drowned the elder.' She clenched her fist. 'Then I marched my parents into the sea and aimed my bow and arrow at them. They tried to say it was for my own good. I shot my father in the throat and then my mother spoke. She told me where they had hired Messiro from. I dragged my mother out of the water, shut her in her home and set it on fire. For ten years I searched for the scarred murderer.'

Karl sat forward, his body dull with sadness.

Rimala sharpened an arrowhead against a rock and threw it to Karl. He fumbled it.

'I didn't even speak to Messiro,' she said. 'He washed his murderous, scarred body in a river, and I hid behind a tree. I shot him through the back of the neck, then sank ten more arrows into his body to make sure.'

Karl sharpened the arrowpoint against his rock.

Rimala's eyes met Karl's. 'My life's mission was done. What else was there? I tried to live normally. Fishing, farming, building, but she's always in my head. Everything reminds me of her, because we shared so much. And anything we didn't share reminds me of her, because I want to share it with her.' Rimala took an arrow from her quiver and dug the point into her finger. 'I took a knife, walked into a river and slit my throat. Bled out, carried along the river staring at the sun. It felt good and final. Then I appeared here. So, that meant the people who broke my heart must be here. I found my parents again. I marched my mother off a cliff and my father took a deadly bath in the burning sea, but his screams didn't sound painful enough. Now Messiro must die again. He doesn't deserve one life, let alone two.'

Karl nodded. 'But what if Mamala is here?'

Rimala shook her head. 'I always ask if anyone fitting her description has been seen, but it's easier to find bad people. They leave a trail of misery.' Rimala gritted her teeth. 'It's time to attack.'

Karl nodded. 'Thank you. For sharing.' He turned to walk back to the others, but Rimala grabbed his arm. She squeezed it and turned him around.

Hatred swept over her face. 'Now you understand. If you get in my way, I won't hesitate to go through you.'

AN ALMIGHTY HEADACHE

'It's very empty,' Freyu said, confused, returning from scouting the base.

Karl poked his head out from behind the rocks. Nobody in the two guard towers, and nobody at the open iron gate. 'You're sure?'

Freyu pointed to the top of a guard tower.

Rimala held up four fingers and pointed to the far end of the base.

Freyu raised her hand to Rimala then turned to the group. 'So that's four guards by the exit we need to go through. And probably some inside buildings we can't check until we're closer. Let's go.'

Rimala climbed down the tower and vanished behind the wall.

There was something scarier about a relatively empty base.

'Are we walking into a trap?' Quizmal stared ahead.

Freyu shook her head. 'The ship's gone, so most of them must have left.'

Luro scratched the scales on her neck. 'It's uncomfortably quiet.'

Had Zianfer taken her army to Ulago?

Freyu led them to the open gate, her curved sword across her chest. Karl followed with Quizmal close to him. Luro stayed at the back, her sword held out to the side and Goblo on her shoulder.

'Feed me,' Goblo said.

Quizmal gave her a rock. She crunched through it, but her stomach didn't light up.

Karl placed his hands on the cold stone walls and peered into the base. Barely a flame's flicker. Rows of wooden dwellings spread like moss and a reservoir filled the distance. Three more guard towers marked the perimeter and a large building that must have been for meetings and dining dominated the bottom of the cliff.

The stone paths were an upgrade on the mud that characterised the Sea Spike.

Freyu called the group in. 'There are four of them, and six of us.'

'Five and a half.' Goblo nodded at Karl.

Karl folded his arms.

Freyu pointed to a second path to their left. 'Karl and Quizmal, you take that path. Me, Luro and Goblo will take the one on the right. We'll approach the four guards from both sides, and with Rimala in the tower, they'll have no chance.' She handed Quizmal her sword and took his hammer.

Karl raised a finger. 'Can we try to capture them instead of slaughtering them?'

Freyu nodded. 'In the Realm of the Dead, it's serve conversation and find mutually beneficial ways to avoid death and serious injury.'

Karl smiled. He and Quizmal crept along the pathway, close to the dwellings. Karl peered in a window, confirmed it was clear and then they moved to the next.

They approached the end of the path and the laughter grew.

Four guards in leather armour sat around a mat and flicked pebbles into a bottle. Their weapons were piled on the mat. Beyond them was the path to the shore and the mountains.

Rimala, in the nearest guard tower, pointed to the other path. Freyu stepped out of hiding.

Quizmal pointed his sword forward, as did Luro. Freyu held the hammer against her hand while Karl raised his palms.

'Hi there,' Karl said. 'Looks like a fun game.'

The guards turned and reached for their weapons.

'Please don't,' Karl warned. 'By the time you grab them, at least two of you will be dead. Actually, three.' He pointed to the guard tower.

Rimala took aim, but Freyu held an arm in the air.

Three of the guards looked towards the smallest one. He stood and they followed. He was as high as Karl's shoulder.

Karl pointed to Rimala. 'She's an incredibly angry, unreasonable person. Move and she'll fire an arrow into your face. I don't want that and I'm sure you don't. So, step away from the weapons, get on your knees and put your hands on your heads, please. We'll tie you up and be on our way, then whoever comes back here will help you. Sound good?'

The small one turned to his fellow guards and nodded. 'That does sound good, actually.'

The other guards agreed.

Karl smiled. 'Thank you for being reasonable.'

'But killing you sounds better.' The guard crouched, grabbed his sword and thrust it towards Karl's stomach.

An arrow pierced the back of the guard's neck and the sword fell at Karl's feet.

Everything spun and Karl's heart hammered his chest. Before he could regain his composure, all four guards were down, arrows in each of them and they exploded into ash. Freyu picked up one of their swords.

Rimala nodded at Karl.

'Is everyone okay?' he asked, catching his breath.

Goblo ate the bottle of pebbles.

Luro pointed behind Karl. Quizmal's eyes widened, panic on his face.

'What?' he said.

He turned and something heavy whacked the side of his head. It was as though something exploded inside his skull.

Everything faded.

Karl's vision blurred. He touched the part of his head that throbbed, and blood covered his fingers.

The clanking of metal, whooshing of swords, piercing of arrows, and cries of angry people clogged his ears.

Karl pushed himself to his knees and his vision started to take shape. Words barely formed in his mind and he couldn't speak.

He swayed and fell. As his vision cleared, a guard rushed towards Luro.

Karl scrambled for a sword from the pile on the mat and staggered forward. He weakly wedged the sword into the guard's side.

His energy left him. He fell onto his back and breathed heavily. The ash that exploded over him confirmed he had ended someone's existence. The guard's leather armour slapped the stone floor.

Another guard stood above Karl and smirked. The guard lifted his sword.

Goblo leapt onto Karl's chest and blasted light into the guard's face then ran off.

The guard stumbled and blinked repeatedly, feeling around. Luro grabbed his hair and yanked him to the floor. She slit his throat and his afterlife exploded into ash.

Luro breathed heavily.

Karl's left eye felt as though it might burst. 'Thank you.'

She nodded and the grunts of battle calmed.

Rimala stood above Karl. 'Welcome to the reality of the Realm of the Dead.' She crouched and picked up a chain whip with a steel ball on the end of it, then walked away.

Karl guessed the blood on the steel ball was his.

Freyu pulled Karl to his feet. 'We should probably patch that up.'

Quizmal wept above a smashed jar where light flies used to be. 'How will I see you?' He touched his head to the stone.

Karl put a hand on Quizmal's shoulder. He reached into his pocket, but broken glass cut his fingers. He pulled out shards of the jar and dead light flies. 'I'm sorry, Quizmal.'

How was he going to know if Sabrinia was okay?

Quizmal sat back, defeated. 'How will I see Questions?'

Karl knelt in front of him, avoiding the glass. 'I promise you we'll see her in person.'

Quizmal didn't respond.

Freyu grabbed Karl's arm. 'Come on.' She glanced at the others. 'We all smell like a donkey-hippo's toilet bucket. Let's wash and see what we can gather. Ideally weapons, food and obviously water.' She sniffed herself and shook her head. 'And hopefully some new clothes.'

Rimala lashed the chain whip at a larger guard's back. He screamed into the night. 'I need to do something first.' She marched the guard towards a wall.

'Rimala!' Freyu called out, but Rimala ignored her.

Freyu walked Karl through Port Larken and to the reservoir. Most of the dwellings were empty and they mostly found junk, but among that junk were some orange trousers, undergarments, a tunic, a needle, some thread, boots, honey, sheets, and some bread. Finally something other than mushrooms.

'It feels like my brain's broken,' Karl groaned.

They approached the reservoir. 'You're lucky it was a wonky swing. It only clipped you.'

Karl shuddered at the thought of what full contact would have done.

Freyu dropped the tunic, orange trousers, undergarments and bread on the stone floor. 'Sit.'

He did and placed the other items down next to them.

Freyu tore the arm off her tunic, leaned over the side of the reservoir and dipped it in the water. She dabbed it against his wound then rubbed honey into it.

He winced and closed his eyes to combat the stinging. 'This is horrible.'

'You're welcome.' Freyu chuckled.

A scream filled the night. No doubt Rimala making friends.

Freyu tutted. 'This bit's going to hurt.' She showed Karl the needle and thread.

'Can't we just leave it open?' he asked.

Freyu held his head. 'Stay still.'

Karl's skin pinched and he was thankful he couldn't see it. He thought about the man he had killed. Probably just trying to find his place in Zianfer's world, too.

Freyu tore an arm off the new tunic and placed it on top of Karl's wound. She bit some thread and tied it around his head and chin, keeping the bandage in place. 'Done,' she said. 'Now get washed up but keep that head dry.' Freyu removed her clothes and dived into the reservoir. She came up for air. 'Goodbye, dirt!'

Karl watched her float for a moment. He didn't feel comfortable taking his clothes off, but he was wearing what felt like a damp carpet. He stood, but hesitated.

'Don't be shy,' Freyu said. 'We're all dead. Who cares what anyone else thinks?' She drank the water as though she was some kind of sea creature.

Karl laughed. 'You could at least turn around.'

She smiled and did.

Karl removed his clothes and lowered himself into the reservoir, keeping his head dry. He scooped some water into his mouth. Even with his dirt in it, it was delicious. The night sun's rays bounced off the water and reminded him of the Land of the Living. It was the first thing that didn't feel tinged with death.

Freyu swam towards him. 'How's the head?'

'A lot better, thanks to you.' He rubbed water over his face and scrubbed the dirt off. 'I guess you're right. In the Realm of the Dead, it's serve death or eat death.' He huffed.

She chuckled. 'Maybe we just need to adapt it as we go. Let's try: in the Realm of the Dead, it's serve non-fatal wounds and offer peace or a violent death.'

Karl chuckled. 'I think that wins for now.'

Freyu's eye locked onto Karl's. 'Thanks for reminding me that the world doesn't have to be full of hate.'

Karl swallowed. 'You, too.' He smiled, but guilt attacked him. He couldn't be happy without Sabrinia. 'Let's get going before more guards come.' He swam away.

Luro rushed up the reservoir's edge. She squeezed the back of her neck. 'I've found some… things.'

Her shaking suggested they weren't good things.

A PEST FOR ALL REALMS

Over twenty swords pinned the giant to the storeroom wall.

Blood ran down his body. His eyes flickered and he groaned.

'Do you think that's Ulago?' Karl asked Luro.

Luro shook her head. 'Paliun said Ulago has white hair and a dragon bite on her neck.'

'Seems Zianfer thinks other giants may point her the right way,' Freyu added.

Karl approached the giant. 'Will you let us help you?'

The giant groaned. 'Please, kill me.'

Not the kind of help Karl wanted to give. 'Is there anything you can tell us that might help us?' he asked.

The giant shook his head. 'Ulago's instructions always carry a mystery.'

Karl scratched his right eyebrow. 'Anything specific?'

Blood dripped from the giant's lip. He screamed.

Karl's heart ached. 'Okay. What's the most painless way to kill you?'

The giant released a long breath. 'A sword through the heart will do just fine. But you have to push it deep.'

Karl swallowed. Freyu offered him her sword. He stared at it. 'I'll do it,' Luro said.

Karl was relieved. 'Yes, you're taller, so you can get a better angle. Good thinking.' He turned to Freyu. 'Let's step back to avoid the ash explosion.'

He and Freyu stepped away.

Luro marched up to the giant.

Karl thought he heard Luro whisper something, but he couldn't be sure.

The giant's eyes widened and the sword jammed into his heart. His face filled with anger before he exploded into a cloud of ash that covered Luro.

She walked past Freyu and Karl. She seemed angry. 'I'll go and wash.' She left.

The giant was a pile of ash on a giant pair of trousers. Such a waste of a majestic creature.

Karl studied the room. The racks were mostly stripped, but some weapons, clothes, and armour remained. 'Let's take what we need and get out of here.'

Karl grabbed a cuirass. The breastplate and backplate were made from the purple nuggets he had spent sunsets hammering a pickaxe against. 'Not really my colour.' He put it on. It was light and the nuggets cooled his bare chest and back. There must have been hundreds of cuirasses before, but now only three remained. He offered one to Freyu, but she declined.

Karl dropped it and took a short sword. He noticed a loose purple nugget on the floor. He picked it up and rolled it in his thumb and forefinger. Frong had told him he used to collect the weird and wonderful stones of the world. He felt they brought him luck. Maybe Karl could give this one to him when he got back. Hopefully it would bring him some good fortune. Karl placed it in his pocket.

'Hello,' Freyu said to a belt of throwing knives. She strapped it on and picked up some arrows for Rimala.

Quizmal rushed in with Goblo. 'Did I find prisoners?' He jangled keys.

Karl and Freyu followed Quizmal into a hut. He opened a trapdoor.

The stench knocked Karl back. 'Might have to have another dip in the reservoir.'

Goblo stopped. 'Don't like.' She ran off.

The others climbed down the stairs into a cellar with a long tunnel of cells built into the stone walls. There must have been over forty. Each contained a prisoner with a sewing needle, thread, and barrel of purple nuggets. They sewed pieces of nugget armour together. Chest plates, trousers, and giant blankets of nuggets.

'We'll free them one by one,' Karl said. 'That way they won't try to attack us.'

Freyu agreed and walked on with Quizmal.

Karl passed a cell when feathers caught his eye. He stopped. Heat surged through his body and his neck tensed. Everything around him muted. He pictured his mother's dying face. He stared at his hands and imagined her blood seeping through his fingers again.

Arazod, curled up on the stone ground, gazed up at him.

He was pathetic, broken, hopeless.

Karl's breaths quickened and his chest could have cracked from the pressure.

Arazod coughed. 'I'll understand if you leave me.'

Leave him? Karl wanted to open the cell and strangle him.

Arazod turned away and rested his head against the wall. 'I'm sorry, for everything.'

Freyu and Quizmal returned to Karl. 'Are you okay?'

Karl grabbed the cell bars and squeezed them so tight his knucklebones could have ripped through his skin. He kept his eyes on Arazod. 'This is the man-hawk who killed my mother. Then helped his sister, Ryza, to kill my friend. Then he took over my home and slaughtered hundreds. He also enslaved Fools and had his miserable ally crush a lionbear's head. Oh, and he forced the woman I love to marry him. Is there anything I'm forgetting, Arazod?'

Arazod nodded. 'I also stopped Ryza burning Oaf's child and saved the day.'

Karl wanted to twist Arazod's beak off. His annoying wheezing seemed to be gone, probably because his wings worked again.

Freyu placed a hand on Karl's shoulder. 'Rimala would stab him through the face.'

Karl swallowed the lump in his throat. Every time he looked at Arazod he saw his own failings. Arazod was a symbol of all that was wrong in his life.

'Bring him to the docks,' Karl said and left the cellar.

RELEASE THE PAIN

Karl knelt on the dock and shoved Arazod's face into the wood.

Arazod groaned but didn't struggle.

'Karl…' Freyu placed her hands to her mouth.

Quizmal grimaced.

Karl stood, placed his boot on Arazod's rope-bound wings, and poked the short sword into the back of his neck. 'We've been in this position before.'

He could end Arazod's second life now and stand in his ash explosion. Last time he let him go it only caused more death.

'I'm truly sorry, Karl,' Arazod coughed.

Karl gritted his teeth. Arazod's apology was as useful as a sandwich made of dragon dung. He kicked Arazod's ribs.

Arazod rolled onto his back. His eyes met Karl's.

Karl shook. He hated this lack of self-control.

He searched for the hatred in Arazod's eyes, but there was nothing. That crazed burning Karl was used to seeing had been extinguished by a cold sadness.

He could jam the sword right through him. Push it deep and pin him to the dock. But then he was no better than him. Maybe it was what Arazod wanted: an easy escape from this rotten world.

Karl pulled the sword away. He cut the rope from around Arazod's chest. 'Get up.'

Arazod rolled to his side and pushed himself up, surprised.

Karl aimed the sword at him. 'Go away. If I ever see you again, I won't spare you.'

Arazod stared at Karl for a moment, then flapped his wings. He hovered above Karl.

Arazod coughed. 'I wish I could take some of my deeds back.'

'Go away!' Karl threw his sword at Arazod, but he flew to the side. The sword splashed into the sea.

Karl's body trembled and his eyes burned. 'Just go away!'

Arazod nodded, turned and flew away.

Karl questioned whether he had done the right thing. He knew his mother and Sabrinia would be proud of him, but it didn't make the pain go away.

'You're a good person, Karl,' Freyu said.

'Am I proud of you?' Quizmal added.

Karl wanted to hit everything. 'Let's get out of here.'

They freed the remaining prisoners. Many decided to stay and guard Port Larken, making it their new home.

Karl returned to the storeroom to get a new short sword. On exiting he found Luro stood in an alleyway staring at the ground, her claws covered in blood.

'Luro? You okay?' He noticed two piles of ash and leather armour in front of her. How did she take two guards on?

She turned. 'Yes. I… after I washed I was attacked. I was fortunate.'

Karl nodded, glad she was fine. 'We're going.'

The group gathered all they needed, from weapons to a barrel of water.

They found Rimala stood over a chained, weeping, bloody

guard. No part of his body had avoided a lashing from the steel ball.

Karl retched.

'Messiro left sunsets ago,' Rimala said. 'He's gone with Zianfer to find the genius giant and today a hundred townsfolk took the ship to join them.'

If Zianfer found Ulago and killed her before they got there, this would all be worthless. Karl doubted they could beat Zianfer in this race, but they had to try. They had to move.

TRIAL AND ERRORS

Zianfer leaned against a stone tree and faced a forest of more, shrouded in mist. Cyrilla flew above it. Hopefully she'd find a solution.

Guards and followers erected tents in the entrance. They would not leave without Ulago's knowledge.

She gazed into the haze, and it stung her head. She stepped back. 'The way to a better life is in this mist. Who would like to be remembered as the one who found the way?'

Nobody volunteered.

She scratched behind her ear.

Messiro approached. 'The leader who sets an example is the leader people will follow.'

He was getting too opinionated, and it annoyed her that he wouldn't make the giant suffer. She didn't like having to do it herself.

'He's right!' a follower said. 'Lead us, oh leader!'

Her followers cheered. Instead of the buzz it normally gave her, she tensed. She couldn't refuse now.

She forced a smile and nodded. 'I will show you there is nothing to fear.'

She entered the stone forest and the mist closed around her. Everything blurred behind the grey and a dull whistling gripped her mind.

The campfire faded as she walked on, but the mist thickened and the whistling intensified. Her nose bled and she was certain white eyes stared at her. She ran back the way she had come and her head throbbed.

Breathing heavily, she stopped against a stone tree. She removed an arrow from her quiver, shredded the bottom of her robe, and cut her thigh.

She stumbled back towards the campfire and burst out of the mist.

'Zianfer!' Salmat ran towards her.

'I'm fine,' she said. 'The mist is just an illusion to help wolves. They're only small but one scratched me.' She approached a table and picked up a potion jar. 'Whoever finds the entrance will have their choice of kingdom when we find the portal.'

Salmat took a sword from a rack and walked into the mist. 'No pesky wolf will harm my leader!'

Several more followers took up weapons and followed.

Zianfer wiped the bloody arrowhead against a cloth.

Messiro stared at her and she smiled back at him.

A MUDDLED MIND

Arazod's wings felt as though they had sacks of sand tied to them. He had no idea where he was flying to, but it was away from where he'd been captured. He could barely keep his eyes open and his wings flapped slower.

The three suns warmed his body, but hunger clouded his thoughts. He'd fly up the mountain ahead, get a view of everything and rest.

His wings struggled. He willed them to keep flapping, but they slowed and so did his mind.

Everything faded and he fell towards a tree.

'What do we do with him?' a woman's voice asked.

Arazod's eyes fluttered open. A shaking old man pointed a dagger at him. An old woman, by a fire, roasted a cut of meat from the wounded croco-baboon at her feet.

'Food?' Arazod asked.

The man turned to the woman. 'Could eat him, too?'

Arazod didn't have the energy to defend himself.

The woman shook her head. 'We've got all this and there ain't much meat on him. A couple of cuts and he's dead.'

The man nodded. 'Your lucky day.' He returned to the woman. She handed him the sword with the meat on it and he took a bite. 'It's great!' He kissed her.

'Beats mushrooms.' She took the sword, ate some meat and nodded her approval. She approached Arazod and held the sword out.

He hesitated, so she shoved the sword closer to his face. 'I won't offer again.'

He pecked at the meat and swallowed. 'Thank you,' he strained.

She pulled the meat off the sword and dropped it into Arazod's claws. 'Enjoy, then be off with you.'

She returned to the croco-baboon. She carefully sliced some meat from the back of its left leg, and it shrieked. She pierced the meat and held it over the fire.

Arazod ate until he felt like he could move without passing out. He stared at the man who had suggested they eat him.

He could rake his eyes out. Or one eye to teach him a lesson.

He caught the thought and scratched his neck. Why did he need to harm them? They had helped him. He could fly away and leave them in peace.

He dug his claws into the soil.

Hurting the man was an urge. A hunger only blood and the high of dominance would satisfy. He stood and stared at the couple, their backs turned. It would be an easy way to get some practice.

His feathers shook. He squeezed his eyes shut and tensed, trying to force the urge out of himself.

He opened his eyes and stepped towards them.

LEAFY HELL

*K*arl woke up to screaming. He felt as though he were imagining it, but the screams became clearer and his heart thumped.

Rimala was berating someone. Probably a leaf for falling on her big toe.

Karl wiped the sleep out of his eyes and stumbled towards the anger.

Rimala aimed her bow and arrow at Quizmal, who was on his knees, weeping.

'We'll die of thirst!' she moaned.

'Am I sorry?' Quizmal blubbed.

Karl stood in front of him and faced Rimala. 'What are you doing?'

'We've got no water thanks to him!'

'Rimala…' Freyu said.

Rimala gritted her teeth and fired an arrow into the tree behind Quizmal. 'We'll never get anywhere with idiots.'

'Couldn't agree more.' Karl stared at her, then noticed the piles of ash with arrows on them around Quizmal.

Karl knelt by him and held his wrists.

Quizmal trembled as though he was freezing. 'Did they say they had light flies? Did they say they would swap them for water?'

Karl's heart ached. He had ripped Quizmal from a life where he had what he needed, which was simply to see his daughter. Now he was a sweaty mess, addicted to light flies.

'Did they lie and attack me?' Quizmal asked.

Karl nodded. 'It's okay.' He glanced at Freyu, who grimaced.

Karl grabbed his waterskin. 'We still have a waterskin each. We'll just have to drink less frequently. And we'll find you more light flies. Don't worry.'

Quizmal shook his head. 'Can we avoid them? Do they muddle my mind?' He buried his head in his hands.

Karl placed a hand on Quizmal's shoulder. This was his fault.

They travelled another two sunsets through more forest and then along the shore. Karl never wanted to see another forest again. The shore was so much better. Breezy, open, and danger was easier to see from further away.

He could also see if Arazod approached. He'd ask Rimala to shoot him out of the sky.

If they made it back to Hastovia he would avoid all forests for at least three hundred sunsets.

When they made it back to Hastovia. When.

The only downside to the shore was walking past eternal water that they couldn't drink. It was as though the Realm of the Dead knew they were thirsty and wanted to tease them.

They arrived at a perfectly sliced line in the mountains. It was the tallest, narrowest, straightest path Karl had ever seen, as though something the size of a world had cut it with a gigantic sword.

They squeezed through in a single line. Karl hoped there

wasn't some sort of cruel creature living at the top of the walls whose favourite hobby was dropping rocks or pouring burning seawater onto those below.

He shuddered at the thought of being back in that water.

The end of the path opened onto an endless sea of white leaves. It would have been beautiful if it didn't stretch so far with nothing else in sight. Every direction he turned, it was leaves and nothing.

Karl sighed. 'I hope the plant is really tall.'

Goblo heaved the white leaves into her mouth. 'Not good.' She threw up.

Karl grimaced. 'Under the night suns, free the frozen berries to light the way. Luro, do you hear anything?' Karl asked.

She stopped and listened. 'Just leaves in the wind.'

Leaves crunched under Karl's steps. 'Sorry to keep asking. It's just a lot more calming when I know there's nothing.'

Luro shrugged. 'The silence is scarier. Means there could be something I can't detect.'

Karl hadn't thought of that. Now he was terrified.

'Why are all the leaves white?' Quizmal asked.

Freyu raised a hand to block the suns. 'These are all dead leaves. We explode into ash. Leaves lose their colour and turn this stony, empty white.'

Everything was so bleak.

'Why are there so many?' Quizmal asked.

Freyu shrugged. 'There's a theory that there's a place called the Forest of Gales in Hastovia, and that the brutal winds carry leaves all the way to a desert where they die. Here is where they are reborn to die again. So, I guess you could call it a leafy desert.'

Karl picked up a leaf and rubbed it between his thumb and fingers. It crumbled. So fragile, like everything here.

'Follow me,' Luro said. 'Paliun's map showed it being this way.' She walked to the north-west.

The leaves vibrated underneath Karl. 'Another afterbirth?' But the movement halted. 'Maybe not.'

'Sometimes that happens,' Freyu said. 'Likely the afterbirth of an insect.'

Karl removed his nugget armour and carried it. The three suns baked his body, and his trousers were like damp sheets wrapped around his legs. He worried his head wound was cooking under the bandage still wrapped around his face.

He dragged his feet through the leaves. The constant crunching became tiresome.

'Anyone else seeing little silver spots?' Freyu asked.

Karl handed her his waterskin. 'Finish it. Sorry that it reeks of my dry mouth.'

She smiled and drank.

Quizmal stepped forward but the leaves gave way and he fell.

'Quizmal!' Karl ran towards the hole.

He hung by his right hand. Beneath him leaves fell into an endless darkness.

'Am I scared?' Quizmal said.

Karl grabbed his forearm. 'I've got you.' He strained but needed help.

Luro knelt and helped to pull Quizmal out.

'Am I okay?' Quizmal asked, pushing himself to his feet.

'Thankfully,' Karl said. 'This is going to sound weird, but we should hold hands. I'll go first and I'll leave my left hand behind, which one of you can grab. That way, if there's another death hole I know I'll get pulled out.' He put his nugget armour back on to keep his hands free.

'I'll go second.' Freyu grabbed Karl's hand. 'I'm probably the lightest here after Goblo.'

Then Quizmal, Luro and Rimala followed.

Goblo climbed onto Luro's shoulder.

'We look like a weird dance troupe,' Karl said.

Freyu chuckled. 'What would we be called?'

Karl kicked some leaves up. 'The Leafy Losers?'

'I'm not a loser,' Rimala grunted from the back.

'You're welcome to suggest something,' Karl said.

'I don't indulge in nonsense,' she replied.

Karl huffed. 'Just trying to lighten the mood.'

Freyu laughed at him.

They walked on, deeper into the endless leaves, now up to Karl's knees. He stopped and squinted. Something formed on the horizon. 'Is that a plant?'

Whatever it was moved.

Freyu tried to work it out. 'Hornet-vulture.'

'What's that?' Quizmal asked.

'I have no idea,' Karl said.

'Why?' Quizmal asked.

'Because I'm seeing it for the first time in both my lives,' he said. 'Don't ask why.'

Quizmal bit his lip.

Karl felt bad. Quizmal had asked more questions than usual over the last few sunsets. It was probably his way of distracting himself from thinking about light flies.

Freyu coughed. 'It shoots spikes from its beak that make people drowsy. Then it waits until the sun warms its victims up so it can have a nice meal.'

'Let's avoid that, then,' Karl said.

Luro shook her head. 'We can't if we want to see the flower it's next to.'

'Of course.' Karl wanted to cry.

There it was. The lone flower standing tall next to its hornet-vulture companion.

Rimala took an arrow from her quiver. 'I'll handle it.' She sprinted towards the beast.

'So, we're no longer worried about endless holes under the leaves?' Karl asked.

The others backed Rimala up. As they neared, the hornet-vulture spotted them.

It shrieked. Rimala's arrow pierced its neck and it choked on its cries. It flew into the air but crashed back down next to the flower. It vanished beneath the leaves.

Rimala nodded. 'Simple.'

Karl studied the stunning flower. It had seven berries of different colours. Blue, white, yellow, red, orange, purple and black. A worm-like creature with two tails was frozen inside each berry. 'What is this?'

Goblo stood by Karl's legs and pulled on his trousers. 'Hungry.' She reached for the plant and held her mouth open.

Karl waved her away. 'No, Goblo. Not for eating.'

Rimala kicked leaves at Goblo. 'Go nowhere near the plant, pest.'

Goblo growled at her.

Freyu touched the berries. 'I've never seen or heard of anything like it.'

'Under the night suns, free the frozen berries to light the way.' Karl stared at the berries. 'Maybe we pull the berries off. That's freeing them, right? Ulago needs to think of better mysteries.'

Leaves vibrated around Karl's ankles. 'Anyone feel that?'

Freyu waved it away. 'Probably the hornet-vulture's ash explosion.'

Karl shrugged and stared at the three suns. 'I guess we wait until night now.'

And that's what they did.

The suns disappeared beyond the horizon of leaves. The leaves shone with such beauty that Karl wished he could share it with Sabrinia. The Realm of the Dead did have its moments.

The night suns rose, and the berries glowed, like small colourful eyes.

Karl repeated Paliun's line. 'Under the night suns, free the frozen berries to light the way.' He pulled the purple berry from the plant and held it to the night suns. The worm creature within it glowed but nothing happened. 'Free the frozen berries. Free the frozen berries.' Saying it over and over didn't change anything.

Quizmal approached the berries. 'Are these drupes instead of berries?'

Karl shrugged. 'I don't think that matters.'

Rimala huffed. 'Hurry it up.'

Karl tutted. 'Thanks for your helpful contribution.' He turned to Luro. 'Did Paliun ever say anything else?'

She shook her head. 'It's what an old goatman boatman told us. He was about to reveal what it really meant but he tripped over his oar, fell into the water and was eaten by a snake-shark.'

Karl grimaced.

Goblo reached her hands up. 'Hungry.'

Karl shooed her away. 'No, Goblo.'

Rimala aimed an arrow at her. 'Last chance.'

Luro raised a finger. 'Wait. I think I hear something.'

The leaves exploded and swirled around them in a giant column. Dust and filth blinded Karl.

He coughed. His eyes stung as though tiny pieces of glass were stuck in them. He wiped and wiped but it didn't help.

'Don't rub your eyes. Keep blinking!' Freyu shouted.

Karl blinked over and over.

Something sharp pierced his calf. He screamed and fell into the leaves.

'Karl!' Freyu called out.

He sat up and squeezed his wounded calf. His vision slowly returned. He hoped he was imagining it.

A kangaroo's body, but an ostrich's legs and three ostrich heads. What in the Realm of the Dead was that? It was about three times Karl's size.

Rimala shot an arrow into its skinny left thigh.

The creature shrieked and turned on her.

An ostrich head reached into the creature's stomach pouch and spat green chunks at Rimala.

She dodged, but smoke rose off the chunks and trapped her in a cloudy cage. Her body twitched and she fell into the leaves.

'No!' Freyu threw knives at the beast's pouch. Green sludge leaked out of holes and burned the leaves.

The monster spat at Freyu.

She dived into the leaves and resurfaced away from the green smoke, but into a swinging ostrich head.

Quizmal sliced the creature's heel. He hacked it again. It buckled but recovered and kicked him away.

Goblo ran to Quizmal and was kicked into the leaves.

Karl's calf bled on the white leaves. He hopped on his foot. 'Hey! Fight me!' He picked up leaves and threw them in the creature's direction, but the leaves blew back into his face. He sighed.

Luro slashed the animal's wounded heel. It shrieked and fell to the side. Luro stabbed it in the thigh.

It spat on Luro's chest and she screamed. She fell into the leaves.

Karl trembled. Please be okay.

The creature limped after him and he hobbled away. It was perhaps the worst chase ever in the history of both realms.

Karl turned and threw his short sword at the large target but still missed.

One of the heads grabbed Karl in its mouth and lifted him. He was helpless.

Another head bit the rim of its pouch and pulled it out. Dark green ooze bubbled and smoked. It was as though someone had jammed cloths used for cleaning toilet buckets into Karl's nostrils.

On Karl's imagined list of how he might die, melting in a bizarre creature's stinking stomach pouch hadn't even made the top fifty.

The kangaroo-ostrich dropped Karl towards the bubbling

ooze, but something grabbed his ankle and threw him into the leaves.

The creature shrieked.

Karl caught his breath and rose to his knees. He lifted his head.

Arazod.

The man-hawk swooped and snatched Quizmal's curved sword. He hacked an ostrich neck, taking a chunk out of it. The other heads pecked at him, but he flew around them.

The beast became tangled in itself.

Arazod chopped at its wounded leg.

All three heads spat at Arazod. He blocked with the sword. Smoke rose from the blade and burned his hand. He dropped the sword and raked his talons down the creature's eyes.

It shrieked and spat.

'A sword, Karl!' Arazod called out.

Karl froze, not sure what to do. Anger filled him.

'Karl! Hurry!' Arazod yelled.

The beast spat more and untangled its heads.

'Hey!' Luro threw her sword to Arazod.

He caught it and drove the blade into the base of the beast's necks, one by one.

It fell forward, its wounded eyes staring at Karl, mere feet away.

A head lashed towards Karl. He fell back.

The beast's eyes faded, and its body exploded into ash and covered Karl.

He coughed and wiped the ash off his face. 'It's like a final insult, isn't it?' A sludgy green pool burned through the leaves.

Karl rose to his knees. He turned around and his heart sank.

The flower was nothing more than a torn stem. With its final bite the beast must have ripped the plant from this realm.

Karl yelled into the nothingness.

IT'S COMPLICATED

$\mathcal{A}$razod stood above Karl. He reached his claw out to help Karl up.

Karl's eyes burned. He kicked Arazod's claw away and dug around in the leaves around the plant's stem, hoping to find a surviving berry.

'Let me join you.' Arazod's feathers fluttered. 'Or I'll follow you and help you when you inevitably come close to death… again.' Arazod walked over to Quizmal and helped him up.

Karl pushed himself to his feet. His calf stung from the bleeding bite. He reached his hand out for the sword and Arazod handed it over. Karl pointed it at him. 'This realm is huge. Can't you go and die on the other side of it?' Karl felt Quizmal's disappointed glance.

Arazod's beak twitched.

Karl expected Arazod to rake his talons down his chest. He wanted him to try, to show everyone his true ways.

Arazod sniffed. 'Give me your waterskins. I'll go and fill them.'

Karl scoffed. 'I'd rather die of thirst.'

Luro handed Arazod her waterskin. 'Thank you.'

Not the united stance Karl was hoping for.

'Can you get me some, too?' Quizmal handed his waterskin over.

Freyu approached and handed hers and Rimala's waterskins to Arazod. She offered Karl a sympathetic glance.

Arazod nodded. 'I'll be back soon. Karl?' Arazod pointed to Karl's waterskin.

Karl turned away. Leaves blew past him and the flapping of wings faded.

'Is Rimala okay?' Karl asked Freyu, desperate to move on.

Freyu nodded. 'She's mumbling about crushing Messiro and her arms are moving. Just temporary paralysis.'

Luro approached Karl. 'Wings could prove useful.'

Karl shook his head. 'He could be the most powerful being in the Realm of the Dead and I'd still tell him to fly into the three suns. If you want me to continue this journey with you, when you get your water we're done with him.'

Luro nodded.

Rimala stood. 'Figured out the berries yet?'

Karl gestured to the non-existent plant. 'Welcome back.'

'You idiots.' Rimala's eyes bulged.

Karl couldn't be bothered to engage with her.

The leaves shook around him. 'If that's another weird kangaroo-ostrich thing I'm going to let it eat me.'

Goblo burst out of the leaves and climbed onto Luro's shoulder. 'Found leaf treasure.'

'Good for you,' Karl said. How were they supposed to find the genius giant?

Rimala stretched and fired an arrow into the distance. She rotated her neck. 'So what now? I need to find Messiro.'

'Leaf treasure,' Goblo repeated.

'We heard you, Goblo,' Karl said.

'I think you should look, Karl,' Luro said.

Karl turned. He could have burst into tears.

Goblo had three berries on her palm. Yellow, blue and red, the frozen creatures inside.

'Goblo, you brilliant little thing.' Karl stretched out his hand. 'Pass them over.'

Goblo smiled. 'Hungry.' She threw the berries into her mouth and swallowed them.

Karl wanted the leaves to swallow him.

'Stupid creature!' Rimala punched Goblo off Luro's shoulder.

Luro shoved Rimala. 'Don't touch her.'

Rimala grabbed Luro around the throat. 'Know your place, scale face.'

Karl stood between them and pried them apart. 'Let's calm down and not accidentally hit me.'

Quizmal pulled Luro back.

'Pathetic bully!' Luro screamed.

Rimala threw Karl out of the way, but Freyu grabbed her arms.

'Calm down, Rimala,' Freyu said. 'Calm down.' She grabbed Rimala's face.

Rimala grasped the tops of Freyu's arms. 'That creature has been useless all along. All it does is eat, expel things from its holes and make weird noises.' Rimala threw Freyu to the side.

Karl stood in front of Rimala and raised his palms. 'To be fair, you just described any one of us.'

Luro pointed at Rimala. 'I'd rather be surrounded by a thousand puking Goblos than you.' She looked around. 'Goblo?'

Quizmal released her. 'Where are you, Goblo?'

Rimala smirked. 'I hope she gets eaten.'

Karl shook his head and turned to Luro. 'Let's look for her. Freyu, you stay here with Captain Happy.' He pointed at Rimala. 'If you want to release your rage, shoot an arrow into the feathered idiot if he comes back.'

❄

Karl and Quizmal trod carefully through the leaves.

'Where are you, Goblo?' Quizmal called out.

Luro disappeared into the distance, taking the west side. Freyu and Rimala became distant specks.

The shift from baking hot to biting cold made Karl worry he was getting sick. 'Hopefully she fires some light into the sky and we'll see her.' Leaves consumed the land in all directions.

Quizmal nodded and kicked some leaves.

Karl didn't want to talk about Arazod, but he wanted to justify himself. 'That flying pest destroyed my life.'

Quizmal nodded. 'Is he trying to help now?'

Karl scoffed. 'He offered to help before, then he knocked Sabrinia unconscious and gave his psychopath sister a gauntlet that shot fire. Because that's what psychopaths need: the ability to burn things that irritate them.'

Quizmal gazed at the leaves. 'Did I want revenge once?'

Karl swallowed.

Quizmal kicked more leaves. 'Did Questions' mother, Quizetta, leave us? Did she find a man who didn't ask her so many questions?'

'Questions never mentioned her mother,' Karl said.

Quizmal nodded. 'Did I spend a thousand sunsets being angry? Did I spread lies about her mother? Did I make Questions dislike her? Did I want to harm Quizetta and her new lover?'

Karl scratched the back of his neck.

'What did that anger do?' Quizmal asked. 'Did it make her or the man suffer? Did it make me suffer? Did I become the negative presence?'

Karl understood what he was getting at, but he didn't need his words. He stared at his sword and imagined plunging it into Arazod's neck.

Quizmal locked eyes with Karl. 'Should you be the person you want others to be?' Quizmal opened his left palm. 'Do you want the world to be better?'

Karl pictured his mother bleeding out and the rage returned. 'I shouldn't have let him go last time. I'll make the world better by snapping that cretin's beak.'

Quizmal welled up. 'Did he show you moments of hope? Do you want to be the one who kills someone's chance to change?'

Arazod wasn't Karl's responsibility, and he was finished with the questions. 'I think we should split up, otherwise we'll never find Goblo.'

Quizmal nodded and broke eye contact.

'Watch out for any holes,' Karl said.

He walked and walked. Crunch, crunch, crunch. Endless crunching and leaves brushing. The thirst gripped his throat.

Quizmal was only trying to help, but Karl didn't want it. He wanted to be allowed to be angry. He needed to let it flow through him.

A faint glow pulsed through some white leaves. Karl approached and listened to Goblo cry. It sounded like a broken horn.

Karl knelt in the leaves. 'Hey, Goblo.'

Goblo sniffed but stayed under the leaves. 'Idiot man angry?'

Karl huffed. 'No, this non-idiot man is not angry with you.'

The leaves rustled and Goblo poked her head out of them. 'Idiot man promise?'

Karl nodded. 'Yeah. Mistakes happen. Some obviously bigger than others. But we'll find another way.'

'Not mistake. Hungry,' Goblo said.

Karl shrugged. 'Sure. No mistake. Hungry.' He had no idea what she was talking about.

Goblo grabbed Karl's hand. 'Tell me time idiot man's mistake.' Goblo wiped her tears and snotty nose on the back of Karl's hand.

Karl grimaced. 'Really, I'm a snot rag now?'

'Tell,' Goblo requested.

Karl chuckled and pulled his hand away. 'One of many, many mistakes happened when I was helping to build a tower. I was meant to hammer a spike through two planks of wood to secure them. I missed and smashed the planks in half. Brought the entire tower down. Finely sculpted stone and nearly a year of work.' He mimed a falling tower.

Goblo laughed. 'Another.'

Karl huffed. 'Reliving one past trauma is enough. Come back, please. We miss you.'

Goblo stared up at Karl. 'Will idiot woman say sorry?'

Karl scratched his cheek. 'I can't promise that. She's a unique kind of idiot. But I can promise you I will keep her far away from you. If she swings a fist again, I'll get in the way.'

Goblo stretched out her hand. Karl placed his hand in hers and she licked it.

'You lick,' she said.

Karl gazed at her with total sincerity. 'Absolutely not.'

Goblo squeezed his hand and glared at him. 'Lick.'

Karl grimaced. Her skin was covered in liquid-filled bumps and blotches of slime. He licked her bumpy hand and retched at the sweaty taste.

Goblo laughed. 'Friends.'

Karl stood and Goblo reached her arms out. This bizarre slimy creature had helped Karl to forget his hatred for a moment.

He grabbed her and put her on his shoulders. 'Friends,' Karl said. He smelled the back of his hand and retched.

Luro hugged Goblo. 'I'm so glad you're safe.'

Quizmal stroked Goblo's head.

Karl kept an eye on Rimala. She stared at Goblo.

He removed the bandage from around his head. 'Once you

get your water from the feathered devil let's find a way out of here.' Karl glanced around. 'I have no idea which way is out, but we'll find it. As long as we stick together.' He locked eyes with Rimala.

'Toilet,' Goblo said and reached for Karl's hand.

'Don't even think about it!' Karl stepped back.

'Sword.' Goblo jumped up and down.

Karl's companions were equally confused. Karl reluctantly handed Goblo his sword.

She swayed with its weight and dropped it into the leaves, then disappeared under them. She strained and groaned.

Rimala huffed and turned away.

Karl turned to Freyu. 'She's using my sword as a toilet bucket, isn't she?'

Quizmal chuckled.

Goblo popped her head out of the leaves, a huge grin on her face. 'Hand.'

'Not a chance,' Karl said.

Goblo whined. 'Hand!'

Quizmal offered his hand.

Goblo pulled it down into the leaves and Quizmal rose with the sword outstretched. Goblo's dung decorated the blade.

Luro winced.

Karl's stomach turned with disgust while his heart filled with hope. Three of the worm-like creatures glowed on top of Goblo's waste. They moved, all faced the north-west and stood on their tails. Their faces glowed brighter than their bodies.

Everyone gathered around and stared, then shuffled back as the smell reached them.

'Are they telling us where to go?' Quizmal asked.

Karl nodded and swallowed the relief. 'I think so.' He took the sword from Quizmal and moved it. The worms turned again, towards the north-west. Karl smiled at Goblo. 'You knew?'

Goblo grinned. 'Clever.'

Karl chuckled. 'Can you get them out of your dung now?' He lowered the blade towards her.

Goblo laughed, stopped laughing, then hid in the leaves.

Karl turned to his allies, who all stepped away from the dung. 'Come on!'

Luro shook her head and Quizmal stepped further back.

Karl huffed. 'Can one of you at least hold the sword?'

Freyu stepped forward and took the grip from Karl, holding it as far away from herself as possible.

Desperate to avoid the dung, Karl pinched the yellow creature, but dung caught under his fingernails.

He groaned and dropped the creature onto his palm, then pinched the red and blue ones.

He retched. 'Goblo, we need to discuss your diet.'

Freyu swung the sword, flinging the dung into the distance.

The creatures turned on Karl's palm and faced the north-west again. 'This is amazing.'

Leaves blew and Arazod descended. 'Your water.' He kept his distance and tossed the waterskins to Luro, Quizmal, Freyu, and then Rimala.

Karl's light heart suddenly weighed more than a castle.

'Am I thankful?' Quizmal asked Arazod.

'I don't know,' Arazod replied. 'Are you?'

'Am I?' Quizmal asked.

Arazod's beak twitched.

Freyu stepped forward. 'Thanks for the water. But our friend doesn't want you here. If you follow us, it won't just be him who tries to kill you. I'm sorry.' Freyu stood next to Karl.

Quizmal shook his head and joined Karl, as did the others, apart from Rimala who stayed where she was.

Arazod nodded and scratched his neck feathers. 'Good luck, then.' He turned away and fanned out his wings.

Karl didn't want his heart to feel so heavy anymore. 'You can come with us.'

Arazod turned around, his beak quivered and the feathers around his eyes trembled.

Quizmal smiled at Karl, placed a hand on his shoulder and bowed his head.

Karl stared at the glowing worm-like creatures on his stinking palm. 'First thing you can do is fly to the north-west and tell us what's waiting for us.'

Arazod nodded and flew away. The group followed.

Karl turned to his friends. 'Don't be surprised if he aligns himself with Zianfer and we run into an army.'

WORMING AROUND

The suns rose as the group walked on plains that stretched to the rocks at the front of the circle of mountains.

A terrifying speck patrolled the peaks: Bat Lover. If she decided to search the plains, they were doomed.

The group stopped when the camp's tents pimpled the horizon. Arazod had returned and warned them that Zianfer's army clogged their way in.

Arazod pointed a claw to the right. 'There's an old fortress on top of that mountain. They also control that.' He pointed to the left of the camp. 'Air webs cover those mountains, so it's the safest way to approach to avoid that flying thing. Then I can fly us one by one, over the air webs to the other side.'

'Thank you, Arazod,' Luro said and scratched her shoulder.

Karl took a breath. He nodded.

'I say we fight our way through,' Rimala said.

'You're welcome to,' Karl replied.

Freyu placed a hand on Rimala's shoulder. 'The right time will come.'

Rimala shrugged Freyu's hand away and scoffed at Karl.

'You'd trust the creature who killed your mother? He'll drop you into the air webs.'

Karl swallowed and reached his right hand out for Freyu's sword.

She handed it over.

Karl stared at the worms on his left palm. 'I agree to him flying *you* all one by one. I'll be walking through the air webs.'

Freyu's eyes widened. 'You can't—'

Karl walked towards the mountain.

The air webs swayed and whipped in the wind. Strings of slimy doom attached to web-like clouds. Karl tried to plan a way through.

'Please, Karl,' Freyu pleaded.

The worms pointed towards the back of the circle of mountains.

He waited for the wind to calm and stepped through one air web. A gust of wind lashed a stringy web towards him. He ducked.

Another gust blew three air webs in his direction. He angled his body into the tiniest of gaps between them and let them pass.

His neck tensed and he sidestepped between more webs. Karl imagined this would make a great form of entertainment for evil people. They could unleash the innocent into a course of air webs, offering freedom should they make it, and the glory of an entertaining death should they not.

It was as though sticky stringy fingers tried to grab him.

Karl checked on the worms. They turned to his left. 'What?' They looked towards the outside of the ring of mountains. Karl continued past one more air web. He faced three that whipped and swayed. He'd have to duck, dive, and dodge to stand a chance.

Karl's hairs stood on end. He reached into his pocket and rubbed the purple nugget for luck.

The worms turned further towards the outside of the circle. He moved his hand and they seemed pretty certain.

Karl turned back to his allies and Rimala and Arazod.

'Are you okay?' Quizmal asked.

Karl avoided air webs and returned to them. 'I think the worms are broken.' Karl showed them. 'It looks like they're pointing to the back of the inner circle, but when I was up there they seem to actually be looking towards the outer part of the north-west.'

Luro scoffed. 'The genius giant.'

'What?' Karl asked.

'What is more genius than making people think you're inside a circle of mountains?' She shook her head.

Karl smiled and nodded. 'Genius giant.'

They followed the worms to the outside of the north-west mountain. Karl turned his hand and the worms turned with it, fixated on one part of the mountain where a single flower grew out of the rocks. The same type of flower as the one in the leafy desert.

Karl approached and stared at it. No berries grew on this one.

The flower smelled like mud just after it rains. Karl blew on the flower, but nothing happened.

'Yank it out of the rocks and see what happens,' Rimala commanded.

'We'll try that useful and destructive suggestion last,' Karl replied.

The worm-creatures glowed brighter. Karl held them closer to the flower and the petals twitched. Karl placed the blue worm on the flower and the petals closed around it. A blue glow pulsed down the stem. The petals opened and the worm was gone.

'Did it eat it?' Quizmal asked.

Karl shrugged. 'Let's wait and see.'

They sat on the rocks and waited as the night suns rose.

Rimala stretched. 'Those worms are useless. Let's attack the camp while it's dark.'

Karl rubbed the large scab on his calf. He was lucky the creature only pinched him with its beak. 'And what about the people who have nothing to do with your revenge?'

Rimala shrugged. 'If you're in the way it's your unlucky day. I don't care what your story is.'

Karl sighed.

Rimala stared at him. 'Do you have an alternative?'

Luro climbed higher up the rocks and pressed her ear to them. 'Quiet.' She felt her way around the rocks and stopped.

The rocks clicked and a tiny hole formed. 'Who are you?' a high-pitched woman's voice asked.

'I'm Luro and I'm looking for the genius giant.' She pulled her tunic over her shoulder scar.

'Not expecting a Luro. Bye.'

'Wait! I'm the one dragiant.' She stood above the hole.

'Let me see. Move your head to the left.'

Luro did.

'Tilt your chin to the sky.'

Luro did.

'Now shake your arms in the air like you don't know why?'

Luro glanced back towards Karl. He shrugged.

Luro shook her arms in the air.

The woman laughed. 'Just a bit of fun. Never thought I'd meet the one dragiant. Hold on.'

The rocks clicked again, and a crack formed. Two rock slabs opened and a white-haired giant with a huge bite mark on her neck poked her head out of a hole and she studied Luro. 'Incredible.'

Luro stared at her.

'Obviously you can't be here with good news. Come in,' Ulago said.

The others approached the hole.

Ulago raised a hand. 'Stay away.' She turned to Luro. 'You can bring one more.'

Luro nodded and pointed to Karl. 'Him.'

Ulago motioned to Karl. 'You're not coming in here with that on.'

'I don't know you well enough to walk around naked.'

Ulago pointed at his nugget armour. 'That devilry. Get it off.'

Karl wanted to complain but thought better of it. He removed his nugget armour and tossed the nugget from his pocket towards a tree. He followed Luro into Ulago's hideout.

A GIANT PROBLEM

They followed Ulago to avoid the traps. She had enough to make the most hardened torturer giddy. There were pits, spike traps, poison arrows waiting to be triggered, and barbed nets. This tunnel of doom suggested she did not want to be found.

'My old cave used to be better. But a drunk idiot found me, so I moved to the outside of the circle and it made for a more fun mystery, right?'

'Not sure fun is the right word,' Karl said.

Her rocky room was gigantic and stretched into the darkness. It smelled like someone hadn't left it in thousands of sunsets.

A giant version of the flower that held the berries grew out of the wall. It could have eaten all of them, and what must have been thousands of worms fed on it. The petals lit the cave in a mixture of blue, yellow, red and green.

A small pool in the right corner collected drops of water from the cave ceiling.

In the left corner, chests overflowed with scrolls and lined the wall.

Bottles, jars, and buckets surrounded a stone table near the flower.

Ulago pointed towards a glow coming out of a hole in the ground. 'Give the berries back to their mother, then stand by the wall next to the hole.'

'Berries?' Karl, confused, approached the hole and stared at the worm creature, bigger than him. It squirmed in a pit of what was either soil or dung. Karl dropped the creatures from his palm into the hole.

Hundreds of worms grew out of the mother's body.

Karl joined Luro by the wall next to the hole.

Ulago approached a stone table and grabbed a jar twice the size of Karl's head. 'Berries is what me and my husband used to call those wormlings, because they taste like berries. My clue was meant for him when he dies.'

She took wooden pincers and reached into the jar. 'These are drupes.' She took out what Karl thought was a berry. He should have listened to Quizmal when he questioned whether they were drupes.

Ulago grabbed a knife. 'I knew people would get confused between the two.' She sliced the drupe open, scooped the inside out and flicked it towards the mother berry.

She rummaged around in the bottles and took one with a clear liquid. She used the pincers to grab a berry and place it in the drupe. 'There was a group of rich people who lived near our kingdom. They used to feed light goblins beans and then when the creature would... release... they'd pick the beans out of the goblin dung and eat them. Said it made them extra delicious to have passed through a light goblin's insides.' She laughed.

Karl grimaced. What was wrong with people? Were there not enough food options in the world?

Ulago poured a drop from the bottle onto the berry. It created a casing and then she sealed the drupe around it. 'My husband would've known to eat the berry and then wait for it to come out the other end. I'll have to replace it now.'

Karl shook his head. 'A weird kangaroo-ostrich tore the plant out of the ground.'

Ulago frowned and let the news settle. She took a breath. 'I suppose you came here to ask me some questions.'

Luro nodded and stared at Ulago. Luro had done a lot of staring. Maybe she was in awe of Ulago.

'Just a few,' Karl said.

'Great.' Ulago stomped on a stone next to her table. The stones under Karl and Luro tipped them into the pit. Their bodies slapped against mud and the worm slowly turned its wriggly body towards them.

'Hey!' Karl moaned. 'What about just one question?'

Ulago poked her head into the pit. 'Living alone all these sunsets has made me a bit edgy. Being the one dragiant gets you an audience. So, tell me what you want, and I'll decide if it's worth your life.'

The worm made a popping sound. It stood on its forked tail and towered over Karl and Luro. Brown foam formed around its toothless mouth.

THE SAME PAGE

Rimala wished they would hurry. Her leg twitched.

The camp was near. Messiro was near.

'They'll be back soon,' Freyu said.

Rimala wanted to know how soon? Every moment they waited gave Messiro a chance to leave the camp.

Freyu sat on the grass. 'If you rush into that camp you'll die, Rimala.' Freyu gazed up at her with the sadness of a wolf-cat not wanting their owner to leave the hut.

As each sunset passed Freyu seemed more pathetic. Softer.

Rimala wished she could be a better friend to Freyu, but their paths were different. It became clearer the more Rimala saw her interact with others.

Messiro had to pay.

Freyu patted the grass next to her.

Rimala removed her bow and quiver. She sat and stretched her legs. She reached for her toes.

'I like these people, Rimala,' Freyu said.

Rimala watched Quizmal feed Goblo some grass while Arazod wrapped himself in his wings and perched on a tree branch.

'They're the first good people we've met,' Freyu added.

Rimala nodded. She knew what Freyu was getting at but hoped she wouldn't say the words.

'Maybe having another chance in the Land of the Living will be good.' Freyu smiled.

Rimala scoffed and stood up. 'My purpose is here.' Nobody understood her pain. Her entire life had been ripped away from her. A thousand more sunsets of love, joy, learning, and exploration with her reason to live.

That was the problem with people. They saw revenge as something holding someone back. But revenge gave Rimala a reason to wake up. What would she do when she finally got her revenge? It didn't matter. First she had to get it.

'If I let Messiro go, I will be saying Mamala's life didn't matter.'

Freyu shook her head. 'Wouldn't Mamala want you to have a good life and to find new happiness? Surely, by letting Messiro go you're saying Mamala does matter. She matters enough for you to live for her.'

Rimala folded her arms. 'Don't speak like you knew her.'

Freyu huffed. 'Well, I'm not getting dragged into hatred anymore, Rimala.'

Rimala narrowed her eyes at Freyu. 'You promised to help me.'

Freyu's eye welled up. 'And I have been. Every sunset. But now I know that helping you is to help you off this path of self-destruction.'

Rimala's breathing quickened. If Freyu's loyalty could be broken by a few people she'd known for barely twenty sunsets, then she was no ally.

Rimala picked up her bow and quiver and walked away.

'Rimala, please,' Freyu said.

'I'm going to find food.' Rimala waved her hand dismissively. 'Maybe it'll make us both less irritable.'

A PORTAL FOR PERSONAL USE

Karl and Luro blabbed their stories while dodging the thankfully slow worm.

Luro pleaded. 'I must return to stop giants and dragaurs from warring.'

Ulago thought about it while allowing the worm to get closer to them. 'Okay then.'

Was it that simple? Karl stared at Ulago. 'So, you'll let us out?'

Ulago nodded. 'She only eats algae and her own muck anyway. The slime is just her kisses.'

Karl grimaced but was also relieved.

Ulago lowered the ladder. 'Thought it would get you to the truth sooner and just wanted to study the dragiant a bit more.' She addressed Luro. 'You look a bit thinner than I expected.'

Luro climbed the ladder. 'The diet in the Realm of the Dead isn't as plentiful as what I'm used to.'

Ulago nodded. 'Fair point. Anyway, can't have dragaurs and giants at war. That war will continue here and then that'll be it. This realm is already a mess.'

Karl climbed the ladder.

'What about you? What are you saving?' Ulago asked.

Karl scratched under his bottom lip. 'Well. I'll be helping.'

Ulago laughed. 'Selfish fool.'

Karl got to the top of the pit. 'I don't have people to unite. I just have people I love.'

Ulago twisted her hair. 'It's okay to be selfish. It's why I created the portal.' She handed them both rags to wipe the muck off. 'You know how to use that?' She pointed to the mind stone as Luro wiped it.

Karl nodded. 'Yeah, cut head, weird eel-spider thing crawls into head, steals memories and wipes mind, then you toss it in a fire to watch them.'

Ulago chuckled. 'It was actually created to preserve the memories of the dying, for loved ones in this realm. Before their final…' She mimed an explosion. 'But obviously people use it for evil and then that's what it becomes known for. What few know is that you can put the memories back. Front of the head removes, but make a cut in the back and the eel-spider puts the memories back! In case someone was dying but then made a recovery.'

Karl grimaced.

'But it only holds one person's memories at a time.' Ulago seemed pleased with her knowledge.

Karl gestured to the stone. 'We were hoping you'd keep it. A crazy person wants to use it to find out about the maze.'

Ulago shook her head and walked over to the rock pool. 'I want nothing to do with it. Now, how do you like your algae? Charred, in a tea, or raw off the rocks?'

Karl's stomach twisted. 'I'll skip this meal, thanks. We're kind of in a hurry.'

Ulago waved him quiet. 'Take a seat. A little chat won't hurt you.'

Karl grimaced as Ulago lowered algae into her mouth. 'I should've never created the portal, but my husband had a brutal sickness. It clutched his body, and sunset by sunset a different piece of him stopped working.' She took a breath. 'The worst thing was how it caught his mind. The happy giant I fell in love with had this eternal misery inside. I couldn't blame him, but I wanted to help. I found a mixture that could work, but it needed a plant that was extinct.'

She shrugged. 'I found the god of nature, Naturais, to see if she had similar plants. But instead, she told me of the Realm of the Dead. She agreed to help me if I used my skills to create a portal so she could bring someone back to the Land of the Living. So, obviously, I killed myself and popped up in this wretched land and me and Naturais got to work.'

She grabbed a jar and plonked it on the table. A yellow orb-like flower sat in a twisted stem cage. 'I found the plant. There's an entire forest of them here! Then we found Naturais' friend, a woodland shaling, in an area where only one tree and a patch of grass remained. Terrifying creature.'

Ulago walked over to her chests, grabbed a scroll and tossed it to Karl.

He unrolled it. A sketch of something that looked like a human made of dirt, surrounded by green and brown flames. 'What does it do?'

'Protects the land it inhabits, as it is born from it. Used to live peacefully, but then people ruined their environment, so they turned hostile. Naturais needed protection for her trees, and this is a creature you never want to mess with. You can only kill it by wiping out its habitat. So anyway, we set to work on a portal.'

Ulago slurped some algae down. 'We found our spot in the dragon's wasteland.'

'Sounds inviting,' Karl commented.

Luro nodded, gripped her cup of algae and focused on every word, never taking her eyes off Ulago.

Ulago smiled. 'I assembled it from focus stones with the help of a dragaur, Klarsa, and Naturais.'

Karl raised a finger.

Ulago nodded. 'Focus stones created from extremity that harness pure, raw energy. Klarsa helped us to retrieve a stone from the depths of a volcano. Naturais from the ground's core, and I created a device to harness the harshest winds. The three of us used our combined strengths to retrieve the final stone from a glacier. With them we had the wind's ferocity and volcanic heat to spark an existence, the natural force to solidify these powers and the cold to create a shell around a focal point. Combined with the spirit passing through it, the spark of energies would restore life in the Land of the Living. Life is all about balancing energy.'

Karl stared, open-mouthed, completely clueless about what any of this meant.

'When I stepped into the portal, a shock blasted me twenty feet into the air and burned my back.' She pulled her shirt up. It looked as though someone had branded a map onto her entire back. 'Something was missing.' She stared at the ceiling a moment and swallowed. She gazed back down at the stone table. 'Anyway, we used our minds and found a way to make it work. But we knew how much chaos the portal would bring.'

Luro nodded.

'So, we created the maze around it, under the land. We knew it would attract all the worst people in the realm, and they'd struggle to find it and die. Didn't stop them trying, though, and when I died again I heard all sorts of horror stories. Decided we needed to guard the maze, so I tamed the invisible dragon and she now guards it.' Ulago showed the bite on her neck.

The cup broke in Luro's hands.

'Are you okay?' Ulago asked.

Luro nodded. 'Sorry. Just feeling the tension.'

Ulago ran her finger along the bite marks. 'Had her teeth in there for a whole sunset before she'd listen to me.'

'I've put my hand in the invisible dragon's dung,' Karl said, remembering when he thought he was grabbing the invisible hat from the reverse tower, but instead grabbed a handful of squishy invisible dung. He couldn't shake the stench until the Great Dragon licked it off him.

Ulago laughed. 'Anyone who comes close to her will be burned to death. Anyway, I got back to my husband and cured him. Only in that time he had fallen in love with our neighbour, who had been looking after him.'

'I'm so sorry,' Karl said.

Ulago shrugged. 'I'm glad I saved him. I've been hoping he sees sense and when he gets here, he'll find me, but that's a little less likely now.'

Karl swallowed. 'So, is there a way around the invisible dragon into this maze of doom?'

Ulago shook her head and walked over to another chest. She gazed at it a moment and opened it. She removed a sack the size of Karl. It contained different coloured ball-shaped rocks. 'I'll take you past her myself.'

Karl's heart lightened and Luro grinned.

'Thank you so much,' Karl said.

'I'll see you home and then finally destroy the portal,' Ulago said. 'But the realm's worst could still be lost down there. Some formed villages while they searched and devilish monsters roam.'

Karl rested his head on his palm. 'But you know a way to avoid the scary things, right?'

Ulago sniffed. 'Yes, but who knows what lurks on the correct path now?' She threw objects out of the chest. She took chain mail from it and stretched it out, comparing it against Karl's body. 'Use this.'

'I have my armour outside,' he said.

Ulago shook her head. 'Those nuggets are a brilliant material. They can resist more than most. However, the rarest materials can pierce them. If that happens, the poison within will kill you. So, it's up to you. Wear this or go back and get your death vest.'

Karl reached out for the chain mail.

Ulago opened the rock doors. 'I'm quite looking forward to being outside again. After a while you get sick of your own smell.'

A chill blew through the entrance and Ulago stopped. She dropped her sack and the coloured rocks rolled around Karl and Luro.

'Ulago?' Karl said.

Her skin glowed blue.

Had Arazod betrayed them?

'Step out slowly with your arms raised or your friends die,' a familiar voice said.

Karl poked his head out of the entrance. Anger gripped his mind.

Zianfer smiled at him.

A LIFE-CHANGING CHOICE

*A*razod carefully flew to a tree closer to the cave entrance. He hid in the thick branches, watched and listened.

His companions were on their knees at the foot of the mountain, surrounded by about twenty guards and a robed woman who must have been Zianfer. She stood above the frozen giant's prone body.

'She said there was a flying one,' Zianfer said.

She didn't seem as powerful as the others had mentioned. He could probably scratch her into shreds with a few swipes.

The ghostly figure with bat-humans studied the forest. Arazod remained still. If she took one step closer, he'd fly away.

A guard entered the cave. A scream echoed into the sky and ash exploded from the tunnel, shaking the branches around him.

The other guards backed away from the mountain.

Freyu wept.

Arazod's throat ached. Her tears reminded him of his own when his sister chopped his wings off. The betrayal and humiliation hurt more than the pieces of him being ripped from his body.

Zianfer approached Quizmal. 'I wish you had stayed in the

Sea Spike. Tell me where the flying one is and I might let you return home.'

Quizmal shook his head. 'Did he abandon us?'

A lump formed in Arazod's throat. Someone he barely knew wanted to help him to survive.

'Of course he fled,' Karl said.

'Let's go,' Zianfer commanded.

The ghostly figure and the guards marched Karl, Luro, Freyu, Goblo, and Quizmal towards the camp. Several guards dragged Ulago's frozen body.

Arazod flew down and stood on the grass. He stared at the purple nugget Karl had tossed away.

He could fly away and find a new life. One that didn't involve being hunted. He definitely preferred being the hunter.

He could shriek to see if there were any other man-hawks nearby. His feathers chilled. They would never help.

That life was over. A life of ridicule, insecurity, and needing to impress unappreciative idiots.

Beyond his appearance he was no longer a man-hawk. It was what he was, not who he was.

He could be whoever he wanted to be. The choice was his.

IT'S THE MEMORIES THAT MATTER

Karl tried to shake free of his restraints, but his wrists were tied behind his back and to his ankles. Even if he could escape the tent, he would only find more trouble.

Zianfer tossed the mind stone onto a fire and watched Ulago's memories. She took her jewels off one by one. Among them was a ring with a red stone, a tube of twigs, and another ring with a cluster of green gems. Karl was sure one of those gave her her strength.

Karl hoped the tent would catch alight and cook Zianfer, even if it meant he burned with her.

She wrote on a parchment. She watched the memories several times and her grin seemed stuck on her face.

Karl tried to get a view of the memories, but she blocked it.

'Finally.' She turned to Karl and rolled up the parchment. 'I have my map. Thank you.'

Tears filled Karl's eyes. He would never get home, and he would never see Sabrinia again. 'You've got what you want. Now give Ulago her memories back.'

Zianfer smiled. 'I don't think so. She's too intelligent.'

Zianfer sat cross-legged in front of Karl. 'I'm not as bad as you think I am.' She scratched her nails into the dirt.

Karl ignored her.

'I only want a fair and structured world. In Hastovia I was a lot like your old king, Sastin.'

Dryness stung Karl's throat.

She smiled. 'We met here. Unfortunately, he died trying to escape. Not my doing. Cyrilla doesn't respond well to being hit.' Zianfer stood and walked to a table. She poured some water into a cup. 'I gave my people everything. Freedom, food, the ability to choose what they wanted in life. Sound familiar?'

She was nothing like King Sastin. Karl took slow breaths.

'But people get greedy. They get bored.' She knelt next to him and held her cup to his face. 'Water?'

He shook his head.

Zianfer poured the water on the fire. 'What I gave them wasn't enough. They wanted more, so they stole. I created laws to protect people, but that still wasn't enough.' She clenched her fist. 'I wanted to avoid violence. I hate it. So, I tried a system of rotation. People did jobs for a certain number of sunsets. That way everyone does everything and nobody feels disadvantaged. You take the good and the bad, knowing everybody is equal.'

'Why are you trying to justify yourself?' Karl asked.

'Because I want you to see the vision is never the problem. The problem is those within it, who struggle to follow.'

Sure, it was up to people to fit into something they didn't want to be part of.

'Even with that fair system some became resentful. They burnt crops in protest.' She poured more water and drank. 'My dear friend Hermin gave everything and believed in me and my vision. It became our vision.' She bit the skin on her thumb. 'But some people hated his loyalty.' She tapped the back of her head. 'They dented his skull with all those shovel blows.' Zianfer swallowed. 'I dragged the couple who did it into the centre of the kingdom for all to see. Do you know what I did?'

'Peeled their skin and weaved it into scarves?' Karl said.

Zianfer scoffed. 'I spared them. To remind people that they had a special place to preserve, and that people get chances to change. Do you know how hard it is to let the killer of someone you love go?'

Karl chuckled. 'Funnily enough, I do.'

Zianfer half-smiled. 'I hoped people would settle. But as I slept, that same couple broke into my home. Tied me up, dragged me to the courtyard. They turned a town on me with promises of riches for all, and they stabbed me. Over and over, and over, and over.' She touched all the different places on her stomach, chest, thighs, and back. 'Then they kindly discarded me on a fire like a piece of junk they wanted to burn from memory. My life ended through screams and flickers of sadistic smiles.'

Karl shook his head. 'I'm sorry those people let you down. But not everyone is awful. An unreasonably high number of people are. But not everyone.'

Zianfer stood by his face. She smelled clean, as though she existed in a different realm to everyone else. 'That unreasonably high number is why I've adapted my vision. People can have lives within a controlled structure. The portal will help me to achieve that.'

Karl didn't want to hear any more.

Zianfer showed him a map where castles were drawn on Hastovia and in the Realm of the Dead. 'When I learned that where people appear in this realm links to where they die in Hastovia, I knew I could build something special. By having access to both worlds, I can send people from Hastovia to specific locations here to bolster our community.'

'Great.' Karl shrugged. 'And how many people will die for your goal?'

Zianfer rolled her map up and sighed. 'They will be remembered as heroes. Thanks to their sacrifice there will be fewer wars, and everyone can live a peaceful, eternal life. Murder is acceptable if it is for a greater cause.'

Karl shook his head. 'Keep telling yourself that.'

Zianfer put her jewels back on her fingers. 'It's like these artefacts. I had to kill to get them, but in using them to build a better world the murders become meaningful.' She showed Karl her hand and pointed to the ring with the red stone. 'This allows me to walk through flame, so rumours spread, and fear makes potential invaders apprehensive, saving lives.' She pointed to the twiggy tube. 'This one means I never have to sleep, so I can be alert, saving lives.'

'That one sounds more like a punishment,' Karl said.

She showed the cluster of green gems. 'And this makes me stronger than anyone you will ever meet, so people are more likely to follow, preventing rebellion, and saving lives.'

She was just another false god.

Karl softened his tone. 'But what about people like me who need freedom? People who want to shape their own lives and don't want to be part of a community? I don't want war or to harm anyone. I just don't want to follow a set path.'

Zianfer's smile darkened. 'And that's why instead of killing people like you, I'll eradicate your memories and make you who I want you to be.' She grabbed the mind stone.

'No!' Karl pleaded. He didn't want to forget them. 'Please!' He imagined Sabrinia, desperate to hold on to her image. The time they kissed in his mother's cave. The night they sat up all night on top of the King's Tower in Flowforn and watched octo-eagles fly out to sea. He regretted the times they argued. It was wasted time. 'Let me remember them, please!'

Zianfer pressed the point of the mind stone to his forehead and cut it.

Karl screamed.

TWISTED

Freyu couldn't control her tears.

Rimala stood over Messiro, on his knees in front of one of the many stone trees. Rope secured his arms behind his back and his ankles.

The distant camp buzzed with celebration.

Goblo, Quizmal and Luro were rope-bound to stone trees, and Ulago, unconscious, had each limb tied to a stone tree.

Rimala punched the side of Messiro's head. She glanced at Freyu. 'Zianfer promised me you'll go free and we can live in her community.'

Freyu didn't recognise Rimala from the person she had spent most of the afterlife with. 'I'd rather die with my friends.'

Rimala scoffed. She fired a barbed arrow into Messiro's left shoulder. He groaned, strained, then collapsed to his side.

Rimala stomped over to him and propped him up against the stone tree.

She walked back and fired another arrow into the same shoulder. He fell to his side again and groaned.

'You killed an innocent, wonderful person!' Rimala fired an arrow into his left thigh.

He strained. 'I'm a warrior for hire. I've killed many.'

Freyu had wondered what Rimala's moment would be like, but the crazed look in her eyes was beyond anything she could have imagined.

Rimala marched towards Messiro. She snapped the arrows, jammed the jagged shafts into his mouth and swirled them around. She knelt opposite him.

Messiro spat the shafts out, his mouth leaking blood.

Rimala took an arrowhead and poked it into Messiro's thigh.

He exhaled. Freyu expected him to scream.

Rimala pushed the arrowpoint further and Messiro's face strained. 'A hut by Lake Sandisa,' she said. 'A beautiful woman, brown hair to her ankles, eyes that sparkled with kindness and joy, two moles side by side, here.' Rimala removed the arrowhead and pressed it to the top of her lip, smearing her mouth with Messiro's blood. 'She never harmed anyone!'

Messiro nodded. 'I remember,' he said calmly. 'Your parents hired me. Told me their daughter was led astray by a child murderer. I was to kill her and leave you the note. They hoped removing her would help you onto a more honest path.'

Rimala stared at him. 'You snapped her neck!'

'Your parents demanded I slaughter her. I showed mercy.' Messiro spat blood onto the stone.

'You think you did a nice thing?' Rimala grabbed his cheeks and squeezed.

Freyu grimaced. 'Rimala…'

Rimala spat in Messiro's face. 'Nothing in your existence is good.' She bashed his head against the stone tree.

Freyu wished she could cover her ears.

Messiro groaned. 'In a mercenary's life, the only good you can do is to make death as pain-free as possible.'

Freyu's heart ached for Rimala's suffering, but she found herself understanding Messiro. What he did was awful, but the real villains were Rimala's parents, the puppeteers of those in weak positions.

Rimala stood. 'I won't be as *good* to you.' She took several steps back.

Messiro bowed his head. 'Do as you must. All that we deserve will find us.'

Freyu closed her eye. She waited to hear the bowstring pulled back, but wood clattered against stone.

She opened her eye and the bow and arrow were on the floor.

Arazod held Rimala over ten feet in the air and dropped her.

Rimala's ankle cracked against the stone.

STICKY SITUATION

reyu gagged Rimala with rope while Quizmal tied her to a stone tree.

'I'm sorry,' Freyu said.

Rimala's eyes burned at Freyu. Her screams were dulled through the gag.

This was for the best.

Arazod grabbed a barbed arrow. 'We should kill her.'

Freyu stood between him and Rimala. 'Please.'

'She'll tell them what happened,' Arazod said.

Freyu shook her head. 'All she can tell them is we escaped, which will be obvious when they find her.'

She reached out for the arrow. Arazod scrunched his beak and handed it over.

Freyu approached Messiro. Blood covered him, yet he seemed at peace. 'What you did was truly terrible.'

He nodded. 'I was taught that life is about walking proudly on the path we are born on.'

Could she trust him? 'So, you chose to follow Zianfer's path?'

More blood dropped from his mouth. 'I believed in her vision to do something good. But she has lost sight of what she once saw clearly.' He shuffled on the stone and stared into Freyu's eye. 'I know the camp, and the weak from the worthy.'

Arazod scratched his talons against the stone. 'We don't need him. I'll fly us out one by one.'

'What about Karl?' Quizmal asked.

'We must free him from the camp,' Freyu added.

'How will you carry her?' Quizmal nodded at Ulago, still unconscious.

Arazod huffed. 'Can't we leave her?'

Freyu shook her head. 'It's our fault she's had her mind wrecked.'

'We can't allow Zianfer to manipulate her into a powerful weapon,' Luro said.

She was right. It would make their already tough task impossible. Freyu knelt and used the barbed arrow to cut Messiro's ropes.

Rimala's muffled shouts tormented her. She couldn't face her, but she had to.

Rimala groaned and grunted, her chest rose and fell.

Freyu's heart ached for her former friend. But Rimala was blind to everything going on outside of her obsession. It made her forget what friendship was.

Messiro struggled to his feet and limped towards Rimala.

Freyu stood in front of him. 'No.'

He raised his right hand. 'I only want to speak.'

Rimala's eyes locked onto him.

Freyu let him through but stood next to him.

Messiro struggled to kneel. 'I'm sorry I am the reason you felt loss. I won't apologise for doing what I needed to in order to survive. But I'm deeply sorry that my survival cost you something dear.'

Rimala kicked out but exhausted herself.

Freyu pulled Messiro away and sat opposite Rimala. 'I wish you would come with us. But I know you won't.'

Rimala ignored her.

Freyu hung her head. 'When we're far away Arazod will return for you.'

'Unlikely,' Arazod muttered and Freyu shot him a disappointed glance.

Messiro held his wounded shoulder and nodded to the left side of the camp. 'Zianfer's tent. Likely your stone and friend are there. The guards in steel and leather armour know how to fight, but the ones in nugget armour are simple followers whose only skill is in blind dedication. However, that brings its own dangers. Avoidance will be tricky with a giant, so I suggest we fight our way through and create a distraction to help your friend.'

Luro nodded. 'I have an idea. Arazod, I need your wings.'

Arazod and Luro retrieved Ulago's sack of coloured stones from her cave and returned. It was the heaviest thing he had ever carried.

Arazod caught his breath and Luro approached Ulago, who stirred.

'Where am I?' Ulago asked. 'And who am I?' She scanned the surroundings. 'What?' She spotted the others. 'And who are you tiny people? Has everyone shrunk?'

'I'll handle this,' Luro said.

She spoke to Ulago while Arazod studied the camp, between two mountainsides. He smirked. 'I need your help,' he told Goblo, who chomped a chunk from a stone tree.

Luro cut Ulago's ropes.

Ulago sat up. 'I'll trust you for now and then decide if I should change my mind.'

'Prepare yourselves,' Arazod told the group. He and Goblo

crept towards the camp. 'There.' He pointed to the left mountainside overlooking the tents. 'Ready?' Arazod flew into the air, spread his wings and flapped them.

Goblo shot light from her stomach at Arazod. His shadow consumed the mountainside. He turned his head, so his beak looked like the mouth of a dragon.

Screams erupted from the camp and several people fled. Arazod chuckled. The screams energised him. He hadn't felt this powerful in a long time.

Luro concentrated.

'Are you listening?' Freyu asked.

She laughed. 'It's like a stampede.' But then her face fell.

'What?' Arazod asked.

'Chirps.'

Arazod nodded. 'If we lose each other, meet in the trees near the giant's home.' He grabbed the bow and quiver of arrows. He flew higher and away from the group.

The bat-humans shrieked. Each pulled the ghostly woman by her hair with one hand and planted the nails of their other hand into her skull.

Her eyes glowed blue.

Arazod flew away and she followed. An icy spike brushed his feathers. He evaded another and swiped a wing between two more spikes. He flew over the forest of stone trees and mist.

The spikes whizzed at him. One grazed his beak.

Freyu followed Messiro through the middle of the camp, mostly deserted apart from a group of guards.

Rimala was such a big part of her afterlife. Maybe she should go back and free her. The person she cared for might still be in there.

The group of guards pointed their spears and swords at Freyu.

Ulago looked down at them. 'You have one chance to prove you're not rotten.'

A guard gritted her teeth. 'Kill the ugly beast!' She threw a spear towards Ulago's thigh.

Ulago smacked it away and turned to Freyu. 'Ugly?'

Freyu shrugged. 'They have poor eyesight and poorer taste. You are beautiful. Majestic, in fact.'

'You now have my trust,' Ulago said.

The guards charged.

Freyu clenched her fists.

Ulago reached into her sack and removed a purple rock. 'Let's see what this does.' She hurled it at the guards.

A cloud of purple exploded and formed a bubble around them. It carried them into the sky.

'Hey!' one yelled and stomped on the bubble.

'Don't do that! We'll break all our bones,' another complained.

Away they floated, debating what to do.

Ulago turned to Luro. 'I made these?'

Luro nodded.

Ulago smiled. 'I'm brilliant.'

The group advanced past many drunk guards, several asleep on the ground. The final row of tents came into view.

Zianfer's voice filled the air. 'Find the enemy!'

Three guards jumped Quizmal.

Freyu pulled her fist back, but Messiro threw two right jabs in a flash and headbutted the third guard.

Freyu had never seen such quick hits. She stared at him.

He nodded. 'I'll be quicker when I don't have arrows inside me.'

They made it to the entrance. Two people blocked their way. A follower in nugget armour pointed her mace at them, while a guard in leather armour aimed an arrow at Ulago.

'Move or I'll eat you,' Ulago said.

The pair exchanged a glance. The one with the bow and arrow placed them on the dirt. 'Don't feel like being chewed today.' She walked away.

The other charged at Ulago. 'For Zianfer!'

Ulago grabbed her and threw her into a tent, bringing it down around people inside it.

Freyu gazed at the blue specks in the sky. 'Our turn to help Arazod do his part.'

Ulago reached into her sack and pulled out a rainbow-coloured rock. 'This looks fun.'

Arazod's wings felt heavy.

The endless screeching tired his mind and the ghostly figure gained speed.

Arazod dodged another couple of ice spikes. He fired an arrow at a bat-human, but they easily dodged.

He fired an arrow at an icy spike, but it did nothing.

Maybe he'd be better off flying into the mist. He steadied himself.

A flash of multi-coloured light filled the sky.

Arazod covered his eyes.

Four chubby birds with tiny wings flapped around the camp. They looked as though they'd been created by stitching fifteen different creatures together.

The ghostly woman turned and flew towards them.

The chubby birds flew up then crashed into tents, barely able to hold their own weight.

This was Arazod's chance. He kept his distance and descended towards Zianfer's tent.

She threw spears at the birds while the ghostly woman blew ice at them.

Arazod's feathers shuddered. He opened the tent.

Karl lay curled up and bound, groggy.

Arazod stood over him. 'I know you hate me, but you have to let me get you out of here.'

Karl scrunched his nose. 'Why do I hate you? I don't even know you.'

Arazod spotted the mind stone on the table. Maybe this was a good thing. He snatched it and tucked it into a pouch on his belt.

He dropped the bow and arrow, crouched and lifted Karl. 'Come with me and I'll tell you everything.'

'Leave me!' Karl struggled, but Arazod cradled him.

Karl wriggled. 'I want to stay with my dear leader.'

'No, you don't,' Arazod replied.

Karl bit Arazod's chest feathers and spat them out.

Arazod fought the urge to shout. He dug his claws into Karl's legs. 'Stop it!'

Karl screamed.

'Shut up!' Arazod said. 'It's not safe here.' He carried Karl out of the tent.

The ghostly woman landed in front of them.

'Are we friends?' Karl asked the ghostly woman.

A chill ran through Arazod's feathers. He gripped Karl and he flew away.

'Why are you doing this?' Karl whined.

'To help you.' Arazod glanced back. The bat-humans flew their ghostly leader towards him.

Karl tried to squirm free. 'I love my leader. Take me back!'

Arazod flew over the air webs halfway up the mountain. He'd never dodge the icy spikes with this whining lump squirming. He was going to die, and Karl wouldn't even appreciate his attempt to save him.

The ghostly woman formed an icy spike.

A sea of air webs waited below.

He could drop Karl, dodge, then catch him if he was fast enough.

It would never work.

'Those things look comfortable,' Karl said.

He could drop Karl, dodge, then fly to safety. His heart raced, pounding at his insides, screaming at him to choose survival.

He dropped Karl, but then gripped Karl's wrist in his talon. He couldn't let him die, not without trying. Maybe this was what idiots meant when they spoke of dying with honour. What a stupid idea. Surely surviving at all costs made more sense.

'Don't let me go!' Karl begged.

The ghostly figure shrieked.

Arazod flew up. An icy spike grazed his left shoulder. It sent a chill through his body, and he nearly let go of Karl.

He had no idea how he'd dodge the next ones. Four icy spikes pointed at them.

'Why is she angry with you?' Karl asked.

The ghostly creature grinned at them. The smile reminded Arazod of himself, enjoying the pain in a victim's eyes more than the activity of killing. That's where the satisfaction was, in the dominance. The ghostly creature placed a hand under her chin.

A yellow cloud exploded around her and her bat-humans. One bat-human struggled to hold her. The other, covered in a yellow stone casing, fell towards the air webs.

Ulago stood on the mountainside, Freyu on her shoulder, cheering.

Arazod's feathers fluttered with a lightness he was unfamiliar with.

Karl pointed to the bat-human in the air webs. 'Lucky it landed in those comfy-looking things.' The web shot a red beam into the sky and a cloud appeared. A shriek burst out of it.

A huge, featherless bird dived as fast as an arrow. Its fanged beak grabbed the bat-human, tore it from the air-webber and flew back into the cloud.

'I'd appreciate it if you didn't dangle me over these things anymore,' Karl said.

The other bat-human shrieked and struggled to keep the ghostly woman airborne. It landed and its shrieks were not of a hunter, but of a sufferer.

Arazod turned and flew away from the awful mountains. They had been lucky. He didn't like relying on luck. He missed having the odds stacked in his favour.

A PAINFUL REMINDER

'Why have you stolen me?' Karl complained, tied up on the mud by the lake.

Arazod grew weary of Karl's whining. 'You were tied up on the floor of a tent. What do you think was going on?'

'Zianfer said she found me with my memory destroyed. She was helping me to remember but needed to keep me tied up for her own protection.' Karl squirmed.

'And you believe that?' Arazod said.

'Well, yes. She told me I was one of her favourite people and we had enjoyed many a picnic together.' Karl sat up. 'Help!'

Arazod covered Karl's mouth. 'Just listen to me for a moment, you imbecile.'

He explained what had happened to Karl, placing particular emphasis on Zianfer being terrible and less emphasis on his and Karl's past. He hoped it would be enough.

'I'm going to remove my claws from your mouth now, so please don't scream,' Arazod said.

Karl nodded.

Arazod removed his claws. He stared at Karl and smiled.

'That all sounds very interesting,' Karl said. 'But Zianfer told me about the portal and that she wants to take me there, as a reward for fighting for her and as an apology for me getting hurt. So, why would she destroy my mind and then help me? She's great. In fact, if you take me back, I'll ask her to let you join us. She has seeds. Birds like seeds, right?'

Arazod huffed. 'I'm a man-hawk.'

Karl looked confused. 'Do they like seeds?'

Arazod ignored him and turned away.

'You know, I'm going to go back to her,' Karl said. 'You can fly me to the end of the realm, but I'll find my way back to her. I'm loyal like that. So, either kill me or let me go.'

Arazod wasn't going to get through to Karl with words.

He pulled the mind stone from the pouch on his belt and showed it to Karl. He didn't want to, but Karl had to see Zianfer was bad, even if it meant seeing that Arazod was worse. 'I'll show you your memories, then you can decide.'

Karl shrugged.

Arazod made a fire. He held the stone over it. Was this a mistake? He turned to Karl. 'You're going to see some bad things. Bad things I did.'

Karl's eyes flickered with worry. 'What are you talking about?'

'You'll see.' Arazod dropped the mind stone into the fire and knelt behind Karl.

They watched Karl's memories. It was one mishap after another. His life had all been in Flowforn. Arazod never thought of the impact of destroying kingdoms. He never thought of the individual lives and the consequences of his actions. To him, lives were small. But all of Karl's early memories were in the walls Arazod had destroyed. They all involved Sabrinia, who Arazod had forced to marry him.

A memory showed Karl looking into water at his own reflection with Sabrinia by his side.

'Who is she?' Karl asked.

Arazod could not bring himself to answer.

Another memory. King Sastin's funeral, the moment Arazod came into his life.

Arazod closed his eyes, but he didn't deserve to look away. How could he expect to change if he couldn't acknowledge what he had done?

He watched. The fire flickered with the image of him and the Fools destroying the courtyard.

'That's you. Why are you destroying everything?' Karl asked.

Arazod had put him through a hellish adventure, and it only got worse. But one thing Karl always managed was to find new friends and allies. There was nobody Arazod could ever call a friend. Oaf was the only creature to ever speak to him normally instead of out of fear or a need for something.

Arazod watched Karl hold his mother in his arms right after Arazod had cut her. 'Who is that woman?'

Arazod's beak twitched.

Then the misery continued, when Arazod and Ryza invaded Flowforn and killed another of Karl's friends. Then Arazod's other betrayal when he handed Ryza the Gauntlet of Seliria. Then Ryza stabbing Karl in the chest.

Karl's memory of Zianfer visiting him in a cell flickered in the fire, then his adventures in the Realm of the Dead up until Zianfer placed the mind stone on his head.

Karl's breathing sped up.

Arazod closed his eyes. 'That woman you saw me marry is Sabrinia, the woman you love. The woman who loves you. And the one I cut who bled in your arms is your mother. I am worse than Zianfer. But she imprisoned you here, enslaved you, and wiped these moments from your mind. She is only slightly less awful than me.'

Karl scratched his head. 'I don't understand. I don't remember those people at all.' His voice broke.

Arazod had felt shocks of remorse before, inconveniences, but this was the first one that hit him hard. Normally he would ruin a life and never see what it would do to that person. They'd be dead or imprisoned, out of sight. But here, this path, Arazod had put Karl on it. Karl would still be in Hastovia if Arazod had never invaded Flowforn.

'You've done terrible things,' Karl said.

'I'm a bad being, Karl. I've tried to be good, then I've impulsively killed and betrayed. It's in me. I enjoy power and dominance. It makes me feel like I'm worth something. Even now, the thought crossed my mind to slash your throat and fly away. It's hard to control, because it's always there and feels as normal as eating. But you can't let Zianfer lead you.'

'But why should I follow you instead?' Karl asked.

Arazod scratched his beak. 'You shouldn't. But there are people you should.'

FALSE HERO

Karl lay on his stomach, face down on a stone table in the giant's home.

They had followed a scaled creature called Luro through the trap-filled cave and assured Karl they could give him his memories back.

He wasn't sure who to trust, but the images in the fire had shown Quizmal helping him, and Freyu patching his wounded head. He wasn't sure what he was meant to feel about what he had seen. The moments looked dramatic, but he only felt confusion.

'I'm not sure if this hurts,' Luro said, holding the mind stone. 'It probably does.'

Quizmal approached Ulago. 'Can I have a parchment and quill?'

Ulago shrugged. 'If you can find them. Probably in that pile.' She pointed to a chest of scrolls.

Quizmal rummaged through it, found some parchment and a quill, sat and began writing while watching.

'I'm not a study,' Karl complained.

'Am I writing the *Is This the Book of Tales 2* for Questions?'

Karl huffed. 'Whatever that is, I need to approve anything that references me.'

'Ready?' Luro asked.

'No.' Karl grabbed the corners of the table and closed his eyes. A sharp pain ran along the back of his head.

Freyu placed a hand on his shoulder. 'It'll be okay.'

Something small moved around on Karl's head. Little feet poked into his skin then went into his mind. He groaned.

He retched and his brain throbbed. An intense warmth filled his head and his eyes stung. 'What's going on?'

'I can't say I know, but I'm sure it's fine,' Freyu said.

Images flooded Karl's mind. The ones he'd seen in the fire, only now more emotions came with them. A sudden longing gripped his heart and his eyes filled with tears.

Wave after wave of joy and misery. Then anger. So much anger and pain. Arazod's face invaded his thoughts. More menacing.

Karl's mind burned. Tears fell and he screamed. The intense heat consumed his face and he passed out.

Karl shivered.

Quizmal knelt in front of him and dabbed his head. 'Are you okay?'

Karl nodded. 'I remember it all.' His heart was heavy. It was as though he'd lived a life of failure and tragedy.

Ulago rummaged through her chests, read scrolls and tossed them. Piles of scrolls surrounded her feet.

'Thank you all,' Karl said. He had nothing else to add and stared at the stone floor. He was lucky. At least he was able to get his memories back. Ulago's were gone, erased when Zianfer stole his.

Luro offered Karl some water from her waterskin. 'We need

to get to the dragon's wasteland and find the maze. But our map of the maze no longer exists.' She nodded her head towards Ulago, who read another scroll and tossed it.

'We won't beat Zianfer to the portal.' Karl struggled to his feet and leaned against the wall. 'She knows exactly how to get there and the way through.'

'But she still has to overcome the invisible dragon.' Luro turned to Ulago. 'You were going to come with us to help us pass her.'

Ulago read another scroll and tossed it. 'No, no. I'm going to stay here. Seems I have those traps for a reason. So, I'll piece together my life and maybe I'll go travelling around this dead world. Who knows?'

'If Zianfer controls the portal you'll be travelling within her world,' Luro said.

'I'll risk it.' She pointed to the bite on her neck. 'If the dragon did this, as you say, I don't fancy Zianfer's chances.' Ulago scanned another scroll, laughed and then dropped it onto the pile. 'Turns out I got kicked out of giant school for throwing a stink flower in the teacher's toilet stall.'

Karl laughed, but nobody else did. He stopped laughing.

Ulago yawned. 'Too much to get through. I'm done. You can take water, any bits and pieces you need and then... you know.' She gestured towards the exit.

Everyone seemed deflated.

Karl approached Ulago. 'The last thing I want to do is follow a powerful lunatic into the mouth of an invisible dragon, but this miserable world could get a whole lot worse if we don't.'

Ulago laughed. 'Are you pretending to be heroic?'

That wasn't the response he had hoped for.

Ulago clasped her hands. 'Imagine that Zianfer knew of no portal but was on her way to find an item that could enslave the Realm of the Dead. Imagine her quest had nothing to do with yours and you could leave this realm to your life and loved ones, because the portal was right there against that wall. Would you give up the chance to leave to stop Zianfer harming others, or would you jump through that portal and disappear, not caring about the rest?'

Karl swallowed. She was right. He stared at the wall where he wished the portal was.

Ulago grinned. 'Exactly. The only reason you want to stop her is because she wants the same thing. So, don't pretend you're being anything other than selfish. What I want, is peace and quiet, and nobody throwing spears at me or calling me ugly. So, if you will…' She gestured to the exit once again.

Karl nodded.

Freyu handed him the mind stone and he placed it in his pocket. 'Let's go.'

Luro leaned into Karl and whispered, 'I'll follow. I want to try to get her to sympathise with my giant side.'

Karl nodded. He and the others left and found Messiro and Arazod waiting outside.

Karl's chest rose and his blood boiled.

Messiro approached, the arrows out of his body and his wounds bandaged. 'I'll accompany you until we find a village.'

Freyu smiled. 'Thank you.'

Karl stared at Arazod, who stared back.

Arazod scratched his talons against the stone. He tossed Karl a purple nugget. 'You left it by a tree.'

Karl stared at it and placed it in his pocket.

Arazod turned around and spread his arms and wings out. 'If you want to, kill me.'

Karl wanted to snap his neck. He tried to be forgiving, to see past all Arazod's deeds, but the pain was too severe.

He walked up to him and stood behind him.

'Thanks for saving me,' Karl said and walked into the forest. It would be better for Arazod to die helping them get to the maze.

BEYOND THE BEARDS

They travelled for sunsets, through another boring forest and along the windy coast. Trees poked out of the purple sea like deformed fingers.

The choky waft of burning twigs became too familiar but was at least less invasive than the sludge that stretched inland. Karl had no interest in wading through whatever that gloop was formed of.

The Realm of the Dead was confusing. It was as though someone had given a child all the pieces of a world and let them smash them together.

He couldn't shake Ulago's words. He was selfish.

At least Zianfer's selfishness was to create a world she thought was good for everyone, even if she was clearly insane. What did he want? To go home and have another chance at living.

But he had died saving others. So the chance to live again was surely made for people like him.

Arazod flew down from the mountains.

Karl's body tensed and his senses shredded. It was an involuntary reaction whenever Arazod neared, as though he was readying himself for something awful to happen.

Arazod pointed a claw over the mountains. 'Her army is at least a sunset ahead of us.'

'So we walk faster.' Luro scratched her shoulder wound.

Freyu dragged her feet. 'Can we rest?'

'Tired,' Goblo said.

'We can't lose ground.' Karl's legs throbbed and his stomach cried out for anything, even some bitter mushrooms.

Arazod pointed behind them. 'It might be a good time to go inland and find shelter.'

A ship pierced the horizon. Either Zianfer was adding to her army, or another one approached and they would wipe each other out. Hopefully.

Karl waded through the nasty sludge as the night suns rose. Arazod flew above the group, holding Goblo and aiming her stomach light ahead.

The stench of damp grass tickled Karl's nostrils. He retched so many times he wished he would throw up already.

Goblo's light scanned the unknown. It flashed over what looked like a head.

Karl's heart tightened and he stopped.

'What?' Freyu asked.

'I saw a… a head. Run!' He slowly pushed through the sludge but stopped as the laughter grew.

He turned and Quizmal chuckled, illuminated by Goblo's light. The head belonged to a statue, and it had sludge up to its shoulders.

'I'll save you, Karl.' Freyu slapped the stone head.

The others laughed. Even Messiro cracked a smile, but it could have been a curved scar catching under the night suns.

Karl's shoulders slumped. 'Well, it's still terrifying.' He returned to them. The statue's face was angry, like a warning. He traced it under the sludge and an outstretched arm pointed away. Other statues poked out of the sludge further into the mess. All aggressive, sunken to different depths and pointing in the same direction.

'A warning to stay away,' Freyu said.

'Nice of them to go to the effort.' Karl noticed another statue, submerged apart from its face and an outstretched arm. It pointed in the opposite direction to the other statues. The face was familiar, but a sculpted stone beard obscured it.

Arazod and Goblo returned.

Arazod squawked, 'There's a village up ahead. Enough food, water and shelter.'

'Then that's where we go,' Luro said.

'Four problems,' Arazod said. 'But I can kill them.'

Karl studied the statue and remembered where he had seen it before. He hoped he wasn't tricking himself. 'Maybe there doesn't have to be any killing.'

'Their swords and horned wolves tell me otherwise,' Arazod replied.

'We need to go this way.' Karl pointed deeper into the sludge and statues.

'But there's nothing over there and we'll lose ground on Zianfer,' Freyu said.

'We need to hurry,' Luro said.

'Trust me,' he said. 'Please.' They stood no chance against Zianfer. They were outnumbered and if that ship had more of her followers, then they had whatever ranked lower than no chance.

But if he was right about this then maybe there was hope.

The others glanced at each other.

Freyu stood next to Karl. 'Don't make me regret this.'

They followed the statues and, judging by their groans it was for longer than they cared to. Goblo was particularly vocal and called Karl idiot man more than he wanted to hear.

'Are you okay?' Quizmal asked Karl.

He nodded and followed another bearded statue that pointed towards a sludgy waterfall.

A gigantic blob occupied the top of it. The sludge rolled off it, forming the rank mess they stood in.

'Idiot man!' Goblo growled.

Karl's heart sank. 'No…' He stared at the statues either side of the waterfall.

Freyu sighed. 'Let's go back.'

Karl approached the waterfall. He stepped through it and coughed up sludge. He wiped the muck from his eyes and hoped when he opened them there was a cave in the rocks.

Nothing.

He stepped back out. One statue pointed to the other, which pointed to the sky. Karl leaned against the one that pointed skyward.

'Come on, Karl,' Luro said.

'What is that?' Quizmal stared at the giant blob.

'Probably something that would rather eat us than meet us,' Karl said. Why was this statue pointing up?

'I'll fly ahead and kill the obstruction,' Arazod said.

'Wait.' Karl studied the statue and the arm. He pulled on it, thinking it might be a lever, but nothing happened.

'What's he doing?' Quizmal asked Luro.

'I think he may be losing himself,' Luro replied.

'Do something!' Karl hit the statue. He was sure. He was so sure. He hit the statue again, not caring that his fists ached. 'Please.'

Freyu approached and placed a hand on his back.

'Nothing makes sense here!' Karl tired of pounding the statue and sat at its base. His heart raced.

Messiro approached him. 'When things do not make sense, it is for us to create sense.'

Karl stared at him with no idea how to respond.

Messiro nodded respectfully and walked away.

Freyu sat next to Karl. 'Sorry.'

'This is an impossible quest,' he said. 'We're stupidly outnumbered and not even a tiny bit as insane.'

Arazod approached.

Karl gritted his teeth. 'Don't even think about trying to say something comforting.'

Arazod pointed up. 'Can I point instead?'

Karl looked up. 'What?'

Arazod flew above them and stood on the statue's head. 'This is not a finger pointing up at the sky. It's a candle, and I doubt it's to illuminate a stroll under the night suns.' Arazod pointed at Goblo. 'Weird goblin thing, show them.'

Goblo grunted. She aimed her light at the arm.

Karl stood and grinned.

Quizmal made a fire and they lit the candle. They waited. Nobody spoke. Quizmal wrote on his parchment and Goblo ate whatever she found on the grass and rocks.

Karl stared at the candle, flickering in the dark. Such a tiny flame held all the hope in Karl's world.

The stone hand glowed, then the arm, and soon the entire statue shone. The group stepped away.

'Perhaps it's a secret entrance,' Luro said.

'Or it's going to come to life and kill us,' Karl suggested.

The blob atop the waterfall turned towards the group.

'Or... it's to alert the blob that its supper is ready.' Karl backed off.

'Wait. I hear something,' Luro said.

She turned and raised her fists.

'Karl?' a familiar voice said.

Karl turned and his eyes filled with tears. Was he imagining it? Maybe the mind stone had scrambled his brain into hallucinating.

Long red hair and eyes that shone with positivity in the darkest times stared back at him.

Hargon. A friendly face from the Land of the Living, from Flowforn. From home.

Hargon grinned, standing next to two Oafs holding long stone spears with intricately designed points.

Karl approached Hargon and squeezed him with all the hope in the realm.

'Steady there, you'll crack my ribs,' Hargon said. 'Wait. Him?' He pointed at Arazod.

Karl nodded. 'Long story. But he's with us, for now.'

Arazod shifted his gaze to the grass.

One of the Oafs removed the candle from the statue and replaced it with a new one.

'Seems we have a lot to catch up on,' Hargon said. 'But first let's get you out of the night. Follow me.' Hargon approached the waterfall.

'I knew it!' Karl said.

Hargon nodded. 'We came a different way, but this is the more fun way back.'

The Oafs jammed their spears into thin slots in the rock wall and turned them. A stone door fell into the sludge and the muck flowed into it. The Oafs stepped in and onto a path to the side of a sludge slide.

'Down we go,' Hargon said.

Karl stared at him.

Hargon shrugged. 'Oafs know how to bring joy into things.'

Luro took Goblo and went first, followed by Messiro.

'I'll fly down,' Arazod said.

'Have you never been on a slide?' Quizmal asked.

Arazod shook his head.

'Is it fun?' Quizmal said.

Arazod stared at him and turned his beak up at it.

Quizmal shrugged and allowed himself to fall back onto the slide and laughed his way down.

Hargon reluctantly approached Arazod. 'It is worth it. And there's enough water down there to wash your feathers.'

Arazod nodded. He sat, folded his wings over himself and slowly pushed himself down. He disappeared into sludgy darkness. His voice faded with him. 'This really is a joy!'

Hargon poked his head out of the rock door and shouted up the waterfall. 'Bye, Jim!'

The blob gargled.

'Lovely blob, that Jim,' Hargon said.

Of course Hargon was friends with a weird blob.

Freyu stared down the slide.

'You okay?' Karl asked.

Freyu nodded. 'Yeah. Yes. Yeah... why wouldn't I be?' She trembled.

'We can go down together,' he suggested.

She nodded and sat. He sat behind her, his legs to the side of hers. She grabbed his hands and pressed them to her stomach.

'Just keep your eyes closed,' Karl said.

He turned to Hargon. 'Could you give us a gentle push?'

Hargon obliged. They slid down. Sludge flew into their faces and Freyu's screams turned to laughter. The cave twisted and turned, and everything was completely dark.

Karl worried his head would crash off a wall. A light formed in the distance, and they sped towards it.

The slide ended and they flew through the air towards a pool.

Karl was flying headfirst into the water, but then dangled above it, held by the sludge.

Karl laughed and wondered if he had stepped into a dream.

The giant, finely sculpted stone castle within the mountain was the sort of thing Karl had imagined as a child, just not while being upside down. It was the kind of place he wished existed in secret for him to escape to.

An Oaf waded through the pool and approached them. She cut through the stringy sludge. Karl and Freyu fell into the water.

A DIFFERENT KIND OF HELP

Karl grabbed Freyu's hand, and she pulled him out of the large rock pool.

'Wasn't that bad, actually,' she said.

Karl nodded. 'Yeah.'

Freyu's wet clothes clung to her and he looked away.

Hargon and the two Oafs left the rock pool and joined them.

They stood in a rocky garden, surrounded by flowers and creatures sculpted out of stone.

Statues of Oafs holding light orbs stood atop towers and illuminated the rocky world. Another statue atop the castle held a candle and glowed a fading white, like the one by the waterfall.

Hargon placed a hand on Karl's shoulder. 'Follow me.'

The group dripped their way through rock doors. Stone rooms lined the walls for as far as Karl could see.

'This is the water floor,' Hargon said.

Bathing pools and drinking buckets filled the space. A room full of barrels of water was tucked away in the corner.

The Oafs left Hargon. One jumped into a bathing pool with other Oafs, while the other walked ahead of the group and vanished around a corner.

Hargon led the group up some stairs. 'This is the dining floor.' They passed the most extensive room Karl had ever seen with a table longer than most ships.

Hargon grabbed some plants from a soil bed. He handed them one each. 'Cavern bush. Much nicer than the mushrooms.'

Karl chewed it. The sour taste numbed his cheeks, but Hargon was right. It was tastier than the mushrooms of doom.

Babies' cries echoed around the stone. 'And up here are the little ones.' Hargon climbed more steps, and they entered a room full of babies in stone cribs, hundreds of them wrapped in rags. The noise was both beautiful and horrible.

'Stupid,' Goblo said.

Karl chuckled. 'Agree with you there.'

Freyu smiled.

Luro grimaced. 'This is one of those times when having a superior sense of hearing is a bad thing.' She stepped out of the room.

Arazod's beak twitched. He probably thought about shredding some babies.

Karl pulled his wet shirt over his nose.

'You get used to it.' Hargon picked a baby up. Karl had no idea whether it was a boy or girl. Hargon gently rocked it and his face lit up.

'May I hold one?' Quizmal asked.

Hargon nodded.

Quizmal lifted a baby and played with it. Karl hadn't seen him this happy the entire journey.

Hargon turned to Karl. 'We try to find any parentless babies and bring them back here. It's weird that they'll never grow up or do anything to help build the place, but we have to help them. Especially with little smiles like this.' Hargon held the baby to his face. 'Yes, yes, we do.'

Hargon offered the baby to Karl.

He stepped back. 'I'm good, thanks.'

Hargon placed the baby back in its crib. 'Even in a place like this they see the joy. Reminds you living is about others.'

Karl smiled. Hargon had such a gentle way of looking at life. It confirmed Karl's desire to get back to Sabrinia. He wanted to live, for her and his friends. To feel the small joys.

Hargon pointed to soiled rags in the corner. 'The Oafs are still trying to perfect the rock nappy. We're low on cloth.' He walked towards more stairs.

Karl peered out of a window hole. The cave stretched into the distance and Oafs excavated it. Sculptures of trees lined pathways and Oafs and people conversed. Some young children and Oafs played a game involving throwing rocks into a hole.

Slides connected many areas of the underground land. This place was a bubble of fun trying to avoid being popped by the world outside.

The Oafs had made a dark cave a place of bright beauty. Karl hoped they would be willing to leave it to help him on his quest.

Hargon opened a door into a tunnel. 'I'll show you the best part.' They walked up a narrow cave slope until they stood on a mountain ledge underneath the night suns.

They overlooked a huge, quiet lake surrounded by mountains and colourful trees that had no place in this grim realm.

It was an image of peace and hope. Air webs over the mountains weren't a danger here, but a form of protection.

Hargon pointed to the water. 'We've got everything we need here. Shows that wherever you go you can find a piece of paradise.'

Karl nodded.

Luro leaned on the rocks and closed her eyes. 'This reminds me of home, even the smell of the sickle leaf.'

Quizmal took out his parchment. 'What do you call this kingdom?'

Hargon shrugged. 'Doesn't have a name. It's whatever you want to call it.'

Quizmal seemed confused and wasn't sure what to write down.

Freyu sat on the edge of the rocks with Goblo while Arazod studied the skies.

Karl inhaled the freshest air but couldn't wipe the worry from his mind.

Hargon smiled at him. 'I get the feeling you're not here for the ambience.'

Hargon, holding a slab of rock and his paint palette, returned, followed by an Oaf with a hump on her back.

Karl knew who she was from Oaf's stories, and a lump formed in his throat. The only Oaf with a humped back. Oaf's mother, Boofa.

She took one look at him, fell to her knees and wept.

'Don't, you'll set me off.' Karl knelt in front of her and placed his hands on her shoulders. 'Is it weird that I feel like we're friends even though we've never met?'

She smiled through the stream of tears and pulled him into a tight hug.

Karl worried his bones would shatter.

'I saw you in the light flies. Cecil loved you,' she said.

The past tense crushed Karl and reminded him he was dead.

'And I still love him. All of them,' Karl said.

Boofa released the hug and stood. Karl did the same and introduced her to everyone.

She paused on Arazod.

He raised a claw. 'I'm... I'm sorry.'

She stared at him, no doubt reliving a moment of misery he was responsible for.

She nodded and her eyes met Quizmal's.

Karl gestured to him. 'Meet—'

'Family,' she said. 'You look like her.'

'Do I wish I could meet your boy?' he asked.

Boofa nodded. 'He's your boy, too, now.'

Quizmal smiled.

While Karl loved this reunion, they didn't have time to soak it in. 'What if you could hug him again and meet your grandchildren?'

Boofa folded her arms.

He told her everything from the portal to Luro, while Hargon sat on the edge of the ledge and painted the lake and mountains under the falling night suns.

Boofa shook her head. 'We had our lives, and now we have our eternal one. Why would we risk such a gift?'

'A gift? Outside of this place is misery and pain. And it'll keep spreading,' Karl said.

Boofa placed a hand on Karl's shoulder. 'Yes, there is misery and pain. But you're choosing to let that be the first thing you see. The world is what you make it.' She leaned on a rock. 'And you're forgetting we don't kill.'

Karl's heart tightened. 'I was kind of hoping you'd consider injuring.'

Boofa smiled at him. A smile of rejection. The kind that carries all the pity but none of the help.

The spark that had returned to Freyu's eye disappeared. Luro stared out across the beauty and her expression shifted to determined anger. Goblo snored. Quizmal rested his head against the rocks and Messiro rubbed his wounded thigh. Arazod wrapped his wings around himself.

They had no chance.

Boofa opened her arms. 'You can stay here with us.'

Hargon stood. 'Yes! You can wait for everyone here. Help build it up and we'll have somewhere even more amazing to welcome them to.'

'Is that a good idea?' Quizmal asked.

Exhaustion flushed over Freyu's face. 'Maybe we should think about it.'

'No, what's wrong with you all?' Karl said.

'I'm with Karl.' Luro scratched her shoulder.

Messiro rubbed his scarred head. 'Time to rest and reflect will give you a clear mind.'

'I don't need a clear mind!' Karl said.

Arazod's wings fluttered. 'No battle is won when exhausted.'

Other than Luro, the others seemed to agree.

Boofa stepped towards the cave entrance. 'I'll show you to your rooms.'

ON THE WINGS OF A FLY

Karl, in new and thankfully dry clothes, stared out of the window hole in his rock room at the top of the castle.

It was lovely. Just because it was constructed didn't make it less lovely. Beautiful sculptures of trees, flowers, and friendly-looking people who weren't wielding weapons.

There was a warmth that felt out of place beneath the land.

He could live here and build with Hargon, but it wasn't what he wanted. He wanted the life he had lost too soon. The life he had sacrificed to give others a chance.

Some of his friends seemed to want to stay, as did Arazod.

He'd let them think until morning, then demand they make a choice. He hoped they would see things his way. Why settle for lovely when you can have amazing?

Hargon poked his head into the room. He held a jar with a light fly in it. 'It's the only one I've got. But thought you might want to see how people are doing?'

Karl wanted it but shook his head. 'Not if it's your last.'

Hargon held it towards him. 'I don't want to dwell anymore. Best to convince myself that they're happy and look forwards.'

Karl nodded and took the jar. 'It really is great to see you.'

'You, too. It's a shame you won't be staying longer.'

Karl smiled. 'You don't know that for sure.'

Hargon chuckled. 'I hope you get what you want, Karl. And stay safe.' He tapped the door frame. 'I recommend watching the other world from the mountain ledge.'

Hargon left.

Karl wanted to watch the light fly, but he couldn't let Quizmal suffer any longer. He approached his room. Quizmal sat on his bed and wrote on his parchment. His face seemed peaceful. Writing gave him joy and focus.

Karl offered him the jar and his eyes widened. 'It's yours.'

Quizmal held it and stared at it. Sadness washed over his face. He offered it back to Karl. 'Is it addictive?'

Karl nodded.

'Is it scary?' Quizmal added.

'Yeah. I guess you're right. Have a good rest.' Karl left the room.

He walked to the ledge and stared at the calming lake. It was as though the air gave him a gentle hug.

Something flew above him, but when he looked it was gone.

He felt light but had a nagging worry this could never last. He could die trying to get back to Sabrinia or stay alive here and wait. But if he stayed something bad would come. It always did. Sitting still never did anything.

Karl stared at the jar. He opened it and pinched the light fly from it. He poured the water onto the rocks.

He thought of Sabrinia and released the fly. It shot into the puddle.

It swam through a stream, against the current as colourful creatures whizzed past it.

It flew over a forest of upside-down trees. Roots blew in the wind.

Smoke rose in the distance and a fiery orange filled the horizon. The fly descended into the roots. The smoke thickened.

Soldiers swung swords at leafy creatures while branches impaled humans and muddy beasts formed from the dirt.

Karl's heart raced. 'Please don't be in this.'

The orange smoke thickened.

Karl concentrated, trying to make out any shape. It was hopeless. 'Come on! Show me!'

He waited.

Black eyes pierced the smoke, and the fly flew closer.

Karl swallowed.

The eyes belonged to a stone creature covered in spikes. It was as tall as a tree and stared into the battle, doing nothing.

He prayed his friends were nowhere near it.

The fly flew right up to its face but then around it and past it.

The orange faded and the smoke rose. The fly followed three sets of tracks formed by hooves.

One track ended with a humped horse stuffed full of arrows next to a beheaded creature, the bottom of it a snake, the top a woman.

Karl retched.

The remaining tracks continued and all the air left Karl's body. Death rode a humped horse with Marlens unconscious on one hump and Frong on the other.

Sabrinia rode the other humped horse away from the forest of roots and definite doom.

They looked ahead and the fly neared. It flew by Sabrinia's side.

Her face was scratched, and her eyes were dull with exhaustion and sadness.

The fly followed them until they stopped on a hill overlooking the shore. They released the humped horses, and when Marlens recovered they continued on foot down to the shore and into a cave.

The group didn't speak. They sat and stared at their blood-stained clothes and the sack between them.

Marlens reached out and held Frong's hand. He strained a smile through his singed beard and rested his head on her shoulder.

Sabrinia spotted the light fly, exhaled and frowned. She stood and approached it.

She swung her hand at it, but it moved. She swung again and again.

'Stop!' Karl yelled. 'It's me!'

Death noticed and grabbed Sabrinia's arm. He spoke to her, and she stared at the fly. She burst into tears.

Frong and Marlens looked over at the fly, too. They waved.

'Hello!' Karl's heart lightened. 'I wish you could hear me.'

Sabrinia clasped her hands. She stared at the fly and mouthed, 'I miss you.' She might have mouthed something else, but Karl was certain it was that.

Karl missed that smile. He wiped his tears with the back of his hand.

Sabrinia walked out to the sand and the fly followed.

She dragged her foot through the sand, writing a message.

Karl waited. A grin stretched his face, awakening muscles he hadn't used in a while.

Hopefully she was writing that they were heading back to Flowforn to avoid all monsters and danger.

Something shimmered in the darkness behind her. It flashed towards the light fly and knocked it to the sand.

'Sabrinia?'

An arrow pierced the sand in front of the light fly and obscured its view.

'Sabrinia! Stupid fly, move around the arrow!'

Blood dotted the sand in front of the arrow.

The fly flickered and died.

Karl stared at the puddle of water, his body shaking uncontrollably. His friends. They couldn't be. Sabrinia couldn't be.

THE WORST WAY

*K*arl rushed through the forest, armed with only a rock. He had to keep moving. He had to get to the portal, no matter what.

The others would understand eventually. He knew the chances of survival were low, and he didn't want to drag them down with him or worry about them.

He sprinted.

A weary old woman, teeth chipped as though she'd tried to eat a statue, stepped in front of him and held a dagger out. 'Stop!' she commanded.

Karl didn't have time for this. 'No.' He sprinted past her, but an old man with an axe stepped in his way. 'Stop or die.'

Karl gritted his teeth and raised the rock. 'You want water? Have it.' He chucked his waterskin at the woman's feet. 'Now get out of the way!'

Two more people emerged from next to Karl: a trembling boy barely strong enough to hold his sword and a girl with a blow pipe.

'We don't want water,' the old man said. 'We want you.'

'We're hungry,' the old woman added.

Karl huffed. 'There's grass all around. Just eat that. Or the leaves. I really need to go.'

He stepped forward and a blow dart whistled past his nose.

'Next one's in the leg,' the girl said.

'On your knees,' the man said.

Karl yelled into the air and dropped to his knees.

The man pulled Karl's hands behind his back and tied rope around his wrists. He stood Karl up and pushed him to walk.

'What's your name?' the man asked.

'Do you always ask the name of your food?'

'Well, you'll be traveling with us a while. See, we can't kill you.' He mimed exploding. 'So, we'll chop off little bits then let you heal.'

Karl's body tensed. What an afterlife.

'Come on. Faster.' The man pushed Karl and he fell face first into the mud and grass.

The girl laughed.

A rock smashed into the side of her head.

Luro punched her in the face, and she dropped the blow pipe.

The woman lunged at Luro, but Goblo fell out of the sky and landed on her back. Quizmal tripped her and Freyu kicked her head.

The man swung his axe at Quizmal.

Messiro leapt towards him and kicked the side of his face. The man fell against a tree.

The boy ran away.

Hargon joined the group, threw everyone some rope and they tied the thugs. He shouted into the forest. 'When we're gone you can come and untie them! We don't want to hurt them.'

'Good thing my ears could hear your whining,' Luro told Karl. She grabbed his face. 'How dare you go without me?' Her eyes carried a fury Karl had only seen in tyrants.

'Sorry,' he said.

She breathed slowly and calmed, then nodded and let go of him.

Freyu untied him. 'We're in this together.'

Karl shook his head. 'But we have no chance.'

'Have we ever had a chance?' Quizmal asked.

He had a point. 'But we're behind. And we're outnumbered by hundreds. There is no way of succeeding, but I have to go. I have to try. Otherwise, I'll always wonder if I could have done it, and she needs me.'

Arazod landed in front of Karl. 'She doesn't need you.'

Karl picked up the man's axe and stepped towards Arazod, but he held his ground and his gaze.

Karl's nose was inches from his beak. 'You have no say in me and her.'

Arazod raised his claws peacefully.

Karl wondered if he'd still rake them down his face.

'She is the strongest being I have ever come across,' Arazod said.

Karl swallowed.

'I invaded her home, and all she cared about was sparing her people. I imprisoned her, and instead of begging forgiveness she threatened to rip my beak off and insulted my singing.'

'To be fair, she was just being honest about the singing,' Karl said.

Arazod's beak twitched. 'There's a line you do not cross.'

Karl shrugged.

'I forced her to marry me, yet she only said yes to save...' Confused, he looked at Hargon. 'To spare...' He pointed at him.

Hargon shook his head. 'I'm not reminding you. You'll just forget again. You're rude.'

'To spare him. She would have happily lost her head if she didn't have to think of others.' Arazod folded his arms. 'She's not like us. I didn't see it at the time, because I was desperate for her to love me. But her power is entirely unique. I've had kings and queens beg me for mercy and offer me their people to spare their own lives.' Arazod scratched his neck feathers. 'But Sabrinia, she offered me herself to spare her people. Even when I left her on top of a statue to fall, she would've probably found a way to swing off it and kick me. She has more power than we could ever understand.'

Karl shook his head. 'It's nice for you to acknowledge how brilliant she is, but last time I saw her arrows were flying at her. I need to get back.'

Arazod laughed. 'Then I feel sorry for whoever fired the arrows. She doesn't need you, Karl. You need her. But if you rush alone towards Zianfer, you'll never see her again.'

Karl gripped the axe handle tight. He couldn't admit Arazod was right. 'I don't care.'

'But we do,' Freyu said.

Quizmal nodded. 'Are we your friends?'

Luro folded her arms. 'We have a shared quest, so share it and the burdens that come with it.'

Messiro nodded. 'I planned to stay in the first place we found, but I shall join you. I made a mistake aligning with Zianfer and her selfish vision. I'd like to correct my error.'

Karl took a breath. If they wanted to waste their lives, then who was he to stop them? 'If you break a limb or find Bat Lover chewing your arm off, don't complain to me.'

Freyu smiled. 'Wouldn't dream of it.'

'And we're not stopping,' he said. 'To look for food, water, anything. This is it. Direct. We're already far behind.'

Arazod fanned his wings out. 'I think I have a way we can get there faster.'

FLYING CAN BE FUN

'No way. Not a chance,' Karl said as the giant sludge blob released a slime bubble that floated into the air. The bubble's colour faded and it became what Karl knew as an air web.

It drifted into the distance and settled above a tree.

Karl retched from the stench of damp grass, sweat, rotten mushrooms and whatever else formed the blob.

Hargon nodded. 'I think Arazod's right. Just means as he's blowing you forward he'll have to fight off the death birds that fly down from the sky, as you'll all be frozen stiff by the sting.'

Karl raised an eyebrow at Arazod and waved some sticky flies away, but they stuck to his hand. 'I'm not putting my life in your claws.'

'Do we have a choice?' Luro asked.

Freyu grimaced. 'So we hang high in the sky, paralysed?'

Hargon nodded.

Quizmal took his parchment and quill. 'Why does the blob make air webs?'

Hargon stroked the giant blob, his hand slightly sinking into it. 'You might not think it looking at him, but Jim used to be one of those cloud birds. When they eat a certain amount they mutate into these blobs to release air webs to try to feed the rest of their family. It's all just nature, really.'

'Terrifying, bizarre nature,' Karl muttered.

Hargon pointed to an air web. 'You could sit on top of it. You won't get paralysed, but it's hard to balance and you might do yourself an injury.'

'How do you know you can sit on top of it?' Karl asked.

'Erm… it just seems logical.' Hargon bit his lip.

Karl smiled at him. 'You tried, didn't you?'

Hargon's shoulders slumped. 'Yes, and I fell and got tangled in the webs. The Oafs had to throw spears at the air-webber that tried to eat me. Then they had to hook the air web and pull it down to the lake to get the stringy bits off me.'

Karl laughed then stared at an air web. They didn't have much of a choice. They would need to put all their hopes in Arazod. Karl turned to him. 'What's to stop you leaving us to get eaten by air-webbers?'

Arazod smirked. 'Nothing.' Arazod flew up and flapped his wings at an air web. It did move fast with a bit of wind behind it.

Karl retched and waved the stench away. He glanced at the group. 'So, I guess we're doing this.'

'Wait,' Boofa said, emerging over the rocks and out of breath. She dropped a sack on the rocks. 'I'm sorry we won't fight with you.'

Karl nodded. 'I understand. When I see Oaf, I'll let him know you're okay.'

Boofa squeezed his arm, but nearly crushed it.

Karl held in the pain. 'Are you sure you don't want to lend us your strength?'

Boofa released his arm and chuckled. She reached into the sack. 'While we won't kill, we'll help you to defend yourselves.' She placed a variety of weapons on the stones. Luro picked up the stone longsword, Goblo grabbed a tiny stone dagger, Freyu strapped a belt of stone throwing knives over her shirt, while Quizmal picked up a stone club.

Messiro sat on the cliff edge and stared at the horizon.

'Do you not want a weapon?' Karl asked him.

Messiro turned to them. 'Life is imperfectly perfect. When I kill, I show respect for life's beauty by using the tools I entered the world with.' He showed Karl his hands.

'What about a bow and arrow?' Karl asked.

Messiro smiled and turned back to the view.

Quizmal took his parchment out and wrote on it.

Arazod flew down to the weapons and studied them.

Karl wasn't comfortable with this at all.

Arazod shrugged. 'It's for your safety.' He took the stone axe and turned it in his claws.

He killed Karl's mother with an axe.

Boofa handed Karl a shield. 'It's not as powerful as the one my boy made you, but I hope it gives you strength.'

Karl placed his left arm through the straps. 'Thank you, Boofa. But, you know, by giving us weapons you're technically contributing to potential death, so you may as well join us.'

Boofa laughed. 'How you use the weapons is up to you. I give them to you for defence and to scare people away. My hands are clean.' She took two potion bottles from inside her gown. 'You might need this. It'll help revitalise the weak.'

'Thanks.' Karl took it and handed it to Freyu.

She approached Messiro and he rubbed some on his wounds.

Luro raked her nails into her shoulder and winced.

'Do you have anything for itches?' Karl asked Boofa.

'I'm fine,' Luro said. 'Just nervous.'

Karl shrugged.

Quizmal approached Boofa. 'Am I thankful our children met?'

Boofa pulled him into the kind of hug Karl longed to have with his loved ones.

He gave them their moment and walked to Hargon, stood on the cliff edge.

'You ready?' Hargon asked.

Karl nodded. 'Not really.'

Arazod flew up and flapped his wings, blowing the first air web down towards Karl.

'Just let it take you,' Hargon told Karl. He choked up. 'Good to see you again.'

Karl hugged him. 'Thank you for everything. I'll see you next time I die.' He chuckled.

Hargon grabbed his shoulders. 'I hope it's not too soon.' He picked up a stone slab, a palette of paint, and his brushes, then sat on the edge of the cliff. 'It'll make a great painting.'

'Just don't give me a big head or abnormally long arms as you used to.' Karl reached into his pocket and clenched the purple nugget, wishing for safety, hoping it made any kind of difference.

He checked the mind stone was carefully tucked into his other pocket.

The bubble floated towards Karl. The stringy slime webbing hung down and pointed towards him. He closed his eyes. 'You ready to defend us, Arazod?'

Arazod chuckled. 'I've been aching to kill something.'

The stench neared and the waft surrounded Karl. His nostrils burned and his eyes stung. He opened his eyes and clutched his shield over his chest.

Stringy slime slapped his face, and a shock consumed his body. He was completely stiff. His thoughts moved but his body stilled. He tried to break through it, but everything was stuck as though turned to stone and disconnected from his mind.

The stringy webs wrapped around his chest and dragged him off the cliff. Arazod flapped his wings at the air web to move it.

Karl hung above the stunning lake, completely helpless.

A red beam shot from his air web and into the clouds. A

shriek shook the sky. Karl willed his body to move so he could cover his face with his shield, but all he could do was stare.

A huge, featherless bird shot at him and opened its fanged beak, showing its jagged teeth.

Arazod flew in front of Karl and hacked at the beast's neck. It bit at Arazod's head, but he dodged and sliced its left wing.

The creature shrieked and fell into the lake with a glorious splash.

Karl hoped this journey wouldn't take long.

Air webs took the rest of his friends as Hargon sat on the edge of the cliff and painted.

Karl hoped to see the painting one day, but a long time from now.

Several red beams shot into the sky and Arazod readied his axe. He flew above the air webs and waited for the holes in the clouds to appear.

'I am the greatest!' Arazod started singing.

Karl realised that the worst thing about being frozen stiff was that he could not cover his ears.

'I am the strongest!'

An air-webber flew towards Luro but Arazod chopped its beak off.

'Fight with me and your life will not be the longest.'

Two air-webbers went for Freyu and Goblo. Arazod threw the axe into the first one's neck then raked his talons over the second's eyes. He flew down and pulled his axe from the falling air-webber, then as the second blindly bit at the air, he chopped its head off.

'Give me all you have, and I might let you go...'

Another two air-webbers aimed for Messiro and Goblo. One opened its beak wider than Karl's entire body. Arazod wedged the axe into its mouth and as the other was about to swipe Goblo, Arazod grabbed its wing and flung it into its friend.

'On second thoughts, no.'

Arazod placed a talon on the air-webber's neck and pulled the axe out and hacked them both until pieces of them splashed into the lake.

Another red beam shot up from Karl's air web. He hoped Arazod would notice, but he was too busy bowing. He was in his element, killing in front of others.

The air-webber's shriek got Arazod's attention. The creature flew at Karl and clamped its beak around his body. Luckily the shield stopped its teeth piercing his chest, but he was sure some snagged his back. It tried to pull him free to take him away, but Arazod hacked at it until it let go and fell.

Arazod smiled at Karl.

Karl hoped this journey would end soon.

Arazod must have killed ten more air-webbers. The last three times beams shot out of the air webs nothing came and the clouds cleared. Karl hoped this calm would last, although Arazod's singing made it a painful experience.

He had screeched through more of his terrible songs: *Pecks in Passing', 'Frisky Force of Feathers', 'Sweet Egg o' Mine',* and Karl's least favourite, *'We Will Flock You.'*

Being unable to move forced Karl to stare at whatever he was faced with.

The Realm of the Dead was far more stunning than Karl would let himself believe. They passed over a river that broke off into what must have been hundreds of streams, making it look like split and frayed veins.

Atop mountains on the horizon, giant stems reached into the sky, with flowers open like platforms. It was as though they offered whatever was on top of them to the suns.

A canyon crack shot water into the air, eternally raining over a desert dotted with stone arches.

Rocks floated above the western sea, as though held in place by a magical force.

Everywhere Karl turned he saw something he had never seen before, but any hint of appreciation was washed away by fear. Was Sabrinia alive? He needed another light fly to put his mind at ease.

This was perilous. They were up against Zianfer, an army of followers, Bat Lover and an invisible dragon. Then there was the small problem of a maze of misery.

Karl wondered what the dragon's wasteland could be. Was it a place dragons went to burn everything for practice? Was it the setting of a great dragon battle? Was it a ruined kingdom and charred villages, victims to an angry dragon?

As mountains formed on the horizon it became clear. They were no ordinary rocky mountains. They were mountain-sized piles of dragon dung. It was a literal wasteland.

That meant there would also be invisible dragon dung.

How would Zianfer and an army of followers beat a dragon? It could wipe them out with one breath.

Karl realised why he had been hacking at purple nuggets in the water for so many sunsets. He wanted to tell Arazod to blow them faster, but he couldn't speak.

His heart filled with dread.

THE RAREST MATERIAL

Zianfer stood in front of hundreds of her followers, all covered head to toe in armour, leg wear, and helmets made of purple nuggets that shimmered in the suns.

Behind her, twenty guards in steel armour were armed with bows and arrows. She turned to Cyrilla, rage in her eyes. She dug her toes into the soil.

The loss of one of her bat-humans would hopefully motivate her further to eradicate opposition from this land.

'When we have the portal, we will find those responsible and bring them to you,' Zianfer said.

Cyrilla dug her teeth into the side of her lip, drawing blood.

Two distant, giant piles of dung stood either side of the entrance.

The invisible dragon was no doubt in front of it.

This land was beautiful. Bright green long and thick grass, flourishing plants, trees of vibrant colours - spoiled by piles of dung, but magical, nonetheless. This was the place in the Realm of the Dead with the most life, yet also with the potential for the most death.

She beat an arrow against her nugget armour and grinned,

proud of her achievements. She coughed and cleared her throat of the tickly dung.

'Today, we will conquer one of the most fearsome beasts ever known and it will mark the greatest day in our history. The day our eternal lives truly begin!'

Her people cheered.

'We will make the Realm of the Dead a place where nobody needs to fear anything.' She turned to three guards and nodded.

They lit torches and approached her.

'This armour makes even the most ferocious, fire-breathing beast your equal.' She spread her arms out.

The guards held the burning torches to her armour.

'Only the rarest materials can pierce your armour.' She laughed as flames did nothing to her. Zianfer nodded at Cyrilla.

Cyrilla's remaining bat-human sat on her head and jammed its nails into her skull. Cyrilla's eyes burned blue, and she spewed blue slime over Zianfer's armour.

Smoke rose off it and covered Zianfer until she was lost in a blue-white cloud.

The crowd murmured, and when the smoke rose, they gasped.

Zianfer smiled at them. 'With this armour, you are invincible!'

They cheered.

'You don't need to run from a dragon ever again. Together, we will live forever!'

Her followers roared and it gave her goosebumps. 'Turn your back on its flame and cover yourselves in the nuggets when the flames rain.'

Guards handed the followers large blankets of purple nuggets, big enough to cover ten people.

Zianfer stared at the dung piles. She picked a flower and let it turn to ash in her hand. 'Let us become the new world.' She walked towards her people, who parted to let her through. She led them towards the dung mountains.

Her heart raced. As they neared, large areas of long grass flattened under thuds.

Her people hesitated. The guards readied their arrows in their bows.

Zianfer reached into a sack, pulled out nugget armour and turned to Rimala.

Rimala shook her head. 'With my wounded ankle, I'll be no good. But I'll help with arrows.' Rimala hobbled to the guards and took a bow and arrow.

Zianfer hated vengeful people. They were always a disappointment. Vengeance needed to be refocused, made useful, not a distraction. What a waste of a warrior.

The flattening grass patches drew closer, and the thuds became louder, accompanied by slow breaths. Smoke rose from what must have been the dragon's mouth.

Zianfer raised her arrow. 'For a forever future!'

Her people rushed towards the smoke.

Zianfer clasped her hands.

Fire swirled behind the smoke.

'Cover!' Zianfer ordered.

Her people hid under the large sheets of nuggets.

Fire rained down and covered everything between the dragon and Zianfer.

She coughed through the ash of burnt nature. As smoke rose, it outlined the beast that now flapped beneath the suns.

The nugget sheets remained still. Zianfer's heart clenched. If her plan didn't work, it was over.

The dragon landed among the flickering flames and the outline of its face aimed at Zianfer. It roared and its wretched breath nearly knocked her over.

Her vision could not be destroyed, but the sheets were eerily still. Her eyes welled up. 'I'm sorry, Hermin,' she muttered. It was all for nothing. She had been wrong.

A sheet shuffled. Then another, and another.

The sheets rose one by one and her people cheered.

Zianfer choked up and smiled. Her heart swelled.

She raised her arrow. 'Kill the beast!'

Her followers rushed the dragon and stabbed at its ankles. Some climbed it and the beast shook them off.

The guards and Rimala fired arrows, but they simply bounced off the dragon's scales.

Zianfer threw arrows; she smiled as they bounced off the dragon's nose and eyelids.

'It's not working,' Rimala moaned.

'Call them back!' a guard said.

Zianfer half-smiled. It was working. She removed her nugget armour and threw it on the burnt grass.

Her followers screamed as the outline of the dragon's mouth snapped them in half. Limbs and bodies flew into the air. Some vanished into the invisible beast or crashed down onto the dirt and exploded into ash.

Guards covered their ears from the screams, but Zianfer absorbed them. It was the music of a new beginning.

Rimala stomped towards Zianfer. 'You wanted me to be with them!' She threw a punch at Zianfer.

Zianfer caught her fist and squeezed it. 'Do not interrupt this moment.' Zianfer pushed Rimala's fist away.

Rimala swung again. Zianfer caught her fist again. 'One warning is all I offer.' She twisted Rimala's wrist.

Rimala screamed and collapsed to her knees. 'Please!'

Zianfer snapped Rimala's wrist back, then kicked her to the ground.

Two guards dragged Rimala away.

The screams stopped and the massacre covered the burning grass. The invisible dragon's blood-covered lips faced Zianfer. Blood dotted the dragon's invisible body as though the droplets floated towards her.

Fire rose around its mouth as it stepped forward. Its feet kicked up the ash of death.

Zianfer smiled and Cyrilla stood next to her.

Guards readied their arrows.

'Don't bother,' Zianfer said.

A greenish-purple fluid flowed from the dragon's mouth. Its invisibility faded and its full, cloudy silver form appeared.

Its scales were perfection, the same size and in perfect lines, like a carefully sewn pattern on a sheet. Its spikes were evenly spaced along its body.

How could the world allow for such beauty and power? It wasn't fair on everything else.

Its silver eyes burned at Zianfer.

She smiled as its lips turned a dull purple. It blinked repeatedly, struggling. It stopped stomping and its feet and wings dragged along the burnt land.

'Closer.' Zianfer waved it towards her.

The dragon groaned and its neck and body turned the same greenish purple as the fluid that fell from its mouth. It took big breaths and stopped.

It rested its face on the dirt and stared ahead. It tried to blow fire, but burning blood dribbled out of its mouth and fizzed against the dirt.

Zianfer approached the beast. She kicked away a broken purple nugget. 'Only the rarest material.' She smiled and stared at the dragon's magical teeth.

She placed a hand on its cold head. 'Rest well.'

Ash exploded all over Zianfer. She wiped her eyes and mouth and grinned.

A single dragon scale glowed on the ground. Zianfer kicked it away.

The entrance between the dung mountains welcomed her.

She took the scroll from inside her undershirt and read the

instructions she'd written. Once they entered, the third path from the right would take them towards her goal.

A guard handed her a robe and she put it on. Her heart was split between the sadness of loss and the joy of what they stood to gain.

'Let's make sure their sacrifice was worth it.' The unifying of worlds was near.

ROOTS

A giant ash cloud signalled Karl's destination. Karl worried they were too late.

Arazod blew them down onto the wasteland.

He hacked at the dangly, slimy webs and freed the group. Once detached, the webs fell off everyone.

Karl lay on the dirt, helpless, and waited for the feeling in his body to return. The first thing that seemed to work was his mouth. 'Never again.'

'Thank you, Arazod,' Freyu said.

Karl avoided Arazod's gaze so he wouldn't have to thank him.

Quizmal's neck slowly turned to Karl. 'How's my hair?'

His three red hairs stood on end. 'Still there, enjoying the air,' Karl said.

Messiro lay facing the sky. 'There is a strange peace in such stillness. Allows you to be with your thoughts.'

Karl disagreed. He retched as the atmosphere filled with the stench of dung, burnt grass, and sticks. 'As soon as we can move, we go.' His left arm and leg were completely stiff.

Freyu tried to stand but her right side gave way and she fell.

Quizmal chuckled. 'What will everyone do when they return to the Land of the Living?'

Karl appreciated his attempt to pass the time.

Luro scratched her shoulder. It seemed to bother her more. 'I'm going to rip my aunt's throat out and build peace. Give the giants their land back and create a shared space for growing crops where we can work together.'

Freyu smiled. 'I'm going to my old village. I'll teach my people to live differently, less wastefully, and I'll write some books on what I've learned, to prepare people for the Realm of the Dead.'

Goblo growled. 'Eat stones.'

Quizmal laughed. 'Will I play with my grandchildren? Will I tell Questions about my adventures and the good friends I've made?'

Karl smiled. His fingers moved.

Messiro kicked his legs, stretching them. 'I will not return. I will prevent Zianfer ruining this land and I'll find somewhere to live and build a community. I've destroyed enough lives.'

Arazod scratched his talons against the dirt. 'The first kingdom my father made me burn down. I'll return there.'

Karl scoffed. 'Want to make sure they all died?'

Arazod ignored him.

Karl caught Freyu's disappointed look.

'What about you, Karl?' Luro asked.

'I'll ask where that forest of roots is and I'll go and find Sabrinia.' Saying it out loud made it clear how pointless this was. Where would he even appear in Hastovia? How far would it be from them? He might not be able to get to where Sabrinia was for hundreds of sunsets.

'Is this land beautiful?' Quizmal asked.

Messiro nodded. 'Maybe it's the name that's the issue.'

'Yeah,' Freyu said. 'Realm of the Dead doesn't exactly suggest a land of happiness.'

Luro agreed. 'Something like the Forever Realm, or Land of Eternal Life would sound more positive.' She strained to fight the stiffness and screamed her frustration into the sky.

While the others debated names, Freyu fell silent. Karl regained some movement and managed to roll over to her.

'Rimala?' he asked.

She blinked. 'Have you ever wanted to help someone but kill them at the same time?'

Karl couldn't nod so gave a thumbs up. 'She made her choice, Freyu. You did all you could. Whatever you think, you didn't fail her.'

Arazod poured water on his wounded forearm. 'Sometimes people can't see a choice. They're blinded by what they believe or what they think is right.'

Karl chuckled. 'Spoken like someone who always makes bad choices.'

Arazod's shoulders fell, and he flew over to the debate about names for the realm.

Karl felt cruel, but why should he? Arazod deserved an eternity of hostility. He switched his mind to the task at hand.

Freyu sniffed. 'Let's change the subject. We might die, so now's a good time to ask me anything.'

Karl looked her in her eye. 'I think you can guess.'

Freyu nodded. 'It happened in this realm. Nothing brave. Nothing special. Just bad luck. I slept under a tree that turned out to be a home for mole-bees.'

Karl grimaced. He didn't know what they were, but they sounded awful.

'Tiny, cute things,' Freyu said. 'But one mistook my eye for a place to dig for food. Got wedged in it. Only way to get it out was to burn it and pull it. Poor creature died and took a chunk of my eye with it.'

Karl winced. Movement returned to his neck. 'I'm so sorry.'

Freyu shrugged. 'It is what it is. I'm the lucky one in this story.' She sighed. 'Do you think I should ask Arazod to sing for us to pass the time?' She smiled.

'Don't you dare.' Karl's legs began to move. His entire body slowly regained its connection to his mind. He stood and walked on, towards the smoke.

His face fell. His worst fear was realised.

Broken purple nuggets and hundreds of weapons covered the land. All these people, wasted. For what? An idea of a perfect world, seen through the eyes of a lunatic.

Freyu stood next to him and shook her head.

Everyone dwelled in the silence of disaster for a moment.

A growl alerted Karl to a pile of dung. He buried his nose in the pit of his elbow.

'What's that?' Quizmal asked.

A bear, half its body in the dung, stared at them and shoved dung into its mouth. The dry waste crumbled and dropped all over its protruding stomach. It growled again.

'Dung bear,' Freyu said. 'Exactly what the name makes you think. It has no interest in us.'

'Don't worry, it's all yours,' Karl assured the bear.

'Yum!' Goblo sprinted and jumped into the dung.

The bear roared and chased her through the foulness.

Karl grimaced. 'If the bear eats her, it's entirely her fault.'

He faced the entrance then addressed the group. 'We're dealing with someone who's happy to dress people in poison nuggets and feed them to a dragon. This is your last chance to turn back and go and live with Boofa and Hargon.'

Freyu stepped forward. 'We're going nowhere.'

Karl swallowed. They might not have been the friends he loved from Hastovia, but that didn't mean they weren't his friends, plus Arazod. 'Thank you all.' He glanced once more at the devastation. He wanted to say something meaningful but had nothing.

They entered a dark path of swirling tree roots; a dizzying, endless spiral that sloped down. It went on so long Karl worried they would fall out of the bottom of the Realm of the Dead.

Karl wanted Goblo to remain at the back so the stench was behind him, but they needed Goblo's light. He wished the tunnel would end, just so he could go a moment without retching.

Finally, the tunnel opened onto a stone platform in a cavern large enough to fit several ships. Seven root paths were separated by root walls that stretched all the way to the ceiling. No chance of a flying shortcut. Only magic could have created this place: a world beneath the dung.

The roots glowed a gentle white, illuminating the maze enough to see, but leaving enough dark to fear what might emerge as they ventured forward.

Messiro studied the roots, searching for footprints.

To their left, a sign:

Your greed will be your end

Arazod jammed his axe into a root wall, but as soon as he pulled his axe out, the roots grew back. 'Looks like no cheating.'

Karl stood on the roots in the middle path. Small roots reached around his feet and up his ankles. Karl yanked his legs free and stepped out of the path. He groaned.

'What's wrong?' Quizmal asked.

Karl pointed to the ceiling of the cavern. Thousands of pained faces frozen in time and deformed by roots stared down at them. 'If we stand still on the roots too long, I think that's where we end up.'

'I'd rather explode into ash,' Freyu said.

Karl threw the purple nugget onto the path. 'Maybe we gather the remaining nuggets from outside and use them to mark our path.'

The roots reached around the nugget.

Karl grabbed it before it was gone and returned it to his pocket. 'Or we don't. Seems they've really thought about how to maximise the awfulness of this place.'

Arazod flew into a path and hovered. He got too close to a wall and roots reached out from them and tried to grab him. He returned and landed on the stone platform.

Goblo stretched her arms towards him to be carried.

Arazod tutted and stepped away from her.

Luro approached everyone. 'We choose a path and we don't stop. We follow whoever is in front.'

'And we don't split up,' Freyu said.

Karl nodded. 'Who wants to lead?' He hoped someone would step forward. Of course nobody did. 'Fine.'

He stared at the seven paths. 'I guess there's only one way to choose.'

'Will you follow your heart?' Quizmal asked.

'What? No.' Karl pointed at the path furthest to his left then moved his finger along them with each word. 'Show me the way, show me the way, so I can fight another day. If you take me along the wrong path, curse words at you I will shout.' His finger ended up back at the first path. 'That one.'

Arazod shook his head. 'That didn't even rhyme! And you had the audacity to mock my singing.'

Goblo spat on Karl's trousers. 'Rubbish.'

'At least I did something!' Karl said.

Messiro shook his head, appalled. 'I would call you an imbecile, but I have no better suggestion and you're the only one who volunteered to lead. They say a fool who is willing to lead is better than a leader too scared to look a fool.'

Karl pointed at Messiro. 'Exactly, Messiro. Exactly.'

Freyu approached the path. 'For any future choices, if you're going to do a terrible rhyme just do it in your head.'

He'd do it out loud just to show them they were being unreasonable.

The group gathered in front of the path furthest left.

Karl took a breath. 'We keep moving. We make it home, or we die.'

He stepped onto the roots.

DEAD WEIGHT

Zianfer stepped off the roots onto stone. Water gushed out of six ceiling cracks into six holes on the ground. They were watery pillars, eternally flowing and fizzing with hot energy. Smoke rose off them.

She recalled Ulago's memory of holding her hand to the water and it burning. 'Don't touch the water unless you enjoy pain,' she said.

Cyrilla's bat-human screeched and clicked.

Cyrilla seemed confused. Her eyes shot around the room, but the bat-human tugged at her and dug its nails into her head to calm her.

Two large rocks were in the corner of the cavern. Zianfer consulted the parchment. The path through a flowing wall of water had a certain allure, although was a route to burns and death. A narrow crack in the cavern could tempt those uninformed to squeeze through but was also incorrect.

Zianfer studied the edges of the wall to her right. A puddle formed, suggesting that water flowed into the room from elsewhere.

She pointed to Rimala and called her over. 'Place your hand in that.' She nodded to the puddle.

Rimala didn't move. She held her broken wrist.

A guard pushed her towards Zianfer, but she turned and kicked the guard.

Zianfer grabbed the back of Rimala's head and slammed her face into the rock wall.

Rimala collapsed.

Zianfer grabbed Rimala's broken wrist and placed it in the puddle.

Rimala screamed but her wrist did not burn.

Zianfer turned to her twenty remaining guards and Cyrilla. 'The good water leads the way.'

She walked over to a rock and gazed at the room from the angle Ulago had in the memory. She stared at her hand and the jewels. She lifted a rock and placed it over the nearest hole. Burning water splashed against the rock and burned holes in her robe. She stepped back.

She grabbed the second rock.

'Let us,' a guard said.

Zianfer laughed. 'That's kind. But it would take four of you.' She smiled, lifted the rock and blocked another hole.

Above the puddle, the rock wall fell into a slot in the ground.

Rimala pushed herself to her feet and stumbled into the path.

Zianfer followed, grabbed her hair and dragged her back into the cavern. 'No!'

She slammed Rimala's face against the wall again.

Rimala groaned and fell to her knees.

Zianfer grabbed the back of Rimala's neck. 'I despise vengeful people. They are blind to the good in front of them and cause nothing but pain wherever they go.'

She remembered those to whom she had shown mercy in the Land of the Living. Those who let the need for revenge at being shamed poison them.

She stepped on Rimala's broken wrist.

Her scream echoed through the cavern.

'Cyrilla, block the entrance.' Zianfer shook her head at Rimala. 'You will die here. I hope your last thought is regret about your behaviour.' She jammed an arrow into Rimala's side.

Cyrilla stood in the entrance and pressed her hands against the walls, holding herself in place.

Zianfer pushed a rock off a hole.

She entered the path and Cyrilla stepped off the entrance. The rock wall rose, blocking Rimala's regretful face.

NATURAL HABITAT

Karl's head throbbed. They rushed through long, winding paths, each one the same. Endless roots twisted. It was dizzying and added to the hopelessness.

'Are we going to be trapped forever?' Quizmal asked.

'I have no idea.' Karl walked towards another choice of three paths.

'Are my legs giving up?' Quizmal asked.

Arazod grabbed him under the arms. 'Here.' He lifted him and flew.

Karl bit his lip. How long could they keep this up? Everyone's heavy breaths suggested energy was depleting.

They turned left into another corridor of roots.

Freyu groaned.

The only person who seemed fine was Luro. She hadn't said much and seemed more focused than ever. Probably thinking about the pressure of what she had to do.

She dug her nails into her shoulder wound.

'The roots are so slow, maybe we can rest?' Freyu asked.

Messiro shook his head. 'Focus the mind. A body in rest is harder to awaken. We can rest when we are away from the roots.'

What if the roots never ended?

Another seven unnecessarily long paths later and Karl hoped his eyes weren't deceiving him. 'Please tell me you all see an open area and a nice comfortable boulder instead of another choice of three paths.'

Freyu cheered and Arazod flew ahead.

Karl lay on the boulder and stared up at the ceiling. Faces of failure stared down. So many. Such desperation to escape this realm and return to their lives.

A growl forced Karl to sit up.

A horned bear charged out of a path.

Freyu threw knives at its legs, and it fell to the roots around the rock. 'Can we have a few moments of peace?'

'Why don't the roots grow around the rock?' Quizmal asked.

Luro shrugged. 'I guess whoever made this place wanted to give people hope to add to the pain.' She scratched at her shoulder.

'Are you sure you're okay?' Karl asked.

She huffed. 'I'll get an ointment for it when we get to Hastovia.' Blood ran down her shoulder and she seemed more irritable.

Karl stared at the paths around the room. 'Fourteen choices. That's ridiculous.'

Small roots grew around the bear and slithered up its hairy body as it tried to drag itself onto the rock.

Messiro stood. 'If we are meant to find our way we will.'

Freyu smiled. 'That sounds nice, but it's not that helpful.'

Messiro nodded. 'In our history we reached a point where the importance of quantity overtook the quality of our sayings.'

Karl chuckled and Quizmal didn't even bother writing that last saying down.

Karl needed to rest, but he needed to get back to Sabrinia more. He understood why the roots moved so slowly; it was to add to the torment. Eventually he would be so tired he'd hope they swallowed him instantly, but the slow swallowing would hammer home what a terrible mistake this was.

Karl studied the paths. One sloped up. Another down. One seemed to extend forever.

'Lost,' Goblo said.

Karl nodded. Their greed would be their end. Was wanting to live again greedy when your life was cut short? Or was it just fair?

The bear disappeared into the roots. Its face emerged among the others in the ceiling.

'I say we take the path that goes up,' Arazod said. 'Better than going deeper into this mess.'

'I say down,' Karl said, partly wanting to disagree but also thinking it would be better. 'If it seems the most torturous way, then it's probably the right way.'

Messiro nodded. 'Perhaps I will use this saying.'

'You're welcome.' Karl stepped onto the roots and approached the paths.

'We could split up,' Luro said.

Karl shook his head. 'Under no circumstances do we split the group.' He returned to the rock.

'We could go towards that greenish brown glow.' Freyu pointed down a long path where the glow emerged from a corner.

'Is it coming towards us?' Quizmal asked.

The glow grew brighter, and a shape hovered at the end of the path. A shadowy figure, surrounded by a greenish brown fire. It didn't move.

Freyu gasped. 'A shaling.'

Karl swallowed and remembered Ulago's scroll. 'Ulago referred to a shaling in these exact words – terrifying creature.'

Freyu nodded. 'I think she was being kind. We run or die.'

'Sounds clear enough.' Karl ran towards the path opposite the shaling.

The crackling of its fire intensified. It sped towards them.

A green and brown flame flew past Karl's head and burned the roots in front of him. They quickly grew back.

'Which way?' Luro yelled. The path split in two.

'Left!' Karl sped around the corner and another flame exploded. The force knocked him against the wall and shook his bones.

He bent to pick up his shield and another fireball hit the root wall. A ringing filled his ears.

Messiro picked Karl's shield up and helped him out of the way.

'The others,' Karl said.

Messiro dragged him along the path. 'They had to go the other way. Quick.'

Karl pulled free and ran back. 'Stick together!'

Another fireball exploded. The green and brown light stunned Karl. His eyes burned and he couldn't focus. Everything was a green and white blur with brown spots.

His head throbbed. He reached his arms out, feeling for anything.

Hands grabbed him but he shook them off. He swung his arms and collided with a face.

'We must move!' Messiro said.

'We can't leave them!' Karl screamed.

Claws grabbed Karl's shoulders and lifted him into the air.

'No!' He tried to kick free, but the claws wouldn't let go.

DO NOT OPEN

Karl's focus slowly returned. He lay on the stone roof of a hut, surrounded by other rock dwellings. A tree stood proudly in the middle of the camp reaching up towards the ceiling, somehow thriving without light from the suns.

They were in another open area, but one where people had set up a home; quite a fancy one. People must have carried the stones here and camped to investigate the maze.

The roots didn't stretch around the stone. It seemed stone was the only thing to resist their grasp.

There were another seven paths to choose from. Karl's heart sank.

Messiro touched his fingers to his bloody lip.

'I'm sorry,' Karl said.

Messiro nodded. He whispered, 'It's okay. I know you didn't mean it. But...' He pointed to a path where the shaling glowed and stared ahead. The roots from the floor and walls danced around it.

Karl's chest tightened. 'Why isn't it moving?' he whispered.

Arazod landed on the roof. 'It's been like that a while,' he muttered.

Messiro leaned into Karl. 'What else did Ulago say about them?'

Karl thought back to their conversation. He raised a finger. 'Terrifying creature.' He raised another finger. 'Protects land it inhabits.' He raised a third finger. 'Hates everything and can only be killed by wiping out its habitat. Don't think we can wipe all of this out.'

Messiro paced the rooftop and studied the surroundings. He removed one of his shoes and pulled his arm back.

Karl leapt to his feet and stood in front of him. He whispered, 'What are you doing?'

'Trust me.' Messiro turned to Arazod. 'If it doesn't work, take him and fly away.'

Karl folded his arms and muttered at Arazod, 'I don't need your help.'

Arazod shrugged.

Messiro shook his head. 'Those who truly need help often deny it.'

Karl huffed. 'Just get on with it.'

Messiro launched his shoe onto the root floor.

The shaling crackled and launched a fireball at it. The shoe burned a green and brown and the shaling approached. It stared at the spot where the shoe was, then stopped again.

Karl and Arazod stared at Messiro.

'Was bringing it closer part of the plan?' Karl whispered.

'Natural habitat,' Messiro replied. 'If anything touches its natural habitat, it senses it. Soil, sticks, leaves, will all alert it.'

'You genius,' Karl said. Then he realised the problem. 'Everywhere is made of roots. We're doomed.'

Arazod moved to the front of the stone roof and scratched his talons against it. 'I'll fly into the path and scratch at the roots until it comes back. You two search the huts for anything useful. When I return, we choose a path and we hurry.'

Messiro nodded.

Arazod flew into the path behind the shaling. As soon as he entered, the roots along the walls reached out and triggered the demon. It shot fireballs at Arazod, but he flew away.

The shaling's flames crackled louder, and it followed him.

Karl and Messiro dropped down onto the roots and quickly leapt onto the hut's stone floor.

There was a chest adorned with diamonds next to a large stone bed. Whoever set this camp up was likely a king or queen, or a really successful thief.

Karl found an old cloak. Inside the pockets, nothing.

Messiro reached into the chest and offered Karl some old seeds.

'I think I'll wait until I get to the Land of the Living.'

Messiro nodded and ate some. 'I'll search the other huts.'

Karl's heart filled with dread as Messiro ran along the roots.

Messiro poked his head out of the hut, a huge smile on his face. 'We have hope.'

Karl followed him to a hut with a giant map scratched into the stone wall. This place was incredible in its awfulness.

One path led to a root desert that seemed to never end. Another to a waterfall that fed into a stream, but the word 'burn' etched over it suggested there would be no swimming to any portal. Maybe a boat? Only one path remained undiscovered.

Arazod hovered in the doorway. 'I took it as far as I could before I forgot how to return.'

'Thank you,' Messiro said.

Karl reluctantly nodded. 'Let's hurry.'

They walked along several long paths, worried at any moment they would hear the shaling's crackling.

They came to a small cave. A boulder blocked its entrance,

and they could finally stop on the stone floor. One long root ran out of the ground then under the boulder and into the cave.

A path ran along the cave's side.

A warning was carved into the stone next to the entrance. Karl touched it and read, 'Do not move the boulder. This is not the way. Danger inside.'

Karl turned to Messiro and Arazod. 'What a stupid sign. Obviously now I'm curious, so we have to move the boulder.'

Arazod's beak twisted. 'As a former professional villain, I would only make that sign so people died thanks to their curiosity.'

Messiro nodded. 'Curiosity killed the horse-witch.'

Karl stared at him.

'I'd categorise that saying as quantity,' Messiro said. 'I must admit I am curious, too.'

Karl pushed the boulder, but it was too heavy. He groaned and strained. Messiro joined but it only moved slightly. They needed more to get it over a bump.

Arazod watched and smiled.

'You could actually help,' Karl said.

'So you need my help?' Arazod folded his arms.

Karl stared at him. He glanced at Messiro, hoping for a solution.

'There is no shame in asking for assistance,' Messiro said.

Karl hated them both. 'Can you help?' he muttered.

Arazod's beak curled into a smile. 'Say please.'

'Don't push your luck,' Karl said. 'Do you want to spend more time in this maze?'

'Fine.' Arazod joined them.

They pushed the boulder over the bump. It rolled away from the entrance, but its momentum took it down the path.

Karl grimaced. 'I hope we don't need to put it back.'

They entered the dark stone room. The air turned stale and was uncomfortably hot.

The long root snaked along the stone floor and up to a shadowy figure slumped against the far wall. The figure was muscular with a sack over its head. A chain as thick as Karl's body bound its arms and wings around its chest. Another bound its legs to the wall. It was a cross between a woman and some kind of beast.

The root split off into several others, trying to consume the figure but unable to. They burned and reformed on the creature's chest.

Her chest rose and fell. How was she alive?

Karl stepped towards her, but Arazod put a claw against his chest. 'This creature is here for a reason.'

'She might know the way,' Karl said.

Messiro studied the room. 'Imprisoned beasts become consumed by hunger, and those who free them become the feast.'

Karl worried this was no beast. He remembered Frong's story of the gods. He reached out from as far back as he could and pinched the sack above the creature's head. He yanked it off, revealing a wolf's face, with eyes so bloodshot the anger alone froze Karl. 'Shardur, the god of shadow and darkness.'

A steel gag stopped her biting.

'I think we should go,' Arazod said.

'A restrained god is one who cannot torture you,' Messiro added.

She tried to burst out of the chains, but they flashed with blue light and shocked her.

Karl jumped back. He raised a hand. 'We don't want to hurt you.' Even if they did, they probably couldn't. 'Can you tell us where the portal is?'

Shardur nodded.

Karl turned back to Messiro and Arazod for approval.

Messiro grimaced and looked away.

Arazod stepped back. 'Let's take her memories instead of talking.'

Karl shook his head. 'We should give her the chance to talk first.'

Arazod's wings fluttered. 'For someone who nearly died so many times then eventually did, you don't understand danger very well, do you?'

'I understand that kindness leads to more kindness, sometimes.' Karl shuffled towards Shardur and wiped the sweat from his neck. The heat radiating from her chilled his body.

He reached the back of the steel gag and removed the pin. He pulled the gag out of her mouth. 'So can you tell us how to get to the portal, please?'

Shardur stared into his eyes and roared.

His ears stung and he fell back.

'Gag her!' Arazod jammed the tips of his wings into his ears.

Messiro fell to his knees and covered his ears. He crawled towards the cave entrance.

Karl tried to put the gag back, but she bit at him and roared again.

'I can't!' Karl's head filled with heat.

The roars continued and she released a stomach-turning howl.

Karl crawled behind her and tried to get the gag in, but she chomped down on it and dropped it at her feet.

There was no way Karl was going near it now.

Arazod and Messiro edged towards the cave entrance.

Karl reached into his pocket and took the mind stone out. He tensed, fighting the hellish noise. 'Fine, I tried the nice way.'

THE DOOR

Zianfer grinned as the portal hummed with colourful energy, the doorway to creating the world she wished for. A root extended from the top of it all the way into the cavern's rocky ceiling.

Cyrilla turned back into the maze, but her bat-human pulled her back by her hair. She growled and tensed.

Zianfer ignored her and walked up the steps.

She touched the stone arch and stared at the focus stones. The different energies came together and throbbed in the middle. It was both fierce and beautiful. The key to a true, unthreatened eternal life.

She turned to her people, the twenty-five who remained. 'Who would like to be the first?'

Several people stepped forward and she smiled.

'Wonderful. One of you will enter, then kill yourselves, so when you reappear here we know it has worked. We need to know what awaits on the other side.'

Everyone stepped back, retracting their excitement.

Zianfer contained her disappointment.

Cyrilla's bat-human clicked more and Cyrilla turned to face the maze again.

'Cyrilla, will you choose a volunteer?' Zianfer asked.

Cyrilla turned to Zianfer, but sadness slapped her face. She back-handed her bat-human and sprinted back into the maze.

'Cyrilla!' What was wrong with her?

Zianfer shook her head. 'Fine.' She pointed to a young guard. 'You. Do this and you'll get to choose whether you lead a fort in this realm or the other.'

The man nervously approached the portal. 'Will… will I also get a pet wolf?' He trembled.

Zianfer nodded. 'Yes.' What a bizarre man.

'Great.' He smiled and stood in the arch. Colourful energy surrounded him and the root throbbed. From the cavern ceiling, a dark red glow pulsed through the root until it hit the stone arch and formed a drop. The drop fell into where the energies met and the colours flashed.

The guard vanished.

Zianfer's heart filled with hope and joy.

FRIENDS WITH CONDITIONS

Freyu, Goblo, Quizmal, and Luro rushed through a stone tunnel.

At least they were off the roots.

They had fallen into this stone pit and had no choice but to follow one path.

'Do you think they're okay?' Quizmal asked.

Freyu nodded. She had to believe it.

'Why?' Quizmal asked.

She wasn't prepared for a follow-up question. 'Well... because they don't give up that easily. And, we're so close to the way home it'll give them that extra push.' She felt lighter thinking about it. 'Before, this was just a possibility, but now we're here I can picture my village's bean and grass nut stew. The steam rising off it and the slight smell of the charred nuts.' She smiled.

Luro scratched her shoulder and closed her eyes. She rocked.

'Why don't you at least try Boofa's potion?' Freyu asked.

Luro shook her head and winced. 'It won't help.'

'How do you know?' Quizmal asked.

'It just won't!' she snapped.

Freyu raised her arms. 'Okay.'

Luro had barely spoken since they fell.

They came to a sharp downward slope, nowhere else to go.

Tiny orange lights blinked at the bottom, probably torches to light the way.

Goblo shone her light onto them.

Eyes.

A boar-like beast, withered and wounded, slumped against the wall. It had the arms and legs of a human, but the head and hooves of a boar.

It was stuck, too wide to fit through any of the three small paths, and too big to get back up the slope.

It pushed itself onto its hooves and grunted.

'It probably thinks we'd make a good meal,' Freyu said. 'But it's slow, so let's slide down and run for that path on the right. Ideally we won't kill it.' She turned to everyone and they nodded. 'I'll go first to distract it.'

She leapt down the slope, trying to stay balanced, and made it. The boar swiped a hoof at her, but Freyu rolled under it.

She turned and held its focus.

It swung its other hoof, but she leapt back.

Her friends made it to the entrance.

Freyu ran for the path, but a lump of sludge wrapped around her ankles and she fell.

She rolled over. Her heart raced.

Muck dripped from the boar's snout.

'Help!' Freyu reached for her throwing knives, but another sludge lump pinned her hand to the stone.

The boar opened its stinking mouth and aimed its chipped jagged teeth at her.

Goblo blinded it and Luro wedged her sword in the beast's neck. She chopped at its head, again and again.

Blood covered Freyu, but Luro was crazed.

'It's done, Luro,' Freyu said.

She kept chopping until the beast burst into ash. She stared at the pile of death a moment then turned and walked into the tunnel. 'We keep moving.'

Quizmal looked as shocked as Freyu. Goblo sniffed ash and grimaced.

Freyu took a moment to catch her breath.

'Come on!' Luro snapped.

They continued along rocky paths and came to a room where water gushed from the ceiling into holes.

Freyu spotted a broken figure with an arrow sticking out of her side. 'Rimala.' Freyu's eye filled with tears.

Rimala tried to shoulder barge a boulder onto a hole. Blood poured out of the cut in her leather armour.

She stared back at Freyu and wept. 'I'm sorry.'

Freyu's sympathy faded under the annoyance at her former friend's betrayal.

'Idiot,' Goblo said, summing it up well.

'Please, help me.' Rimala lay down and groaned.

Freyu turned to Quizmal.

'Will I support whatever you choose?' Quizmal said.

Luro studied the paths, not bothered by Rimala.

Freyu approached Rimala and knelt. They had been through so much in this realm. It wouldn't be right to leave it without her.

She placed the potion Boofa gave her on the stones.

Rimala stared at it.

'Drop this idiotic quest for revenge,' Freyu said.

Rimala stared at her and gritted her teeth.

Freyu took a breath. 'I want my friend back. I want to find that portal and return to the Land of the Living with that friend. I want to show her my village and a peaceful life, one where she can find new purpose.'

Rimala's eyes closed then opened again. She reached for the potion, but Freyu pulled it away.

'Messiro travelled with us,' Freyu said.

Rimala groaned and her eyes widened.

'He helped us. If we see him, you swear to me you don't let it get in the way of us getting home.'

Rimala cried.

Freyu swallowed. 'He did a terrible deed, but he was not the one behind it. He was the hands, others were the arms and intention.'

Rimala's stare still carried hatred, but it softened. 'I promise.'

Freyu snapped the arrow in Rimala's side, opened Boofa's potion and poured it on Rimala's wound.

Rimala screamed and sweat soaked her.

Freyu slowly pulled the arrow out, trying not to shred any flesh. The bloody arrowhead clanked against the stone.

The potion sealed Rimala's wound.

'We need to keep moving,' Luro said. 'I think it's this way.' She stared at the path behind the waterfall.

'No.' Rimala nodded at the rock. 'Push it over that hole. A secret way.'

Freyu and Luro pushed the rock over the hole. Splashes of water burned Freyu.

Freyu turned to Rimala, who hopped onto her good leg. She pulled Freyu into a hug. 'Thank you.'

Freyu squeezed her. She finally had her friend back.

A SINISTER CREATION

Karl walked to the front of the stone hut's roof and stared at the tree in the middle of the camp. 'Be careful,' he told Arazod.

Messiro nodded to Arazod.

Arazod's beak twitched. 'I hoped to never see it again.' He flew into the path.

They waited and Arazod brought the shaling back. He hovered in front of the tree; as soon as he touched a claw to the bark, the shaling fired.

Arazod flew out of the way, but the explosion knocked him onto the roots.

Karl's neck tensed.

The shaling turned to Arazod.

'Help!' Arazod yelled.

Karl could jump down and pull him into the stone home, but he froze.

Messiro snatched Karl's shield and leapt off the roof and in front of Arazod.

A fireball hit the shield, knocking him back.

Arazod recovered, grabbed Messiro and flew them onto the roof.

The tree burned a beautiful green and brown.

The shaling froze, waiting for movement.

Arazod stood and whispered, 'I'll get it away.' He flew back into the narrow path, the roots diverting the shaling.

Karl stared at Messiro. 'Sorry. I—'

'Come on.' Messiro jumped off the roof.

Karl tossed the mind stone into the fire and watched Shardur's life.

He watched a memory Frong had read out to him from the book, *The Godly Godsfolk: Third Edition*. Shardur helped the other gods to imprison Death. They used a magic relic that contained Death's lover, Illuminus.

Once Death was imprisoned, the gods argued over what to do with the Soul of Illuminus.

Shardur took it and hid it. She couldn't destroy the woman she secretly loved. She returned to the Realm of the Dead a shell of a god, wounded by her wrongdoing.

A lot of memories were of Shardur moping around and suffering, just getting through the day. Then she found a new lover. A human.

They lived peacefully. The terrifying being from the third edition of the book was definitely misrepresented. Whoever wrote that book needed a talking to as there seemed to be a few skewed details presented as facts. Shardur was a being full of love.

Shardur's favourite thing seemed to be flying her lover to high points in the realm and having meals as the night suns rose.

Karl chuckled at the beautiful simplicity of love.

Another romantic night on a floating rock was quite steamy, and the silence between Karl and Messiro became uncomfortable.

In the next memory, Shardur walked through a forest and

found her lover by a stream. A large bat-human chewed on her chest. Shardur leapt at the creature, but it turned into mist and floated into the wound on her lover's body.

Shardur tried to revive her lover, but she foamed at the mouth and her body froze. Shardur carried her back to their home and placed her on a table outside. She rushed inside to grab herbs and potion bottles, but when she returned her lover floated away, carried by two smaller bat-humans. She stared back with a crazed look in her eyes, flipping between joy and pain.

Bat Lover.

Shardur's memories became an endless search all over the Realm of the Dead. But there was never a moment of hope, just people shaking their heads and frowning. Shardur gave up. She spent her days sat outside their home gazing at the sky.

Then one day she was approached by Ulago, a twiggy being that must have been Naturais, and an angry looking half-dragon, half-human, who must have been Klarsa.

They were friends, and they created the portal together.

Shardur beamed at the sight of the portal, but then the others betrayed her. They overpowered Shardur. She fought back valiantly with swift strikes, but Klarsa breathed fire until Shardur was blinded by black smoke. Then Naturais wrapped her in branches while Ulago restrained her with magical chains.

Karl felt sick.

They created the maze from the inside out and walked Shardur through it to the stone room.

Naturais covered Shardur in roots; one in particular fed off her. The group walked out of the room and Ulago sealed it with the boulder. Before the final push she grinned at Shardur. Not a shred of remorse.

The remaining memories were of the root attached to Shardur flowing with blood towards the entrance to the stone room.

The memories ended and started again.

The pain of betrayal flooded through Karl. Those Shardur had trusted used her. They probably gave her hope she would find a way to save her lover, then they made it even harder for her to ever see her again.

They denied her a life and moments of happiness, because they felt their moments were more important.

Karl thought about his mother and how he only knew her briefly, and the moments with Sabrinia that were spent fighting for their lives.

Arazod returned.

Karl turned to him. 'Thanks for your help, but know that I can't ever forgive you.'

Arazod looked down at the roots and nodded. 'Let's get off these roots before it comes back.'

Messiro shook his head at Karl and walked on. 'Follow me.'

They approached the path along the side of the mountain by Shardur's cave. The root snaking into the cave throbbed a dark red.

Karl stopped. 'We need to give her the memories back.'

Arazod chuckled then realised Karl was serious. 'Why?'

'She's suffered enough. And while her life was horrible, we can't take the moments of happiness from her. Other beings have done that.'

Arazod shrugged. 'If we must.'

Karl entered and approached Shardur, an empty, confused presence, drained of all emotion and purpose.

He cut the back of Shardur's head with the stone and the eel-spider crawled into her wound.

A clicking drew Karl's attention.

Bat Lover kicked Arazod against the stone wall and scratched Messiro's eyes.

He writhed on the floor, holding his face.

Karl raised a hand. 'We're trying to help.'

Bat Lover's normally expressionless face fell at the sight of Shardur.

Karl checked the mind stone; the spider was deep in Shardur's head. 'Come on.'

The bat-human dug its nails into Bat Lover's head. She tried to push it away, but it fought back and dug them in deeper. The expressionless face returned under the blue glow in her eyes.

She placed her hand under her chin.

Karl gazed at the mind stone again. The eel-spider crawled out of Shardur's head wound.

Karl snatched the mind stone and ran.

Bat Lover blew her icy mist at Messiro, but Karl pulled him out of the way.

The trio fled the cave, but Bat Lover chased them and fired icy spikes at them.

Karl blocked several with his shield, but she fired more. He backed towards the edge of the mountain path. His feet shuffled against the roots. Nothing below but spiky rocks.

Messiro wiped the blood from his eyes and leapt at Bat Lover. She blocked his punches and whacked him into the wall.

Karl turned to Arazod, who flew into the path they came from.

'Coward!' Karl shouted. That's who he was and always would be.

Bat Lover stood over Messiro and placed her hand under her chin. The bat-human shrieked.

Karl swung his shield at the bat-human and knocked it off Bat Lover.

She faced him and seemed dazed. She turned back to the cave entrance and ran towards it.

The bat-human caught up and dug its nails into her head again and her fury shifted back to Karl.

He retreated. 'I was trying to give her the memories back.'

Karl hoped Shardur had recovered and would remember. Maybe she could get through to Bat Lover.

Karl's foot brushed the edge of the path. It couldn't end here. He was so close.

Messiro struggled to stand.

Bat Lover stood inches from Karl and grinned. Blood fell out of her cut lip.

A shriek distracted her.

The shaling.

Arazod flew behind Karl, lifted him and headed towards Messiro.

The shaling shot a fireball at Bat Lover.

She blew icy mist back, but the fireball hit her. She staggered.

Arazod, Karl, and Messiro ran along the mountain path, away from the battle.

Karl turned back, his heart pounding. He wanted to help Bat Lover to break free.

She charged the shaling and they grappled.

This wasn't his fight. 'Let's keep going.'

He faced the path that narrowed with pits full of spikes either side of it.

CHANGING MINDSET

Freyu stepped into a giant cavern.

Other paths leading into the cavern were so high they were clearly designed to torture people by being so close, yet unable to get to the portal without risking falling to their deaths.

Another path was across a steel bridge above a burning stream.

At the far end of the cavern were roughly fifty wide stone steps. Zianfer stood at the top, in front of the portal.

It fizzed with power. How could such a thing send someone back to their life?

Zianfer applauded as a man climbed out of a muddy hole in the stone floor. She pulled him to his feet.

Freyu gestured for everyone to remain silent.

Zianfer stepped towards the portal. 'While today we lost many, we have gained so much. We will never forget their sacrifice, because we will always remember the day we came to command life and death.'

Her guards and remaining followers cheered.

'Do we have a plan?' Quizmal whispered.

Freyu scratched her head. 'Not really, but we should probably stop her entering that portal.'

They could approach from the sides rather than reveal themselves at the bottom of the steps.

There were only five of them and at least twenty or so guards. It was a huge risk, but they had to do something. Her arms tensed.

She spotted Karl, Messiro, and Arazod over the other side of the stairs, peering out of the rocks. A grin dominated her face and her limbs tingled.

'We have hope,' she told her friends. She waved to get Karl's attention without alerting the guards.

Rimala broke from the group and hobbled towards Messiro, not caring that she'd be seen.

'Rimala!' Freyu called her back and chased her.

Messiro spotted Rimala. He ran across the hot steel bridge and back into the maze.

Rimala tried to follow but Freyu grabbed her arm.

Rimala drove her elbow into Freyu's cheek. 'Get off me!'

Freyu wouldn't let go, but Rimala elbowed her again and again.

The blows hurt a lot less than the death of their friendship. Freyu released her.

Rimala's eyes shot hatred back at her and she followed Messiro.

Freyu's heart clenched. There was no saving Rimala from herself. She had to accept it.

She turned back to see Zianfer at the top of the steps smiling at her.

Zianfer pulled an arrow from her quiver and launched it at Freyu.

Karl stepped in front of her and lifted his shield. The arrow smashed against it.

'Thank you,' she said.

But Karl groaned.

Freyu looked down. A second arrow was wedged in Karl's ankle. He dropped his shield.

Freyu tried to pull him away, but another arrow pierced his chest.

Freyu screamed and Karl flopped to the floor.

'Capture them!' Zianfer ordered.

Her guards and followers charged.

Arazod flew into a high path entrance.

Guards stood in front of the portal while others charged the group.

Quizmal clubbed a follower's head, knocking him over the side of the steps.

Others charged and Goblo blasted light into their eyes.

Freyu threw knives as quickly as she could. One pierced a guard's shoulder, and he dropped his weapon. But the numbers would tell.

They had no chance.

Where was Luro?

Maybe she was a pile of ash somewhere in the maze.

Karl bled on the stone floor. The battle happened around him, as though he was decoration to the chaos. He would likely explode into ash soon.

Arazod could fly through the portal, but Zianfer would probably throw an arrow through him.

He could flee, go back and find a different life in this miserable land. Maybe there was something else for him.

But what if this fight wasn't over? What if this fight was only over because he believed it was? What if he could make a difference – a good one?

His feathers trembled and his beak twitched. It was as though his nature fought against the idea of taking such a big risk. It didn't seem to make a difference if he helped or not. Karl always reminded him how much he hated him.

Arazod's heart hardened and his feathers chilled. He started walking away, but the battle cries stopped him. He recognised Freyu's shouts. He felt Quizmal's groans and the strange gargling noise that Goblo made.

Who cared what Karl thought? The deeds weren't good because someone said they were; they were good because of what they were.

Arazod took a breath. He turned and stood at the edge of the path.

Freyu, Quizmal, and Goblo stood back-to-back, trying to evade capture.

Karl's body jerked and he grimaced. Hopeless.

Arazod expected Karl to cast him a farewell glance of disappointment, but he didn't. He stared as though he was full of regret.

Arazod nodded at Karl and crossed his arm over his chest.

Karl reached for his shield. A guard approached him.

Arazod flew down and swung his axe into the guard's neck, leaving it wedged there.

He grabbed Karl's body. 'Use whatever you have left to shield us.'

Arazod pulled Karl's back to his chest and flew towards the portal.

Guards shot arrows that deflected off the shield and another couple stuck in Karl's legs.

'I can't,' Karl strained.

'Stop being pathetic!' Arazod commanded.

Zianfer drew her arm back and threw an arrow at Arazod's face. Karl raised the shield and the arrow skimmed off its rim and brushed Arazod's head feathers. His heart raced.

Karl's shield dropped to the floor along with his purple nugget and the mind stone. His arms dangled by his sides.

'Hold on, Karl! A moment more.'

Arazod flew over the portal and dropped Karl into it.

Karl's body crashed off the hard floor and he lay in the arch, broken and stuffed with arrows.

The colourful energy closed around Karl and flashed.

He vanished.

HOW MANY LIVES LEFT?

$\mathcal{K}$arl's eyes opened. He lay on top of a mountain outside a wooden hut.

A camel-goat rubbed its face against his cheek and licked his ear with its rough tongue.

Arrows poked out of Karl's limbs and his breathing slowed. Every movement stung. He moved his right arm, but it felt as though it could rip.

Arazod was a genius. Karl chuckled through the pain. He'd die and be back in the battle, arrow-free and healed.

The door to the wooden hut opened and a tiny old woman stared at Karl. 'Another one?' She waved the camel-goat away. 'I left the city for the mountains so I wouldn't have to bother with idiot folks and now I've had one idiot appear out of nowhere, use my toilet bucket then stab himself.' She pointed to a corpse by the mountainside. 'And now an idiot covered in arrows. Nobody gets covered in arrows unless they've been really stupid.' She shook her head.

Karl coughed up blood. 'Don't worry, I won't be here long.'

The warmth drained from his body, and he faded. It wasn't as bad as the first time he died when he had a blade in his chest, but it was still awful. The pain left the tips of his fingers and toes and worked through his limbs and into his torso. The intensity grew as the pain surrounded his heart. His thoughts blurred into darkness and his heart gave one final agonising beat.

Karl coughed and grasped through dirt towards the bursts of light. The arrows were gone from his body and the aches, too.

He emerged from a muddy hole behind the portal.

Goblo blinded guards but they closed in.

Freyu, Quizmal, and Goblo surrendered.

Karl used the distraction to crawl behind a rock.

Guards pointed their bows up at paths in the cavern, likely seeking Arazod.

Zianfer closed in on Karl's friends as the guards restrained them.

She grabbed Quizmal's face. 'You were with me from the beginning.'

Quizmal nodded. 'Did I mean to hurt you?'

Zianfer nodded. 'I know.' She released his face. 'But I can't have people with different goals. It's where things begin to go wrong.'

Arazod grabbed Karl and flew him into a path high up the cavern wall.

'Thank you,' Karl said.

Arazod nodded.

Zianfer stood in front of the portal. She paced before Goblo, Quizmal, and Freyu, on their knees on top of the stairs.

She gestured to the portal. 'You can join us, or die here, in front of the chance at another life.'

Arazod turned to Karl. 'Ready to go again?'

Karl swallowed. 'No.'

'Me neither.' Arazod grabbed Karl and they flew towards Zianfer.

She noticed and drew an arrow.

'Goblo! Light!' Karl shouted.

Goblo blasted light at Zianfer and she recoiled. Before she could adjust and aim, Arazod flew Karl into Zianfer and the three of them landed in the portal. The energy consumed them and shot them into the Land of the Living.

Karl and Zianfer crashed onto the mountain while Arazod flew above them.

The tiny old woman was sunbathing on the roof of her hut and sat up. She folded her arms. 'This is not okay!'

Zianfer grabbed an arrow and stabbed at Karl, but he dodged and tackled her to the stones.

They rolled into the camel-goat. It bleated and moved away, then spat at them.

Zianfer overpowered Karl and grabbed his throat. She was too strong.

Arazod swooped down and kicked her off him.

Soldiers appeared out of nothingness and attacked Karl and Arazod.

The old woman leapt off her roof. 'Right, enough of this.' She entered the hut and re-emerged holding a whip.

She lashed three guards and Arazod scratched them. He flew up and kicked two off the mountainside.

Karl punched a guard, who dropped his sword. Karl picked it up and thrust it into the side of the man's armour. It was easier to kill knowing it wasn't really killing, just sending someone to the second life. At least, that's how he justified it.

The woman whipped Karl's legs from underneath him. 'Clear off!'

Karl caught his breath and got up. 'Trust me, I want to.'

The woman whipped Zianfer, who caught the whip around her wrist and yanked it away.

'I'm off for a nap then.' The woman entered her hut and slammed the door.

A guard thrust her sword at Karl. He deflected it, and her momentum took her into a tree.

Arazod grabbed her in his talons and dropped her off the mountain.

The same guards appeared again out of thin air.

'They'll just keep coming,' Zianfer said. 'You cannot win.'

Karl and Arazod backed towards the mountain's edge.

The guards closed in, led by Zianfer.

She smiled at Arazod. 'I remember you from his memories.' She turned to Karl. 'Why would you fight with the creature who brought you so much pain?'

Karl could lunge at her, but he'd likely fail.

Zianfer placed her left hand on her chest. 'I know vengeance is for idiots, but those who betray will do it again. It's in them, a part of who they are, like a sickness. I tried to give those who betrayed me another chance, but they simply found a worse way to deceive me.'

If they came any closer Karl would fight his way out. 'Sometimes people realise they've made mistakes. Then, yes, maybe they make some more, and further ones after that, but then they realise and try to put them right.'

Zianfer chuckled and turned to Arazod. 'Join me. I need more leaders and with your experience, and wings, you could be a valuable member of the new world.'

Arazod's beak twitched.

'What else are you going to do? Die alongside someone who hates you?' She smirked.

Karl laughed. 'Why would anyone want to live in your vision? You let hundreds of your people get eaten by a dragon.'

Zianfer's eyes widened. 'It was for a cause!'

'It was for selfishness and fear of people having choices,' Karl said. 'So let's have the fight we're meant to have.' He raised his sword, but Arazod knocked it out of his hand and wrapped his arm around Karl's neck.

Karl's heart raced. He grabbed Arazod's arm, but Arazod poked a claw into his neck.

'What are you doing?' Karl said.

Zianfer grinned.

Arazod grabbed Karl's sword in his talons, threw it up and caught it in his claws.

Karl's eyes welled up. He stopped struggling. There was no point anymore. The world always reminded him that good things don't last. 'Just do it. I knew you'd never change. You're always after the easy way out.'

'I accept your offer,' Arazod told Zianfer. 'But I want a base high in the mountains and any man-hawks we find will be placed under my command.'

Zianfer nodded. 'Of course.'

Arazod's beak pressed against Karl's ear. 'You've done nothing but belittle me. You're no better than the man-hawks who shunned me.' Arazod raked his talons down the back of Karl's right knee and pushed him onto the ground. 'Finally, I get to kill you. I'll send you back to the guards in the Realm of the Dead. When they end your second life, I want you to remember this moment. *I* killed you. Remember *where we stood* in your final moments.'

Karl no longer cared.

The sword sliced through his neck.

LIFE CYCLE

Karl gasped for air and pulled himself out of another muddy rebirth in the corner of the cavern. Dying was exhausting and misery consumed his heart. He wanted to dip Arazod in the burning sea and listen to his screams.

He touched his neck, his head fully reattached.

A guard pointed his sword at Karl. 'Join the others.' The guard nodded to Freyu, Goblo, and Quizmal, still on their knees.

He marched Karl towards his friends. Karl spotted his shield in front of the portal.

They passed it, and with nothing to lose, Karl shoved the guard, who slipped on the shield and stumbled into the portal.

Karl picked up his shield and blocked a guard's thrust.

Their sword dropped in front of Freyu.

She grabbed it and they battled their captors.

Freyu, Quizmal, and Goblo ran back to the bottom of the steps to retrieve their weapons. The guards and followers chased them.

Another follower swung her spear at Karl. He blocked and whacked her head. He threw her into the portal.

Karl spotted his purple nugget and the mind stone. He rubbed the nugget for good luck, then placed it and the mind stone back in his pockets.

Two guards raised their swords and charged at him.

QUICK THINKER

Arazod stared down at Karl's detached head. His dead expression was more of disappointment than anger.

'A pleasure to have you with us,' Zianfer said. 'We shall build an army at all the key points in the lands, dominating both worlds. You are now integral to that.' She reached out her ring-covered hand to shake Arazod's. 'My flying general.'

Arazod's beak curled into a smile and his feathers fluttered. He grabbed Zianfer's hand in his claw. 'I'm more of a leader than a follower.' He drove his sword through Zianfer's heart.

The guards charged at him.

He hoped Karl would do his part.

TRUE TO FORM

*K*arl blocked thrust after swing and the guards tired.

Another swung lazily and Karl dodged and pulled the guard into the other. He pushed them both into the portal and took a moment to catch his breath.

The ground was covered in muddy rebirth holes. Karl spotted a stray arrow and picked it up.

He turned to join his friends and promised himself if Arazod turned up he'd jam the arrow into his eye and twist it around.

The ground shook. Another rebirth.

He pointed the arrow at the hole. He gritted his teeth and hoped it was the feathered idiot.

A left hand emerged, adorned with jewels. Zianfer.

She would surely send her guards before her to secure her rebirth.

Karl's heart clenched. *Remember where we stood in your final moments.*

Zianfer stared up at Karl. She opened her mouth to shout, but Karl jammed the arrow into her neck.

Blood drained out of her wound.

Karl grabbed her hair and yanked her out of the muddy hole. He dragged her towards the portal.

She coughed words through the blood, barely able to get them out. 'All… I wanted… was a peaceful world. You could… have joined it.' She swiped for his ankle, but he moved and kicked her.

'You wanted control and became blind to what peace is. I'm sorry.' Karl stood over her body and called out to her guards. 'She's done. There's no need to follow anymore.' He yanked the arrow out of her throat and jammed it back in.

The guards charged at him.

'No! That's not the reaction,' Karl said. 'This is all meant to stop.'

Zianfer aimed a bloody smile at him. 'They love me.' Her expression changed to a deep sadness. 'Sorry, Hermin.' She exploded into ash. All that remained were her rings and clothes.

Ten different weapons came towards Karl. Which would he try to dodge first? The spear? Then the sword would get him. The axe? The weird spiked club thing would poke holes in his body.

He backed away but a burning gale knocked him over. He shielded his eyes from the red blaze and one by one the guards burned and exploded into ash. Like a drum beat. Boom, boom, boom. People exploded out of existence.

The weapons that were aimed at Karl clattered against the stone, smoke rising from them.

Luro landed in front of Karl, but with wings. The scar on her shoulder was gone, replaced by a glowing scale.

'Luro?' Karl said.

The others cheered.

She shook her head. 'Use my real name: Klarsa.'

Karl had no idea what was happening, but he was incredibly dizzy and desperate to sleep.

'Ulago is nothing but a crook and a liar,' she said.

'I know,' Karl said. 'I've seen Shardur's memories. I've seen what you all did.'

Klarsa touched the focus stones around the portal. 'When we realised the portal wouldn't work without the blood of a god, we made a deal to restrain Shardur. We could have used some of her blood and all left together, but Ulago felt the portal needed to always be functioning, in case she died again. She had to have an immortal attached to it. I could reconcile it, because I would get to live again. But they betrayed me, too.' Klarsa flew and stood atop the portal and pulled on the root.

Karl backed away from the portal, close to a rock he could take cover behind should she unleash more fire. 'So, your aunt?'

She fanned her wings out. 'A tale. When we first created this, I wanted to return to kill my parents. The only dragiant is my sister. I was from my father's affair with another dragaur. I was shame, a painful reminder. They knew I hated my sister and opposed their dreams of how to build peace. I know peace is an invitation for invasion and with other dragaurs I planned to usurp them. My parents learned of my plan and murdered me. Poisoned me.'

Karl locked eyes with her and shuddered. She had a look he had seen in so many tyrants before. Blind belief and determination.

Klarsa flew down and stood in between Karl and the rock he had noted as a safe place. 'Naturais supported my goal and I confided in her about my true intention, to eradicate giants and any future dragiants. Dragaurs are best at their purest, and we don't need a union with giants. They offer nothing.'

Karl stepped back. 'But you're a dragiant. Ulago confirmed it in her cave. Surely you can see the good in it?'

Klarsa walked in front of the portal, placed a claw on it and leaned against it. She smiled at him. 'I'm not.'

Guards climbed from mud holes. Klarsa breathed fire onto them.

She scratched her shoulder scale. 'We were meant to betray Ulago when the portal was working. But Naturais told her. They tore my power scale from my shoulder and hid it here. A dragon's power scale never dies. We all have one that is the source of our magic and our flight.' She stroked the scale. 'Then they blindfolded me and took me into the Land of the Living so I wouldn't even know where to kill myself to appear here.' She took a large breath. 'They left me on a boat in the middle of the sea. They hoped that maybe stripped of my power I would also be stripped of my anger. Giants are a stain.'

Karl shook his head. She was crazier than Zianfer. He placed his foot on Zianfer's rings and dragged them towards him.

Klarsa walked towards Karl, who stepped off the rings. 'It hurt to change my form. But I'd never find Ulago otherwise. She would know. And nobody would suspect the one true dragiant of being Klarsa.'

Karl shook his head. 'Paliun died for you, because he thought you were doing something good. You wept for him.'

Klarsa chuckled. 'I gave the old fool purpose. I cried because his power was remarkable, and I needed it.'

The rings were too close to her paw. Karl backed down the steps.

Klarsa folded her arms. 'Because I appreciate your help, I will give you a choice. Leave the maze or die here.'

Karl swallowed. 'What about we all go through the portal and live our lives? And maybe yours could be a bit more peaceful?'

Klarsa chuckled. 'It's sad, but I knew your answer would be one that means I have to kill you.' Klarsa kicked him in the chest and he collapsed. The air fled from his lungs and blood dotted his chest.

Goblo ran up to Klarsa and held her arms out. 'Friend.'

Klarsa grinned at Goblo. 'I do like you, but I don't need you.' She booted her into the wall.

It felt like a stone slab was inside Karl's chest. It took everything to crawl.

Klarsa breathed fire at Quizmal. He ducked behind a rock then re-emerged touching his head.

'How is my hair?' he asked Karl.

Karl bit his lip at the sight of the empty skin desert. 'If anything, you look more mature now.'

Quizmal's face dropped. He charged Klarsa and raised his club. A wing whacked him away.

Freyu threw knives at Klarsa but they hit her scales and fell.

Klarsa flew down the steps at Freyu and kicked her over.

Freyu got to her feet and scrambled up the steps to take cover in a mud hole.

Karl crawled towards Zianfer's rings. A few more feet.

Klarsa stood at the bottom of the steps and gazed up. Her stomach and throat glowed orange. Smoke rose off her scales.

Karl stretched his hand towards the rings.

Klarsa breathed fire up the steps.

He retracted his hand and squeezed into the mud hole with Freyu.

They stared at each other, sweating, both completely lost.

Heat and smoke choked the air.

Wings flapped and Klarsa landed above them. She smiled.

'Thanks for everything,' Karl told Freyu.

She nodded and held his hand.

Karl prayed Sabrinia and the others were okay. He closed his eyes, but Klarsa groaned.

Arazod scratched her face and pulled at her wings.

'Get off me!' she moaned.

Karl turned to Freyu. 'In the Realm of the Dead, some people are too crazy to reason with, and in that case, death is appropriate.'

'It's a bit long but the sentiment is right,' she said.

They climbed out of the hole.

Freyu threw knives at Klarsa's scale, trying to dislodge it.

Karl ran to Zianfer's rings and put them on his left hand. Strength surged through his limbs.

Klarsa grabbed Arazod's wings and slammed him against the wall. She torched one of his wings and he screamed.

She held him against the floor and scratched his body.

He shrieked as feathers shredded.

Klarsa drew her left claw back, but Karl grabbed her wrist in his right hand, amazed at his strength.

'How?' she said.

She turned and tried to pull free but couldn't. She drew her head back to bite Karl, but he drove his left hand at her neck and squeezed it.

She raked her free claws across his face. It stung and his cheeks bled, but he wouldn't let go. He fought the pain as the heat rose through Klarsa's neck.

She opened her mouth and drew her head back.

'Goblo!' Karl yelled.

Goblo blasted light into Klarsa's face and she recoiled.

Karl released her left wrist, reached into his pocket and grabbed the purple nugget, then jammed his fist into her mouth.

She bit down and tore into his forearm. She ripped the skin and crunched through bone.

Karl screamed and fell to the floor. His right hand and wrist had left him.

He writhed and turned away from the bloody mess that was once part of a limb.

Klarsa laughed at him. She chewed his fist and wrist and swallowed them. 'Nicer than mushrooms.' She stood over Karl and raised her foot, but then she coughed. Then coughed again.

She clawed at her throat.

Green and purple liquid dripped from her mouth, and she fell to her knees. 'What have you done?'

Karl shuffled away, barely conscious.

She wheezed and gasped. She stumbled towards the portal, trying to get back to the Land of the Living.

Arazod picked up his axe and swung it at her legs. She fell and he placed a talon on her back. 'No.'

'Get off!' she demanded and stretched for the portal.

Quizmal stumbled over. He knelt by her head. His bottom lip trembled. 'Am I sad about this?'

She coughed. 'Shut up.'

Goblo stood next to her head and shone light into her eyes.

She tried to swipe Goblo away. 'Idiots!'

Quizmal held his hand out and Freyu handed him a knife.

He jammed the knife into Klarsa's scale and cut it from her shoulder.

She screamed. Her wings retracted into her body and her scales shrank.

Quizmal flung the scale away.

Freyu ran up to Karl and stared at his wound.

'I'm fine.' He glanced at the mess. 'I'm not fine.'

Freyu tore her tunic and wrapped it around the wound.

Arazod dragged Klarsa down the steps. Her head bashed off each one.

'The plague of giants cannot spread!' she cried.

Arazod dragged her over the steel bridge and to the roots that led back into the maze. He placed a talon on her back and pressed her into them.

She groaned.

Karl could stop Arazod, but why?

The roots slithered around Klarsa. Her weak groans faded, and the roots pulled her into the ground.

Karl stared at the faces on the cavern ceiling.

Klarsa's twisted expression joined them.

'Hang on, Karl,' Freyu said. She dragged him towards the portal.

Karl's heart slowed and he faded.

Freyu slapped his face. 'Stay awake.'

He groaned. Everything was blurry. The portal felt sunsets away.

Arazod lifted him. 'You ready to die one more time?'

Karl nodded. 'I think I'm addicted to it.'

Arazod carried him through the portal and placed him on his feet. He fell to his knees.

The old woman swept bodies over the edge of the mountain and noticed Karl and Arazod. 'Just have the land! I'll move!'

Karl shook his head. 'No need. A couple more trips and we'll be gone for good.'

'Pests!' she said. 'Stop bleeding everywhere.'

Karl laughed and turned to Arazod. 'Want to kill me again?' He stared at his severed head from the last time he had died.

Arazod's beak curled into a smirk. 'Why don't you kill me first? I think I deserve it.'

Karl laughed and cried. He picked up a sword by one of the dead soldiers.

'Thank you,' Karl said.

Arazod's eyes filled with tears. He knelt and bent his head forward. 'Don't enjoy it too much.'

Karl smiled. He found the strength to stand and lifted the sword. 'I'm not left-handed. So, sorry if this takes a couple of goes.'

Arazod winced and closed his eyes.

Karl brought the sword down. Arazod's head came clean off.

Karl retched. He approached the old woman and held out the sword. 'Could you? Please?'

She took the sword. 'Gladly, you pest.' She drove it into his stomach several times.

SAME BUT DIFFERENT

Karl climbed out of his nine hundredth mud hole, his arm back. He gasped and took a moment.

Arazod stood with the others, his wings healed from the burning.

Freyu smiled. 'We did it.'

Quizmal grinned. 'Shall we go through one final time?'

Karl took a breath and stared at the energy. Magical, incredible, but a plague. 'I'm going to stay here.'

Freyu folded her arms. 'Does going through that portal too many times make you go mad?'

Karl turned to Arazod. 'You're right. Sabrinia doesn't need me. And what am I going to do? Run around the world hoping I find her alive?'

Arazod nodded.

Karl leaned on the portal arch. 'Instead of chasing what I had, I'm going to make this place incredible for when it's their time to join me. Destroying this portal is one way to calm greedy people down a little bit. Might stop them having grand ideas that mean mass death.'

Quizmal stood by Karl. 'Can I help you?'

'What about Questions?' Karl asked.

'Does she have her own life now? Shall I create a nice home for her to have here? Shall I give her a *This is the Book of Tales in the Realm of the Dead*?' He shrugged.

Karl choked up.

Freyu placed a hand on his shoulder. 'Well, I'm still going. Really want a decent meal.' She walked towards the portal but turned around. 'Just joking. Maybe I can help here, too.'

Goblo ate some rocks.

They turned to Arazod, who hung his head.

'Do what you need to do, Arazod,' Karl said.

Arazod's feathers fluttered. 'It's not that. I worry, Karl. Part of me loved cutting your head off. It's in me.' His shoulders fell. 'Every sunset there are moments. Moments I have to fight urges to hurt.'

'But you fight them,' Karl said. 'We all have bad thoughts.'

Arazod shook his head. 'Sometimes. You have bad thoughts, sometimes. I have good thoughts sometimes. I want you to wipe my mind so I can start again.'

Karl's heart ached. 'But—'

Arazod raised a claw. 'I want to start again, without my father and Ryza in my mind. I want to start from nothing.'

'So you want to stay with us?' Freyu asked.

Arazod scratched his talons against the stone floor. 'I want to be wiped away and sent back. Completely new. Like Arazod never existed. Just tell me we saved the world, so I know I did one good thing, and then send me off. I don't want my name either.'

Karl touched the mind stone in his pocket. He wanted Arazod to keep fighting.

'What shall we call you when you awaken?' Quizmal asked.

Arazod shrugged. 'I've always been drawn to the name Dennis.'

Karl raised an eyebrow. Maybe Arazod just needed to know

he had support. 'We can help you fight it. We can remind you every day.'

Arazod exhaled and shook his head. 'I'm exhausted.'

Karl swallowed. He would never completely understand Arazod's struggle, so he had to let him decide. 'Dennis the manhawk it is.' Karl removed the mind stone from his pocket. 'I forgive you,' he told Arazod.

Arazod's beak twitched.

'I'm not just saying it because you helped,' Karl said. 'I forgave you long ago and it makes me angry. Makes me feel like I'm disrespecting my mother, Sabrinia, Sags, everyone. But I know they would want me to forgive.'

Arazod stared at Karl. He wiped a wing over his eyes. 'Thank you.'

Karl hugged him. 'I'm only hugging you because you won't remember.'

Arazod laughed, but it was more of a shriek. A horrible noise. He steadied himself. 'When I awaken, ask me what I want to do. If I give any hint of being evil, please kill me.' He lay down.

Karl knelt by Arazod. There was no way he could kill him. Not after everything. He ran the sharp end of the mind stone over his forehead. The blood trickled down his feathers and he closed his eyes.

'Thank you, all,' Arazod said. 'And you, especially,' he told Karl.

Karl swallowed.

The eel-spider entered Arazod's forehead. A blank expression gradually took hold of him and he fell unconscious. The spider returned to its stone and Karl's tears fell onto it.

Freyu and Quizmal placed their hands on Karl's shoulders.

They waited for Arazod to reawaken. Freyu held Karl's sword out to him, but he refused it. 'Let's not have the first thing he sees be a weapon.'

People could change, or at least fight their urges. Maybe it was an ongoing battle, but Arazod showed he could win. Karl wished he had the desire to continue the fight.

Karl turned to Freyu. 'You can go into the portal, then kill yourself if you want your eye back.'

She stared at the portal but shook her head. 'I like me this way.' She smiled. 'And I don't much like the idea of having to kill myself to come back.'

Karl shrugged. 'You get used to it.'

Arazod stirred and looked around. 'What?' He glanced at the trio and Goblo, who still ate rocks. 'What's going on?'

Karl stepped forward and offered his arm to pull Arazod up.

Arazod stared at it a moment, then took it and stood. 'Thank you.'

'Your name is Dennis,' Karl said. He informed him he had lost his memory, but that they had saved the world. He described the battle and the Realm of the Dead. Arazod listened and nodded along.

Arazod scratched his neck. 'It's a shame I don't remember that.' He smelled himself and retched. 'These feathers need a good soak.'

Karl nodded. 'What do you plan to do when you get back to the Land of the Living?'

Arazod licked his beak. 'First, wash myself. And I'm hungry. So, I'll eat and then maybe just fly around, find a nice high place to take in the world and feel a breeze on my feathers. It's a bit stuffy down here.'

Karl placed a hand on Arazod's shoulder. He knew Arazod would be fine. 'Have a good life.'

Arazod smiled and walked towards the portal. A flash of energy later and he was gone, out of Karl's life.

NOT SO BAD

Shardur's cries grew louder as Karl and the others approached the stone room. Part of Karl wanted to leave her and get out of the maze, but she had suffered so much. He'd always regret it and then when overcome with guilt he would likely come back anyway. He realised he might as well save himself going through that process.

The shaling stood at the edge of the root path, waiting to be disturbed.

'Do not touch anything that isn't stone,' Karl whispered.

They entered the stone room and Karl's heart sank.

Bat Lover was face down, burned and crawling towards Shardur.

Shardur pulled against the chains but the energy in them zapped her.

The bat-human, wings withered, crawled towards Bat Lover and dug its nails into her head.

'Get off her, parasite!' Shardur screamed.

Karl's bones shook. He dragged the bat-human off Bat Lover.

It shrieked and clicked.

'Can I?' Quizmal asked Karl and held his hand out.

Karl handed him the sword.

Quizmal jammed it into the bat-human's back and the clicking and squeals died out with the monster. It exploded into ash.

Shardur stared at Karl.

'How can we free you?' Karl asked.

Shardur shook her head. 'You need magic.'

Karl nodded. 'Maybe I have something.' He showed her the rings on his fingers. 'Do you promise not to kill us?'

'My only interest is Lorena.' Shardur stared at her lover.

Karl understood that feeling. 'I hope this works. And we need to destroy the portal. Freeing you from it isn't enough; those stones need to go.'

Shardur nodded. 'After so many sunsets of misery that would bring me great pleasure.'

Karl pulled at the chains around Shardur's chest, and they zapped him and Shardur.

He recoiled, then tried again. He fought the shock and yanked the enchanted steel but failed.

Shardur glared at him.

'Goblo eat!' Goblo ran up to the chains and bit them off Shardur's chest.

Karl threw his arms up in the air. 'What else could you have made a lot easier?'

Goblo ran out of the stone room.

Shardur's arms and wings were free. She yanked the chains off her legs, grabbed the root attached to her chest and pulled it out of her. She bit it into pieces and spat it out.

The root slithered out of the room.

Shardur ran to Lorena, sat by her and placed her in her lap. 'You found me.'

Lorena smiled up at Shardur; the crazed look fought with whoever she really was. 'Even with my mind clouded by those creatures, everything drove me to you.'

Shardur stroked her face.

Lorena's body jerked. 'But I did bad things to get here. I helped bad people, because I heard about your search and thought you were in the Land of the Living. My mind still hurts. It's as though someone is forever screaming, breaking my...'

Shardur held Lorena's face into her chest. 'You found me. We get to have another moment.'

Lorena's breathing slowed and her blood covered Shardur's forearms.

It reminded Karl of his final moments with his mother. He nodded to Quizmal and Freyu. They left the cave.

They waited, avoiding anything that could trigger the shaling.

Shardur's weeping and pained scream would haunt Karl forever.

ROAD TO NOWHERE

Karl stepped back while Shardur ripped the focus stones from the portal.

'I helped Ulago so I could capture Lorena, bring her to the Land of the Living and take her to the healing waters of Sembalis to remove the parasite. But the three vile beasts used me.'

Shardur spotted Klarsa's scale and picked it up. 'The magical energy of dragon scales can feed our land. Let Klarsa do some good. She'd hate that.' Shardur smiled and tucked the scale into her wings.

'I'm sorry about what happened,' Karl said.

Shardur tossed the focus stones into the burning water. 'I will honour Lorena by doing what we set out to do, making the Realm of the Dead better than the Land of the Living.'

Karl liked the sound of that. 'Maybe we can help each other.'

Shardur flew them all out of the maze. Thankfully, they never saw the shaling.

Shardur spotted the invisible dragon's scale and picked it up. 'Two scales. While we have lost much, luck has cast us a favourable glance.'

The group wanted to make signs, so Shardur flew away and

returned with some wood. They made several warnings leading up to the maze entrance. Karl carved the words as neatly as he could using the sword, but they looked crooked and awful.

They read in order of approach:

There is no portal anymore.

We destroyed it because it made people stupid.

If you enter you will probably die. Don't bother.

Seriously, go and do something better.

Are the hundreds of swords and pieces of armour on the dirt not enough of a hint that this place is terrible?

Fine. Greedy idiot or idiots.

Karl took one last look at the mountains of dung. He regretted not going home for a moment but realised he had had his time. He had lived his life and now he could live his death.

He smiled. It was oddly freeing.

Freyu stared at the entrance, probably thinking about Rimala.

'Shall we go in and find them?' Karl asked.

Freyu shook her head. 'It's the best place for her. I just hope Messiro finds his way out.'

Karl nodded.

BUILD IT FOR THEM

$\mathcal{K}$arl stood on the dock at Port Larken, where he had flung his sword at Arazod and freed several prisoners.

The suns set and made the purple water glow as though the sea were made entirely of magic.

The calm, burning waters washed around the wooden posts holding the dock up. He tried to ignore the clanging of construction.

His heart was heavy, but he assured himself he had made the right decision. He questioned himself every sunset. Part of him worried that if he didn't question himself then it would mean he didn't care.

He rolled Zianfer's rings around his fingers. The only one he ever removed was the twiggy one that would let him stay awake forever, because he wanted to sleep. It was the only time he could forget.

He turned to face the centre of Port Larken.

Oafs and those who used to be prisoners carried large stones, fortifying the walls, upgrading the wooden huts to stone, and making more towers.

Karl walked back towards the stone storeroom.

Hargon approached him holding two cups of water.

'Thanks.' Karl took one and walked with him along a path of stone huts.

Hargon brushed his long red hair behind his ears. 'The Oafs have finished the sculptures between here and our place. What next?'

They turned a corner and found several farms. Blue grass grew, along with mushrooms that looked a lot more appetising and flowers that Karl had no idea about.

Shardur stared at a sculpture of Lorena that Boofa finished making. Klarsa's scale shimmered in Lorena's foot, feeding the soil with its magic.

'It's perfect,' Shardur said, and Boofa beamed.

Freyu blew her hair out of her face and placed some flowers in a basket. She handed the basket to Goblo. 'This is to go to Beryl for the soup, understood?'

Goblo nodded. 'Belly.'

Freyu folded her arms. 'No. Beryl. You can eat from what she makes, or why not eat some of the gigantic pile of rocks?'

Goblo nodded. 'Belly.' She ran off with the bucket.

Freyu shook her head and laughed. She grabbed a sack and approached Karl and Shardur. 'Here. Quizmal said he was ready.' She wiped the sweat off her face. 'Don't be gone too long.'

They entered the storeroom where Quizmal marked the maps of the Realm of the Dead and Hastovia. 'What shall we rename it to?' he asked.

Karl had tried to think of a name for a while, but nothing made sense. Afterlife was boring. Afterdeath was miserable. Land of new life. As inspiring as an old, damp sock. 'Not sure yet.'

'Should you go to these places?' Quizmal drew their attention to castles on the map of Hastovia, and the circles he had carved on the map of the Realm of the Dead.

Karl nodded. They would hopefully find more people and bring them to Port Larken before anything sinister got to them.

'Ready to go?' Shardur asked. She fanned out her wings and Karl strapped seven sacks of grass to her belt.

'Hold on tight,' Shardur said.

Karl wrapped his arms around her neck, and she flew them out of the storeroom.

They had visited six forts and finally arrived where Karl had been reborn, paralleled with Flowforn.

The Oafs carved messages on the inside and outside of its walls.

If you are reading this, sorry, you are dead. But also, you are alive again!

You will find food and water on the second floor. Every three sunsets somebody comes to restock the place and bring people to a proper home.

This is a place of peace. If you are a war person, please leave, or else a scary flying wolf woman will eat you.

Thanks!

'Perfect,' Karl said.

'Still not sure I like being called scary,' Shardur said.

'Ferocious?' Karl handed the sack of grass to an Oaf. 'The water is on a ship on its way.'

The Oaf nodded and took the sack of grass.

Karl placed a hand on the Oaf's arm. 'Have there been any new arrivals?' He was never sure whether he wanted the answer to be yes or no.

The Oaf shook her head.

Karl sighed.

Shardur placed her claw on his shoulder. 'Don't think your sadness has gone unnoticed.'

'That obvious?' he said.

'Come with me,' she said.

'Is this the day you finally kill me and reveal you're truly evil?'

Shardur laughed. Then she pulled an angry face and stared at him. 'Maybe.'

Karl shuddered. 'Don't do that.'

Shardur flew them back to Port Larken and dropped him at the reservoir.

She howled.

Karl gazed around, worried what might emerge from the shadows under the night suns.

Freyu, Goblo, Hargon, and Quizmal approached.

Quizmal had something behind his back.

Karl folded his arms. 'I really hate surprises. They often end with me being betrayed.'

Quizmal held out a jar with a light fly in it.

Karl's heart raced.

Freyu grinned. 'When we got everyone out of the Sea Spike, we found Zianfer's stash.'

Karl took the jar.

'Happy watching,' Hargon said. 'I'd quite like to know if she's okay, too.'

Karl swallowed and placed his hand on top of the jar, but then stopped himself. 'I don't know. I'd rather think she survived than learn she didn't.'

Shardur shook her head. 'There is nothing worse than wondering. Trust me.'

Karl pulled the wooden plug out of the jar and pinched the light fly by the wings. He handed the jar back to Quizmal.

Karl knelt at the rim of the reservoir.

Goblo fired light at it.

Karl closed his eyes, thought of Sabrinia, and released the light fly.

It glowed, flew into the air, and shot into the water. A gigantic image formed on the reservoir.

The fly rushed through the sea, its wings flapping at the frantic pace of Karl's heart.

The creature burst out in the middle of the ocean. It stopped a moment and took the surroundings in, as though unsure of where to go.

A lump formed in Karl's throat. Maybe it didn't know where to go because the person he wanted to see wasn't there.

The light fly flew over water for an age.

'Boring,' Goblo said.

Karl stayed focused on the water but appreciated Freyu's tut.

The fly finally saw a mountain. As a forest came into view so did a sandy shore that curved around forever.

Three figures walked along it towards a port town.

Karl's neck tensed and a smile consumed his face. Tears filled his eyes.

She walked with Marlens and Death, who carried several sacks.

No sign of Frong though.

Karl swallowed.

The fly hovered in front of Sabrinia and she stopped walking. She turned to Death and Marlens and pointed to the fly. Death nodded and Sabrinia grinned.

She raised a finger, crouched down and ran her finger through the sand.

Marlens and Death waved at the fly. Death stopped waving and sat down while Marlens continued to wave for far too long.

Sabrinia pointed to the message.

I love you

Karl nodded. 'I love you, too.'
Goblo coughed. 'Can't hear. Idiot.'
Karl huffed.
Sabrinia wiped the message and wrote more.
A figure leapt high behind the group and laughter burst out of Karl. Frong was okay. He was clearly loving his new belt relic and brought the group fruit and berries.
'They're all okay!' Karl turned to his friends.
Quizmal smiled.
Sabrinia finished her next message.

We found my mother. She's great but bizarre

Karl wiped his eyes.
She raised a finger and wiped the message out.
Karl turned to the others. 'She's slow at writing these. You don't have to wait.'
Shardur nodded. 'Thank you for this mercy.'
'Can we go and check the southern fort?' Quizmal asked Shardur.
She got on her hands and knees. Quizmal climbed on and she flew away.
Freyu smiled. 'I've got nothing better to do. And I need to stop Goblo being a pest.'
Karl turned back to the water. Sabrinia had finished her latest message.

A god has been taking innocent people and making beasts out of them.
We found the power to get to her

She spoke to Death, who threw her a jar from the sack. It contained what looked like leeches, but they had fins.

She placed one on her neck and walked into the sea up to her neck. She turned and spoke to Frong.

Karl couldn't lip read clearly enough.

The fly hovered around the water and then followed Sabrinia into it.

She walked along the seabed backwards, waving the fly towards her and smiling.

Karl laughed, his heart full. She had so much of the world to explore. It hurt, but he was happy for her.

She walked out of the sea, pulled the leech off her, grimaced and handed it back to Death.

Frong finished writing something in the sand.

We are going to kill Octorion in her underwater castle. I love you

Frong pointed at himself and the 'I love you' part.

Karl's smile could have ripped through his cheeks.

Sabrinia tried to write one last thing as the fly flickered.

Karl waited. Tears dropped from his chin. 'A bit longer, fly. Please.'

See you when it's my time
  Good luck and be careful. It's a strange world out there

Karl's body tingled. 'Wait until you see this world.' He thought about marking where the light fly was. A port town, a high mountain, a dense forest. He could find it on the map of Hastovia, match it to the Realm of the Dead and build a fort.

He couldn't follow her forever.

She had her journey to complete. Just because he wasn't on it, it didn't mean he wasn't part of it. She would always be a part of his, too.

The fly hovered lower and Sabrinia, saddened, waved. She wiped her eyes. Frong put an arm around her, and she rested her head on his shoulder.

He offered her his beard to wipe her tears but she waved it away.

Karl stared, absorbing every piece of her, wanting to freeze it in his memory.

The image on the water faded and Goblo's light drew back.

Karl felt hollow.

'It's okay,' Freyu said. 'We have loads more light flies in a cave. Zianfer had so many.'

Karl shook his head. 'It's too scary. We should let the light flies go. It's not fair they die so we can see a piece of our old lives.'

'Are you sure?' she asked.

He knew he would regret it, but he had to let go. 'The most important thing is I have the memories.'

Thinking about memories always drew his thoughts to the mind stone, which was now in a box under his bed.

One day he might watch Arazod's memories, but he wasn't sure Arazod would want him to.

Karl rolled his trousers up, sat on the edge of the reservoir and dipped his ankles into the cold water.

Freyu joined him.

'I think I have a name for this place,' he said.

Freyu kicked the water. 'Go on then.'

Karl smiled at her. 'Foreverlands.'

Freyu stifled a laugh. 'Terrible.'

'It's not!'

'It really is.'

'Land of Forever?' he suggested.

'I say we keep thinking on it.' She lay back and looked up at the night suns.

Karl joined her. He worried that when Sabrinia's time came

they might have missed out on too many experiences. Maybe she would no longer love him. What if he no longer loved her?

The best thing he could do was take what she taught him and preserve their love that way. By making the world better for everyone.

The End...

ACKNOWLEDGMENTS

Thank you for reading this and I'm assuming the series so far, otherwise this would have likely been confusing in places and pretty terrible.

When I started writing this series it was an out and out very stupid comedy. To the point there was no story. So, I reworked the first book for ages to put the characters first and the response has been amazing. Thank you. I've been lucky so many people have found a character to care about in these groups of fools.

Thank you for the kind words, encouragement, and desire to actually read the words that I've written.

I have to thank the editor, Nick Hodgson, who is patient, brilliant and pushes me to be better at this. She's excellent and if you're ever in need of an editor seek her out. She can be found at root-and-branch-editing.com

I'd also like to thank Amanda Rutter, a fantastic proofreader.

I also want to thank the cover designer of the originals, Basia Tran. She takes my dreadful suggestions, waves her magic pen or whatever she uses and makes the covers something I could not have imagined in my tiny mind. Her creativity makes me worry she would also make a better writer than me. You can see more of her awesome work at basiatran.com. I had to change the covers to be more consistent, as I'd only found her after book one, but you can see her covers over on my website as they deserve to exist forever.

Thank you, Pixie Britton, the brilliant author of the Kill or Cure series and a good friend. If you like zombies and strong female characters, get it. She's been a great sounding board and reads early drafts of this where she encourages me to be less of a robot.

I want to thank the Laurens. My first proper review from someone who didn't know me was from Lauren and it came at a time when I wanted to bin the whole series, but she genuinely seemed to like it, and not just out of politeness. Or she's an incredible actor. Then she introduced me to another Lauren who reviewed it who also seemed to like it. They're great people whose encouragement made me write book three. They are legends and a credit to all Laurens, giving Laurens a good rep everywhere.

Adam Croft has done nothing, so he deserves no thanks. In fact, he deserves booing for sending me a life-sized cardboard cut-out of Richard Osman that ruins the ambience in my garage.

The biggest thanks goes to my wife, Cinthia. She's brilliant, patient, and listens to me waffle through these nonsense story-lines constantly. I'm lucky I met her and that she let me take her to a restaurant that was clearly a money laundering operation on our first date.

Thanks also to my parents, who have no idea what I do for a living and still pretend that they do.

My final thanks goes to the weird and wonderful characters who have jumped around in my head for so many years. I never knew when I started this that they would grow into the people they became and that I'd do more than one book. Books four and five will come, but for now they need a break. I think I've put them through enough pain, and they need some time to relax into their new lives.

You can keep up to date with what's next at www.mark-boutros.com and I'll update those who care via my newsletter, which you can sign up to at www.mark-boutros.com/crew

For now, all I can keep saying is thank you. And good luck and be careful, it's a strange world out there.

- *Mark*

ABOUT THE AUTHOR

Mark Boutros is an International Emmy nominated and PAGE International award-winning writer who has written for Disney, the Cartoon Network, Sky One, the BBC and Sky Arts.

He was born in London and still dreams of leaving it for a mountain where he can grow his own food and not be asked to do things.

If you want to know more about Mark visit
www.mark-boutros.com

Instagram: @markboutroswrites
Facebook: www.facebook.com/MarkBoutrosWrites